VALLEY OF THE BROKEN

K. F. BAUGH

ALSO BY K. F. BAUGH

Miss You Once Again

Granny Bob's Homestyle Cooking:
Recipes With a Southern Flavor

There are more things in heaven and earth, Horatio,
Than are dreamt of in your philosophy.

- *Hamlet (1.5.167-8)*,
Hamlet to Horatio

ACKNOWLEDGMENTS

This book nearly died several times and owes its existence to a fantastic group of rescuers.

My special thanks to the *Here Be Dragons* writing group: Andy, Ben, Joe and Josh. The flame was almost dead when I joined up with you guys; thanks for bringing it back to life. Your expertise and encouragement has been my writing salvation.

Thank you Chris Bassett for helping me understand what trauma victims go through in the aftermath of their experiences. Thank you Dominic Henry and Jaci Wells for reading through my manuscript for any cultural insensitivities or inaccuracies. Thank you Teresa Schuemann for explaining the complexities of small town law enforcement and rescue operations (although I'm sure I still didn't get it quite right). Thank you Kerrie Flanagan for your support and advice on publishing; you are a fountain of wisdom.

Thank you also to the members of my family (both natural and naturalized) who have supported me in a plethora of ways: Mom and Dad, Katie and Dave, Joey and Lauren, Jon and Laura, Dave and Sharilyn. Also, Jennifer

Kutzik, Jeannine Davison, Lesley Bodley, Jenny Sundstedt, Chuck Harrelson, and April Moore. Thank you Haddie for reading through the final(ish) draft and giving it to me straight up. Thank you Gideon for always making me laugh. And thank you Jim for everything--you make all this possible.

Lastly, thank you Gothic, Colorado for being so quirky that you spawned the imaginings of this book. And are you really sure it's just the marmots ... really?

CHAPTER ONE

None of them noticed it at first, as the noise wove itself into the fabric of normal night sounds. Emily heard the rustling of sleeping bags and the sighs of Gus, her bearlike, shaggy dog, as he cuddled next to her and her brother Daniel. From outside the tent came the murmur of her parents' voices while they drank their beers by the flickering campfire.

Slowly the sound worked its way into the tent, a strange guttural grunt followed by a snarl. Gus tensed and answered with a growl of his own.

"What's that?" Daniel sat up in his sleeping bag. "A wolf?"

"No, there aren't any wolves here." Emily struggled to roll over in her child's sleeping bag. It was almost too small for her lanky nine-year old frame.

"But it sounds like a wolf." Daniel inched closer to her.

Emily sighed. They went through this every time her parents took them camping, even though Daniel was seven now and should have known better. "Remember what Dad said? That all the animals are more scared of us than we are of them."

"But look at Gus. He's really angry."

"It's probably just a—"

Hackles raised, the dog scrambled to his feet and crept along the edge of the tent, eerily illuminated by the campfire light. Despite the increasing intensity of Gus's growls, Emily also noticed her parents had fallen silent.

"Get in the tent, Sara." Her father's voice cut through the darkness, loud and sharp.

"Oh my God," Emily's mother gasped. "Where's the gun? No, NO!"

Her mother's screams twisted around the terrible roars until Emily could no longer distinguish one from the other. Gus launched himself through the rainfly, zippers ripping aside at the force of his leap.

"Mom, DAD!" Emily struggled to escape the tight cocoon of the sleeping bag, her fingers searching frantically for the zipper she couldn't see.

"I'm coming, Mom!" Daniel cried, and Emily saw his backlit form scramble through the billowing tent opening. Emily found the zipper and jerked hard, but it jammed. She thrashed and writhed, trying to escape the material that held her in its unyielding embrace. Her family's wails of pain and fear tore through the air, and the light of the campfire suddenly vanished.

"Daniel, where are you? Come back!" Emily cried, but Gus's barking drowned out her fear-weakened voice. Something battered the side of the tent, then leapt up barking. Emily finally kicked the sleeping bag free, and Gus's barks ended in a high-pitched squeal, followed by the popping sound of the tent poles giving way. Silky nylon smothered Emily's face, and a heavy weight landed on her chest, crushing the breath from her lungs.

She tried to scream as pain collapsed the left side of her

body, but no sound escaped her gasping mouth. A dark chuckle echoed in the haunting silence. When the nylon slipped from her face, Emily blinked, trying to make out the towering form before her, but her blurred vision made it impossible. An opaque mass came closer and closer. Lights exploded in her eyes before blackness overcame them. She was blind.

The pain that had raged along her left leg, arm, and rib cage ebbed, now replaced with a gentle warmth. A strange detachment enveloped Emily, and the terror of moments before waned.

Even though she couldn't see, her remaining senses took over. She heard a blast of wind whip through the pine trees. Tent fabric tickled her forehead and tucked around her. Shivers of heat tingled through her dead-weight limbs. Whispers came from behind, then moved to surround her. Emily felt weightless; up, up she floated, leaving the carnage of the campsite far below.

The whispers dimmed when howls of rage echoed from far away. The layers of nylon untangled from around Emily's face. Something soft like feathers or petals brushed her cheek and then gently tugged her mouth open. When a ragged breath stabbed through her lungs, Emily blinked, and the faint white light of the moon slowly came back into focus.

Silvery figures, pulsing with internal light, danced along the edge of her vision. The wind gusted over her face, and Emily's eyelids grew heavy. The light of the broken half-moon faded, and darkness overwhelmed her.

Ten Years Later ...

"Stop, Gus." Sage tried to push the dog back to the foot

of her bed, but he nudged and strained against her outstretched arms until Sage finally slumped back against her pillow and succumbed to his frenzied licking.

"Enough." Firmly tugging the dog to her side, Sage reached down and pulled the threadbare blanket up from where it had tangled around her ankles. As it settled around the two of them, the shaggy dog finally gave a contented sigh and relaxed against her.

"Did I wake you up? You don't have to be my sleep guardian, you know. The dreams always pass."

Gus replied with something halfway between a snort and a growl.

"Fine." Sage rolled over and plumped her pillow. Feathers strained through the worn seams and pricked at her fingers. She swallowed, then winced at the pain in her raw throat. "Was I screaming? Is that why you woke me?"

Gus didn't answer this time, and Sage tried to remember the dim images. They flashed like snapshots in her mind, then disappeared, as they always did. The color and terror were already starting to fade away, like those brightly colored prayer flags the tourists left on the mountain tops. It only took a few weeks of the altitude-intensified sun for the things to look like washed out rags.

Unable to keep the images from vanishing, Sage gave up and tried to focus instead on Gus's regular breathing. Perhaps its comforting rhythm would lull her back to sleep as it so often had in the past. It wasn't long, however, before murmuring voices and the occasional childish squeal pulled her from the squeaky, narrow bed. Sage rose and peered through her window. On the street beneath her, she saw people dressed in bright colors pulling out folding chairs and opening portable coolers.

"A parade. But it's not—" She dropped the dingy plastic

blinds and walked to the faded calendar hanging next to her closet. She flipped through several outdated months and smacked her hand against the wall.

"The Fourth of July? Already?" She returned to the window and peered at the expanding crowd of onlookers. Even more of them had set up folding chairs along the parade route. Children and dogs wove excitedly between the clumps of red, white, and blue revelers. Sage checked the clock. Before long the first float would appear at the east end of Main Street.

Sage sighed and turned away. She'd have to slip out the back alley before the day's festivities grew more elaborate and the tourist-saturated holiday crowds completely clogged any escape route from town.

Gathering her tangled, dark hair in a ponytail, she nudged the quilt-covered dog with her foot. "Hey, wake up." Gus moaned, but did not move. "I'm serious. We've got to get out of here while we can." Sage pulled on a pair of worn jeans and dug through a pile of clothes on the chair. After smelling the armpits, she settled on an old ski team T-shirt for her base layer and a soft flannel shirt for the outer one.

Gus finally slithered from his place under the blanket and stretched his long, mutt-mixed limbs with languid grace. After his doggie yoga, he shook out his shaggy, gray and cream marled fur and sat before Sage with a petulant glare. Despite his unnatural longevity and other impressive abilities, the dog still had a stubborn streak. He was especially protective of his sleep schedule.

Sage opened the bedroom door. "Go grab a drink," she ordered. "I'm almost done packing."

Sage surveyed her crowded closet. The sleeping bag and moldy tent were still in the back of her Jeep from her last trip, but Sage quickly gathered the rest of her camping supplies. Most of them were second-hand or scavenged from departing tourists: a propane burner, freeze dried noodles and granola bars, matches, a water bottle, sunscreen, a rusty hatchet for firewood, and a game knife. Each item was quickly organized into its proper place in an ancient gear bin. Next, she shoved a few changes of clothes and a waterproof shell into a battered duffle bag.

She snuck down to the mudroom at the back of the house and set the gear bin and duffle bag by the backdoor. Gus's dog food was the only thing she still needed to pack. The dog came and laid down at her feet while she scooped several cupfuls from the bag in the laundry room and dumped them into a plastic container.

"You can eat in a minute. But first I need to check if Liddy's here," Sage whispered and crept to the large bedroom at the front of the house.

The steady tick, tick of the kitchen clock was the only sound Sage could detect as she crept across the musty, creaking floorboards. Dirty dishes filled the sink and threatened to overflow onto the countertop next to it. Scattered papers and files lay in a confused heap on the kitchen table, along with an overturned wine bottle. Liddy must have been doing the bills last night.

At the threshold of Liddy's bedroom, Sage stopped to listen. A rattly, irregular snore sounded from behind the door, and Sage gently pushed it open. Liddy lay sprawled across her bed, still fully clothed. Sage pulled down the shades and covered the older woman with one of her gypsy-like blankets—ragged and colorful, just like her foster mom.

Sage scribbled a quick note on a piece of scrap paper and set it on Liddy's night stand. After a moment's hesitation, she put a bottle of aspirin on top of it. That would increase the probability of Liddy finding it when she woke up.

Returning to the back of the house where Gus guarded her things, Sage shouldered her gear and pulled the rickety door closed behind them but didn't bother to lock it. Neither she nor Liddy ever did. The dilapidated 1800s home was the block's eyesore, and no one was down enough on their luck to break into it. The only thing of any value was the red and black patterned Navajo rug next to Sage's bed, probably disguised as it usually was by the pile of dirty laundry that lay on top of it. Despite this, the rug, a parting gift from Grandfather Benally, was one of her most treasured possessions. The other was her new name, also a gift from Grandfather, the kindest man she'd ever met.

Tears clouded her eyes, and Sage roughly wiped them on her flannel sleeve. "Let's hit the road, Gus," she snapped, louder than she intended, but Gus didn't seem to notice. His tags jingled as he danced around her, reveling in their familiar routine of escape.

They walked to the small detached garage, Gus nosing his way through the door. He leapt into the front passenger seat of the battered, topless Jeep as Sage packed her gear in the trunk. Sunglasses and cowboy hat in place, she barely made it out of the garage before she had to slam on her breaks. A toxic-looking pink parade float blocked the gravel driveway.

For a second she considered ramming it. Surely all that pink needed to be put out of its misery.

"Stay, Gus," she ordered and hopped out of the car.

Sage walked around the dusty truck then back to the float, trying to find the owner, but her gaze kept being drawn to the strange creation in front of her. Large and rectangular, it filled the entire bed of a trailer. Peaks and valleys, green pipe cleaner trees, and popsicle houses dotted the surface, but it was the dark red stain that slashed through several papier mâché peaks that caught Sage's attention. When she leaned closer to inspect it, her stomach tightened. It looked like a river of blood.

"What kind of freak makes a float with blood on it?" Sage asked the emptiness around her. She leaned close again, and the river began to flow. Panic pulled her into its embrace, and Sage let out a ragged gasp.

"Hello? Can you hear me? Are you alright?"

Sage flinched and jumped away. Yanking her sunglasses off, she blinked as the backlit form before her blurred into focus. A tall, dark-haired man reached out to steady her, but Sage jerked out of reach.

"So what's the deal with your float?" Sage said, backing away. "It's kind of sick."

"Sick?" He glanced at the float.

"Yeah," Sage shook her head. "You know, with all the blood?" She pointed at the pink and red monstrosity.

"I don't understand." The man stepped up to the truck bed and traced his fingers over the top. "It's just a topographical map of the Black Mills and Oriel Valleys. The rivers and roads are marked. But there's no blood."

Sage followed him and looked at the float. The red had disappeared, leaving normal blue rivers and brown trails in its place. Embarrassment gnawed at her stomach. She should have known the blood wasn't real. Who made a float with blood on it?

Gus chose this moment to make an appearance and raced, tail wagging, to her side. The dog nosed her hand, helping to still the panic that thrashed at the corners of her mind. Sage stroked his silky soft ears and closed her eyes. It was time to figure out a Plan B for escape, somewhere within hiking distance. But that wouldn't work either. All the trails around town would be saturated with visiting mountain bikers and hikers.

"You're blocking my driveway," she blurted out. "I need you to move, now."

"Sorry. The parade organizers told us to wait here." The man looked around the back alley crammed with other floats and shrugged. "It's so packed now, I don't think I can move."

Sage noticed a few creases at the edge of his eyes, ones that adorned any adult who'd lived at this high altitude longer than a few years. They contrasted sharply with his broad shoulders and jet-black hair. The steady blue of his irises bored into her, and she looked away.

"I've got to get out of here," Sage said, trying to keep her voice steady. "Before this stupid parade jams up the whole town." Maybe she'd just take off on foot.

The man cleared his throat and crossed his arms. "Not a fan of the parade then?"

"Not really." Sage turned away. "Wish all these tourists would stay down in the flatlands where they belong."

"Guess you must be the town patriot." The man chuckled and held out his hand to Gus, who, after a moment's hesitation, raised his paw to shake it. "And is this your sidekick?"

Sage replaced her sunglasses. "Don't take it personally. Gus loves everybody."

"Like his owner, huh?" He smiled, but Sage only shrugged. "Listen, I really am sorry. If I could move out of your way, I would." He turned and nodded to the other trucks and floats, all parked within inches of each other.

"Whatever." Gus quickly returned to Sage's side,

nudging her hand once more. She buried it in the reassuring warmth of his thick fur.

"Mr. Tim," a young tween ran up and tugged on the man's shirt. "The parade guy said they're about ready to begin."

"Get the rest of the kids to gather around the float. Make sure everyone has their bags of candy, but tell them to toss it sparingly. That's all we've got."

Kids suddenly swarmed around the float, and the waiting vehicles' engines roared to life. Sage let out a ragged sigh. In just a few minutes she'd be free.

"Come on, Gus," she said. "Let's get out of here."

"Hey wait." The man took a step toward her. "I was so distracted by your ... greeting that I forgot to introduce myself. I'm--"

"*Mr. Tim.* Yeah, I heard." Sage said, walking backwards toward the Jeep. "Are you a school teacher?" It had been nearly two years since she graduated from the small, mountain town high school, but she thought she would have remembered him. Maybe he was new.

"Something like that," Tim said, his voice nearly drowned out by the din of the vehicles. "And you are?"

Several horns blared and motors raced. The drivers in the long line of trucks and floats were feverish to begin. They were all trapped, including Sage, until this guy moved his float out of the way.

"Look Mr. Tim, could you just move your damn float?"

"I don't see why not," Tim said, leaning against the truck. "But I still didn't catch that name." He ran his hand over the hood's chipped paint, seemingly oblivious to the horns that now blared through the alley.

She knew he wouldn't move until she answered. "It's Sage."

The man waved to Gus. "Nice to meet you." Then he glanced at Sage and winked. "You too, I guess."

Sage watched from her rearview mirror as his truck and the others slowly pulled out of the alley. The minutes dragged by, but finally, only dust motes danced along the dirt road.

She glared at Gus and jerked the car into reverse. "Well, that was cute."

Gus turned away from her and hung his head out the passenger window.

Sage poked him in the back. "Next time some stranger bothers me, I expect you to show a little more teeth and a lot less tongue."

Acknowledging her with a brief, panting smile, Gus returned to his station at the open window. Sage shook her head, but gave the dog a rough back scratch before she turned her attention to the road and escaping Black Mills.

CHAPTER TWO

Hours later, surrounded by the empty miles of a vast wilderness preserve, Sage lay in her sleeping bag and studied the night sky. The panic she'd felt in town had abated after half a day of hard hiking, and her exhausted body felt as if it had become one with the meadow beneath her.

The cloudless night allowed her a perfect view of the glistening panorama above her, something which never ceased to quiet her thoughts, no matter how chaotic. Stars pulsed and glowed, shadowed by the dim outline of mountain peaks and an occasional wisp of cloud as it raced across the moon.

"The Great Bear's tail is moving east," Sage murmured to herself. "She's traveling back to her fall home."

The impression of another sky, one filled with only with confusion and loss, wrapped around her, and she burrowed deeper into her sleeping bag. Gus whined next to her, able to sense the tortuous thoughts that danced at the edge of Sage's consciousness.

"It's all right, boy," she whispered, surprised by the hazy remembrance. Like a sealed vault, her mind had locked away all the details of that night. Occasionally, vague impressions and momentary pictures flashed before her, but they slipped away before Sage could grasp any lasting detail. No matter how hard she tried, she couldn't untangle the event from mental oblivion, and from the few hints the social services people had let slide during her youth, maybe she was better off not knowing.

A twig snapped in the thicket next to her. Sage closed her eyes, and the image of a fox appeared in her mind. The young mother carried a limp black squirrel in her mouth, her mind focused on the four kits back at the den whose bellies would be filled with this prize. When the fox paused several feet away from the small camp, alarmed by the human and canine scents, Sage entered the fox's thoughts. *Ignore us*, she mentally urged. *Go back to your home. Feed your young.*

Sage watched the fox blink several times in the moonlight before returning to her homeward path. Once the fox passed beyond the boundaries of Sage's mind, she opened her eyes to study the stars once more. This ability to sense other creatures and communicate with them was another irrevocable change brought on by that night so long ago. The skill came in especially handy when campsite visitors were of the less benign variety, like bears, mountain lions, or coyotes.

The quiet of the evening disappeared as the Wind whipped through the pine trees, sounding like the rush of a spring-swollen waterfall. It whirled through the neighboring aspen leaves and changed to the clapping of a million leafy hands. Last, it settled on the heavy lupine blossoms next to her and sent their gentle fragrance toward her like a kiss.

"Hello, Broken One," it whispered.

Sage sighed, feeling exhausted. "Hello, Wind. Tonight? I don't feel like talking."

"You are always weary of talking. Except with your dog. You would be content to talk to him the rest of your lifetimes."

"That's because he never talks back." Sage brushed the hair from her eyes. "A highly underrated quality."

"There is never silence for those who listen. You must realize that by now."

"Blame it on my upbringing. I was taught only humans could talk."

"The downfall of all your kind," the voice breathed into her ear.

"Fine. Let's hurry up and get to the point." Sage sat up in the darkness, head pounding with the dull ache that had nagged her since she left town.

The Wind remained silent.

"Please, just tell me."

"There's been two more," it sighed in her ear, the words coming out as a soft wail. "And their blood cries out."

"Blood?" Sage asked, the bloody rivers of the float flashed into her mind.

"Yes, blood. It cries out from places that can no longer be hidden."

"Do I need to find something?"

"Many things. The time is coming for you to protect all who live within this valley."

Sage thought back to the tasks the Wind had given her in the past. "I don't understand. All the animals?"

"As yet you've only protected the four-legged ones. A change is at hand."

Sage pondered its words. Over the years, she'd learned to listen for cries the Wind brought her. Disturbances in the air or even water. Human interference was usually at fault when a creature suffered, but many times it wasn't through malicious intent, only carelessness. A bear who'd grown too aggressive from food left by local campers, despite the plethora of signs that warned against doing so. An animal maimed by a speeding car on the highway. A deer with Chronic Wasting Disease that threatened to infect the entire herd. Some of the creatures she relocated, others she freed and nursed back to health. A few she put out of their misery as gently as possible, according to the directions of the Wind.

But a change? She liked the way things worked now. The Wind whispered a need, then the desire to restore balance consumed Sage, like an itch that needed to be scratched. Once she'd done so, a euphoric sense of peace filled her, at least for a few hours. It was the only time she felt something like happiness.

"What does this *change* mean?" Sage asked. "I don't understand."

"You will," the Wind whispered and caressed her cheek one last time. "Be careful, Broken One." Its voice faded. "Truth has been hidden by your dark dreams these many years. Your heart has slept, but now it is time to awaken."

Sage shrugged and shifted in her sleeping bag. *Her heart.* Its job was to pump blood, nothing else. And aside from its interruption about twenty years ago, it usually did the job just fine.

AFTER SEVERAL DAYS OF HIKING, ROCK CLIMBING, AND the life-giving solitude of the mountains, Sage packed up her gear and drove away from the wilderness area and back toward Black Mills and civilization. When she was only an hour away, her car temperature suddenly spiked, and the dashboard's emergency light came on. Sage pulled over to the side of the road and opened the hood. It took several minutes, but once the steam cleared away, she quickly spotted the problem. A coolant hose had detached from the engine, and the last of the antifreeze was dribbling out.

Gus pressed against her leg, and she looked down at him. "Guess that last rough patch was too much for this old thing. Do we have any water left?"

Walking back to the car, she collected her last two canteens and poured the remaining contents into the engine, but it wasn't enough. Sage drummed her blackened fingers against the wheel well and looked over the landscape around her. No streams, no ponds. Her gaze caught a wooden shack down in the valley below her. Oriel.

Gus let out a low growl. "I know, buddy. I hate it too, but I just need enough water to tide us over until we get home."

Sage gathered up all her water containers and trudged down the hill. Once a uranium mine, the now renamed Oriel Biological Research Station, or OBRS, only allowed full-time scientists and support staff to live in the tiny community that clothed itself in artificially aged wooden slats and false fronts. Despite the mining shack-like appearance of the buildings, most of them were only 20-30 years old and housed state-of-the-art scientific bling and pretentious grad students. She had visited it on a few school field trips and hated every minute of it.

A bell jingled as Sage, followed by Gus, entered the tiny convenience store. A woman dressed from head to toe in Oriel Biological Research Station tourist gear organized a tower of coffee mugs emblazoned with an *I* ♥ *OBRS* logo.

She turned to Sage with a bright smile, one which quickly mutated into a grimace. "That dog should be on a leash. Dogs are only allowed on the designated pathways between the restrooms, store, and medical cabin. We all love our pets, but here they are considered an invasive species and detrimental to the overall health of the--"

"Yeah, fine." Sage held up her containers. "I just need some water, and then I promise my dog and I will be gone."

Slamming a coffee mug on the counter, the woman turned and strode toward them. Gus stepped in front of Sage and single rumbling growl halted the woman's approach.

"He doesn't like the word *leash*," Sage said and watched as a string of disturbing emotions, all of which seemed disproportionate to the situation, played across the woman's face.

The woman moved within inches of Sage. "If you don't get off this property in the next five seconds--"

"Serena!" A voice barked from the shadows of a nearby closet. Both the woman and Sage turned.

"That's enough," the voice continued. "You're being rude to our guest."

Serena's hands fluttered to her chest. "I'm sorry, sir. I just know how dogs--"

A tall, broad chested man glided from the closet and shushed Serena's protest with a quick glance. "Please go back to whatever you were doing."

Serena nodded and beat a hasty retreat to the mugs she'd been stacking when Sage first entered the store.

The man, clothed in an *I* ♥ *OBRS* T-shirt, glided in front of Sage and stopped. "You'll have to excuse Serena." He smiled slightly. "She takes her job *very* seriously." He whispered and winked at Sage.

Sage took a step back, and Gus settled at her feet. "I know you. You're Terrance Storm."

The man held up his hands and shrugged. "Guilty as charged."

"The director of this whole place, right?"

"Have we met?" He took another step toward Sage and studied her more closely.

"Here and there on the trails." Sage answered, vaguely. In fact, they'd met multiple times when Storm was in the backcountry with his grad students. As a lowly local, she'd barely merited his attention. "I live in Black Mills."

"Ahh," Storm responded, his tone now disinterested. "And what, exactly, are you doing here?"

Sage held up her canteens. "Like I told Serena, I just need a refill on my water and then I'll get out of here."

Storm glanced between her and Gus; a grin carved itself across his features again. "There's a water pump out by the dumpsters. You are welcome to use it. But please remember that your dog should be on a leash. Dogs are only allowed on the designated pathways between the restrooms, store, and medical cabin. We all love our pets, but here they are considered an invasive species and detrimental to the overall health of the delicate mountain ecosystem."

"No problem," Sage muttered. Gus wound around her legs, and she nearly tripped on her way out the door. "What a bunch of weirdos."

It didn't take her long to find the bright orange water spigot behind the building. She lifted the handle and waited several moments before a stream poured into her gallon jug.

"Excuse me, miss."

Sage turned and saw a lanky college-aged kid in cut-off jeans, a threadbare T-shirt, and hiking boots.

"Dogs are only allowed on the designated pathways

between the restrooms, store, and medical cabin. We all love our pets, but--"

"I know!" Sage snapped. "I have to fill up my water, but then we'll get the hell out of here. I promise."

"Sorry." His face broke into an embarrassed smile. "They're really strict about stuff here. I just moved in a month ago, and I'm still trying to figure out all the rules. There's so many."

An actual, normal person! Sage thought, but then again, he'd only been here a few months. It wouldn't last. She set down the first jug and began to fill the second.

"So, new guy, what is it you scientists actually do here?" It was a question Sage always asked the few times she'd been forced to stop in Oriel, and she'd never gotten a straight answer.

"We research the life cycle and changing habits of marmots."

"Marmots, huh?" Sage picked up the last water container. "So this whole town, all your equipment, all these scientists, they're all for ... marmots?"

"They're a fascinating and informative species, one that's incredibly sensitive and able to alert us of upcoming challenges facing our planet. Because of their acute receptiveness to climate change—"

"Nope. Heard all this before." Sage gathered her now full containers. "Thought I might get a straight answer from a newbie, but I guess not."

"If you'd like more information, I can take you--"

"No thanks." Sage took a step backward. "Good luck." She said, feeling almost sorry for him.

"Thanks." His shoulders slumped, and he turned away. "Please remember that dog should be on a leash. Dogs are only allowed ..." His voice trailed off as he moved away.

Sage whistled for Gus to follow and, despite the weight of the water, she ran nearly the whole way to her car. Wasting no time, she emptied the jugs into her engine. Gus whined. She looked down at where he sat, near her feet.

"I'm almost done." She emptied the last of the water.

Gus shot into the car after her when Sage opened the door, and they both let out a sigh of relief when the engine finally roared to life after several false starts. The Jeep's wheels shot fountains of gravel as Sage made her rapid retreat out of the Oriel Valley and back to Black Mills.

CHAPTER THREE

Once at home, Sage opened the screen door, calling Liddy's name while Gus darted past her legs and raced up the stairs in the direction of Sage's bedroom. Dropping her bags, she wandered into the kitchen. The dirty dishes had been cleaned. Now cans of paint, brushes, and other supplies crowded the counter space.

Sage shoved one container aside and scanned through the mail, looking for anything addressed to her. Most of it was for Liddy or junk, but the headline of the day-old Sunday newspaper caught her eye. She sat on a wobbly barstool and read.

Two Local Teens Still Missing

Shaun Colter and Tabitha Smalley disappeared around the time of Thursday night's fireworks celebration. The Sheriff's Department and Search and Rescue have widened their search from the Black Mills area to include the Oriel Valley and the area surrounding Shelton Reservoir after a local man recalled seeing Colter's car traveling north on Highway 15.

Speak of the devil, Sage frowned. Having just left the place in broad daylight, she couldn't imagine driving around it at night. Did the scientists chase you with pitchforks once the sun went down? Sage read on.

Dr. Terrance Storm, Science Director of the Oriel Biological Research Station (OBRS), has appointed a liaison to coordinate with local officials. OBRS is working closely with the Highdale County's Sheriff's Department in their continuing effort to locate the missing teens. Storm offered the use of the laboratory's low-flying, military grade helicopter and all-terrain vehicles for the search.

Storm said, "OBRS's thoughts and hopes are united with our neighbors in Black Mills. We will continue to offer support in any way we can, thankful for the continued symbiotic relationship between our two communities."

"*Symbiotic relationship?*" Sage snorted. "Whatever that means."

Tossing the newspaper to the counter, Sage found a chipped glass in the kitchen cabinet and filled it with tap water. While she sipped, her mind pictured the teens driving their car around deserted mountain roads, illuminated by the eerie glow of Black Mills's fireworks. She glanced at the paper once more and shook her head. For their sake, Sage hoped that Shaun and Tabitha hadn't gotten lost around Oriel. What a disturbing place to wander. Unless you were a marmot.

A few hours later, after she'd showered and unpacked, Sage paced the floor. Gus opened one eye from the bed, where he'd remained comatose since their arrival home, but otherwise refused to acknowledge her presence. Sage wished she could join him. Even though she was physically tired, nervous energy buzzed inside her like an over-caffeinated high, and she couldn't stay still.

Her stomach rumbled, and Sage almost laughed with the relief of something to do. She needed to restock her tiny supply cabinet with dry goods for her next mountain excursion. Grabbing a backpack, she gave Gus an ear scratch and headed for the grocery store.

A large, unconcerned Husky trotted down the middle of the deserted main street. Gray-blue mountain peaks towered above the clapboard wooden buildings that lined the sidewalk. Only a few stores were open. With the temporary lull in business, most locals chose to be somewhere else: a wildflower-strewn alpine meadow or whispering pine forest. Even if they had to cater to the tourists most weekends in order to earn their daily bread, the residents of Black Mills accepted the rest of the week as a gift of nature and solitude.

Evidence of upcoming events, however, papered community boards and storefront windows. Hidden under an advertisement for the upcoming Honey Festival, Sage saw a flier for the Black Mills Health Fair/Dental Clinic and the Summer Nights Half Marathon. She wouldn't attend either but made a mental note to remind Liddy about them.

The door jingled as she entered Black Mills's Grocery Stop. Sage nodded to a checker who looked up from her magazine. The girl's gaze quickly slid back to her reading.

Hoping her favorite energy bars were in, Sage walked

straight to the snack aisle on the far side of the store. Her gaze fell on the familiar cardboard box. Empty again. Did no one else in Black Mills enjoy white chocolate and macadamia nuts? She'd have to settle for another flavor.

"Sage, honey, is that you?"

"Liddy," Sage smiled and allowed herself to be pulled into the older woman's arms and crushed against the barrel-sized chest. She shifted her face to Liddy's shoulder. "I was at the house all morning, but I didn't see you."

Liddy gave her one last squeeze and pushed back. "I was up at the Daydreamer Cabin. We have some new folks coming in this weekend, and I needed to get it all cleaned up." She smiled and gestured to the ratty oversized T-shirt and dingy sweatpants. "Some of the shingles on the front porch overhang are loose. Think you could take a look at that and get it fixed this week?"

Sage rolled her eyes. "Liddy, that roof is hanging on with dental floss and chewing gum. I keep telling you, if you don't replace the whole thing soon, it'll blow away with the next strong wind."

"I know, sweetie, but couldn't you please work your magic on it one more time?" Liddy ran her fingers through her disheveled salt and pepper curls. "I just replaced some old pipes at the Joyful Cabin and don't have any extra cash right now."

"Fine. I'll see what I can do," Sage sighed, aware that Liddy never had any extra cash. Despite Sage's constant harping about long-term upkeep on the rental cabins, Liddy gave away nearly as much money as she earned. The older woman had the tenderest heart of anyone Sage knew, which was the main reason Liddy's was the only foster home Sage hadn't run away from. It was also the reason why Sage continued to live with her, helping with the never-ending list of repairs needed on Liddy's rentals, ones which Liddy found harder and harder to take care of on her own. The older woman had helped Sage when she needed it most. That was something Sage would never forget even though Liddy often drove her crazy.

"Where's Gus?"

"Back at the house," Sage answered.

Liddy followed Sage around as she did her shopping and caught her up on all the local news, not that she really cared. When she wasn't away in the mountains or helping Liddy with her rentals, Sage kept to herself. After several minutes of mindless chatter, Liddy brought up Shaun and Tabitha.

"I've got a bad feeling about those two," Liddy said, shaking her head. "They're locals, born and raised. They wouldn't get lost in either Black Mills or that area around Oriel."

"Excuse me, Liddy." A voice came from behind them. Elena Goodrich, the town librarian and city council member, stood with her cart next to them. "Can you move? I need to get to the cereal behind you."

"We were just talking about Tabitha and Shaun." Liddy said, ignoring Elena's request. "I was telling Sage there's no way they could be lost. The school takes so many field trips up to that neck of the woods, the kids have that place memorized by the time they're out of grade school. It doesn't make any kind of sense."

"Well, the authorities in charge of the case feel--"

"And then," Liddy interrupted Elena, "I talked to Fred Conners today, and he said Search and Rescue discovered Shaun's car a few miles up from the reservoir."

"It didn't say that in the paper," Sage said.

"They found it late last night," Elena snapped. "Sheriff

Davis told us not to say anything. Fred should have kept his big mouth closed."

"Were they in an accident?" Liddy asked.

Elena eyed the two of them stonily for several seconds. Then she shrugged. "Since Fred blabbed everything else, I guess it's alright to tell you. Sheriff Davis said the doors were left wide open, and the battery's dead. But there weren't any signs of an accident or struggle."

"Well, that still doesn't sound good," Liddy said. "My heart just breaks for their parents."

Even Elena's sour expression turned glum at this observation.

"And both of them such good kids too," Liddy shook her head. "Tabitha's been accepted to some fancy Ivy League school out east, and Shaun had a full-ride scholarship to some big Midwestern school. Sweet boy that he is, he gave the scholarship up to take over at his daddy's restaurant. Enos Colter's been in bad health you know, so Shaun said he'd run the restaurant until his dad was feeling better. Course, there's no better for old age—"

"He gave up his scholarship?" Sage cut in, knowing Liddy could ramble for hours. "But he was amazing. Everyone said he was going to be a legend."

"Honey, that's the truth. There was barely room in the bleachers for us ordinary folks at times, what with all the college scouts hanging around with their jaws down to the ground. But Tabitha was just the same with school. From what her mother said, she pretty much had her pick of what school she wanted to attend." Liddy pulled a tissue from her pocket and dabbed at her eyes.

"Why were they out together?" Sage asked, briefly touching Liddy's arm. "Were they a couple?"

"Not as I know of." Liddy took a deep breath. "Just friends."

After another few moments of grieved silence, Sage spoke. "Well, I'd better get back to my shopping. I have a collapsing roof to check on."

"I need to go too. We have another incident meeting scheduled for this afternoon," Elena said. She grabbed a box of cereal and tossed it into her cart. "But first, I've agreed to be with Sheriff Davis when he meets with the parents to update them." She grimaced. "If the two of you could keep your *insider information* quiet until after we break the news to the parents, I'm sure we'd all appreciate it."

Sage and Liddy watched her walk briskly away.

"She's a grumpy old fart, but I feel bad for her. Meeting with the parents would break anyone's heart." Liddy turned and pulled Sage into another bear hug. "Now, I know you're little Miss *Hermit of the Woods*, but promise me you'll be careful out there, wherever it is you wander off to."

Sage bristled. "I'm fine, Liddy. You know I live *out there* more than I live in town. I can take care of myself."

"Now don't get all prickly. Of course you can take care of yourself. You've been doing it since they dropped your little fourteen-year old butt on my doorstep--"

"Fifteen."

"What?" Liddy asked.

"Fifteen. I was fifteen," Sage said, louder this time.

"Fine. Your fifteen-year old butt. The point is ..." Liddy paused and dabbed at her eyes again. "The point is, I want you to be safe, honey. And happy."

"I can promise safe," Sage said and patted the older woman on the shoulder. "Now stop worrying. Gus wouldn't let anything happen to me."

Liddy nodded, pulled Sage into one more hug before her phone beeped and she had to rush away to another landlord emergency. Sage crouched back down, absently clutched a few bars and considered the information Elena had shared.

Even with her loner ways, Sage remembered Shaun and Tabitha. They'd been sophomores when she was a senior. Sage hadn't seen much of them, but everybody knew everybody in a small mountain town high school. Not to mention that it would have been nearly impossible to miss the shining reputations of Shaun and Tabitha.

They were in countless newspaper articles, won every town award, were at every community gathering. Sage also knew they came from safe homes with good parents. The kids who won everything and got scholarships to fancy colleges always came from homes like that. A wave of bitterness washed through her. Maybe their perfect little lives hadn't prepared them for whatever they'd faced in Oriel.

Suddenly her vision dimmed, and Sage's mind swam with dark images of a deserted car and muffled screams.

Go now! Something deep within her gut clenched then pulsed through her chest with an electric jolt that shot Sage to her feet. Dropping the granola bars, she abandoned her shopping and raced back down the street toward Gus and her Jeep. Sean and Tabitha were in terrible danger. Their suffering burned through her consciousness, her body, almost as if it were her own.

As she sprinted down the street, the 4x4 trails around Oriel appeared in Sage's mind like a topographical map. She knew the entire area better than most, at least as well as the Search and Rescue teams that were combing the area. Maybe she could explore a few places that the authorities had overlooked.

CHAPTER FOUR

The sun burned high in the midday sky as Sage wound her way through the disappearing, almost forgotten, logging and mining roads that ringed the rims of the Oriel valley. Ancient aspen, taller here than anywhere she'd ever seen, arched graceful arms to create a rippling green canopy above stark white trunks. In the fall, this would be a pathway of gold, something that looked like it came from the imagination of an artist. But thanks to the condition of the ragged trails and the brevity of human memory, deer, mountain lion, and other wildlife would be the sole beneficiaries of the beauty.

When she saw a meadow through the fluttering aspen leaves, Sage pulled off the road to give the tense muscles in her neck and shoulders a rest. Even though she knew the route, navigating potholes, boulders, and washouts took a toll on her body. She had barely rolled to a stop when Gus leapt from the half door and dashed into the woods.

"Don't go too far!" Sage hollered after him before grabbing her water bottle.

She opened the lid and leaned against the hood of her

car. A breeze sent loose tendrils of dark hair across Sage's cheek and forehead. The forest fell silent and suddenly a picture appeared in her mind: a cave with a glassy pool in front of it, pieces of clothing strewn about the edge of the water, and turbulent pockets of mud and dirty snow marked the edges, hinting at a struggle. Sage tried to turn her mind's eye back toward the opening of the cave, but something stopped her. A jagged rush of screams and terror sliced through her. And blood, everywhere blood.

Sage took a gulp of cold air and opened her eyes. "Oh, Wind," she whispered. "Please don't let it be that bad."

Birdsong returned. A squirrel chattered from the trees above her, but the Wind, aside from its gentle sigh through the leaves, remained silent.

"Come on, Gus," Sage hollered. "It's time to go."

The words were barely out of her mouth before she heard the jingle of dog tags and Gus reappeared. Sage opened her door and the dog hopped across her seat, over to the passenger's side.

About an hour later, Sage suddenly felt the urge to stop. Ahead, she saw a small pullout area and nosed the Jeep over the last few feet of the rugged trail.

Sage found her ragged topographical map in the glove compartment and studied it. After several minutes, she decided she was near one of the old uranium mines. It lay a couple of miles behind the Shelton Reservoir, near the ridge that separated the Black Mills and Oriel Valleys.

After she climbed from the car with Gus, Sage tried to silence her thoughts. She had no idea what to do from here. It was time for the Wind to lead her. She knew from past experience that if she listened, the Wind would usually take her where she was needed.

But never to people, the thought interrupted. Sage

remembered what had the Wind told her the other night. "A change is coming ... as yet, it's only been four legged ones."

Her stomach clenched. The vision she'd seen earlier didn't seem to hint at protection or help. Instead, it cried *death*. Still, she had to try. Suffering, even if it wasn't hers, filled her with visceral, debilitating agitation.

Sage took a deep breath and felt a tug toward the swishing pines at her right, along with a deep foreboding. Hesitantly, she turned back to the Jeep and pulled out a backpack filled with water, some food, and a light jacket. She put a flashlight in the pocket of her cargo pants and slipped a game knife onto her belt.

"Forgetting anything?" She turned to Gus. He gave a half-hearted wave of his tail and trotted to the tree line. Sage took a deep breath and followed.

After several hundred yards of overgrown brush, the forest began to clear. Gus had found some kind of path. On its little used twists and turns, she noticed signs of recent foot traffic: a broken shrub branch, a hardened footprint in the mud, trampled grass, scattered leaves. As she walked further, dread uncurled in her stomach. Gus, who had been running out of sight, returned to her side.

"You feel it too, buddy?" She whispered. Gus whined but continued his steady pace.

After one last bend, they walked into an opening encircled by a large buttress of rock. A deep, dusty depression lay in front of the old mine. The entrance was barred with rotten wood planks and a sign that leaned crazily to one side.

"Dan e eep ou," was all that remained of the sign's original warning.

A vague sense of déjà vu filled Sage as she scanned the

clearing. It looked so similar to the place the Wind had shown her in the vision, but there was no snow or mud here. She crouched and ran her fingers over the hardened, dusty ground. She traced several sets of footprints, at least five that she could identify as separate and distinct. There was, however, no sign of a struggle. All the footprints led to the rotted planks in front of the old mine.

The Wind rushed through the evergreens around her, sounding like the crash of a large waterfall. The scent of pine pollen filled the air, and a woodpecker hammered a staccato beat that accompanied the rustling branches. All normal, peaceful forest sounds, but the misgiving in her stomach grew. Gus whimpered and leaned against her.

Sage stood. She pulled a flashlight from her pocket and tested it, even though she'd replaced the batteries that morning. *You're stalling,* she told herself. The realization didn't sit well.

Sage approached the entrance and peered under a board into the darkness. All encompassing, the gloom gulped the flashlight's beam greedily like a living thing, the glow swallowed only inches from her hand. She knew with every fiber of her being that something evil lay within the mine. But she also knew she had to go in.

Gus whined again. She gently hooked his collar with her fingers and led him toward the trees at the edge of the clearing.

Sage dropped the backpack from her shoulders and set it next to the dog. She rummaged through it until she found her flannel shirt. "This might be bad. You okay to go in with me? You can stay out here if you want."

Gus moaned, licked his lips, but stayed glued to her side.

"Good boy." Sage scratched his ears and turned back.

"Stay close, Gus." The two returned to the rotting boards at the entrance. After several minutes of prying, one finally came loose. Sage threw it to the ground, but something caught her attention. Crouching to study the board more closely, she noticed a row of shiny nails. They glinted in the afternoon sun, and in comparison to the rust-covered originals, were obviously new.

Sage gulped and continued to rip away rotten pieces of wood until she made an opening that Gus could jump through. She then squeezed her lithe frame through the small, jagged opening. A terrible odor greeted her, and it was all she could do not to gag. Placing her nose in the crook of her elbow, she held out her light. Its thin beam reflected off an underground stream that ran along the left edge of the mine shaft tunnel. The trickling water continued into the yawning darkness, past what her beam could illuminate.

Grazing her fingers against the cold, damp stone to her left, Sage walked slowly forward. The temperature dropped at least fifteen degrees inside the chamber, and she was glad for her flannel shirt. The gurgle of the small stream was distinct in the tunnel, then suddenly it wasn't. The space to her right had opened up into a large cavern. She flicked the flashlight toward the gaping emptiness.

Something skittered across the beam's edge, and Sage trailed the light after it. A pair of yellow orbs appeared. When they flicked away, another pair blinked to life, then another and another. The muffled quiet of the cave dissolved and growls surged in a chorus of menace. Gus returned their angry greeting with his own.

Coyotes, at least a dozen of them. The wavering gleam of the flashlight caught the remains of a bloody feast at the pack's feet, which they circled around protectively. Sage hushed Gus and forced herself to hold the flashlight beam steady. She watched the largest coyote from the corner of her eye and took a slow, deliberate step away.

"It's okay, guys," she spoke in a soft, soothing tone. "We're not here to disturb you. Or hurt you." Sage calmed her pounding heart. She had faced coyotes before. They were rarely brave enough to follow their growls with anything other than a hasty retreat. It wasn't in their nature to attack anything much larger than themselves. Sage focused her mental energy on the group. *You are safe. Your kill is safe. Ignore me.*

Another snarl, more fierce than the others, erupted and the coyotes quickly moved to cut off the path toward the entrance of the mine. Gus stepped in front of Sage, hackles raised, and squared off with the lead coyote.

Why aren't they listening? Sage stumbled over a piece of rotted wood. Confusion battled with the tenuous link she had tried to establish with the coyotes. Instead of responding to her, as animals usually did, they herded her and Gus backward, toward the yawning dark tunnel that went deeper into the mountain. The coyotes snapped at her legs when she tried to inch back toward the entrance of the mine.

Be calm. Go back to your kill. We will leave. She reassured them, but it was no use. Something was blocking her communication with them. Their aggression, if anything, intensified, and the pack continued to force her and Gus deeper into the cold, musty mineshaft.

Sage switched the flashlight to her left hand and, giving up on any connection with the hostile animals, pulled the knife out of its sheath on her hip. The stream filled the entire pathway now, and she struggled not to slip over the icy rocks. One large coyote darted toward her and tore at the bare skin on her shins. Crying out, she stumbled over a pile of rubble, barely catching herself against the damp, slimy wall. Fear licked at her stomach like growing flames. Sage knew the coyotes would be on her in a second if she fell.

An almost deafening growl echoed over the others, and the beam of Sage's flashlight began to flicker. Moments later it went out entirely, and panic surged through her. She shook it desperately but nothing happened.

Sage clenched the knife in her right hand, the butt of the flashlight in her left, knowing they were all but useless against a hoard of predators who could smell and probably even see her. She felt Gus dart from her side. An eruption of angry snarls and barking sounded from back toward the large opening where they'd first discovered the coyotes. Sage sensed that Gus was trying to lure the pack away from her.

Her shoulders drooped in relief, but suddenly a slash of teeth cut against her leg, and Sage beat at it with her flashlight. The animal hesitated. She screamed and stabbed at it with the knife before it finally retreated, but she sensed it was still only a few feet away. A loud growl confirmed her fears.

Sage backed up again. Her head and elbows cracked against the narrowing shaft as she stumbled in the darkness, wondering how much longer the tunnel continued. Another couple feet, and her back struck something hard. Had the coyote led her to a dead end? Snarling and snapping at her legs, she felt it draw closer and closer.

Desperate for escape, Sage careened to her left and lost her balance as the rocky floor disappeared from underneath her feet. Her legs shot out from under her, and she slid down. Loose gravel ricocheted off her face and upraised hands, tearing against her legs. Pinwheeling her arms, she dropped both her knife and flashlight and groped frantically into the darkness. Her hands struck against a jagged ledge. Sage grabbed at it with a choking sob, and her legs kicked at vast emptiness beneath her.

Panic pried its way into her chest. So this was how it ended? And where was the Wind now that she really needed it? Regret, followed by a rage so strong it made her shake, bubbled up inside Sage. Her entire life had been one tragedy after another. A cosmic joke with this pitiful grand finale.

The coyote fell silent. After a moment, a grating, rasping laugh echoed against the impenetrable walls and into the emptiness below her, pulling Sage from her wild thoughts. She tightened her grip on the slippery ledge.

"Hello? Is someone up there?"

The terrible stench, the one she'd smelled when she first entered the cave, overwhelmed her. Her eyes strained in the darkness, and two glowing red pricks of light appeared.

"If you can hear me, help. Please!"

A shower of gravel rained down on her, followed by larger stones, ones that almost seemed to be aimed at her head and hands.

Sage screamed as a large rock smashed her weakening fingers against their tenuous hold. Adrenaline exploded in her veins, and Sage's rock climbing skills took over. Pulling herself up, she hooked her left forearm and leg over the rim of the ledge. Desperate fingers found a crack in the wall above. She slid her right hand into it before tensing it into a fist to anchor herself into the cliff. Sage used her body's momentum to swing her other knee over the lip of the overhang.

A roar neither animal nor human ripped through the air, followed by a whooshing sound. Something small and powerful, like a silent bullet, slammed into Sage's left shoulder. The pain was debilitating: liquid fire that radiated from the point of impact through the rest of her body.

Sage slipped back over the edge. All that suspended her from the vast emptiness below was her clenched fist wedged in the crack above. She tried to raise her left arm, but it dangled uselessly by her side, still burning from whatever had shot it.

She could barely breathe against the pain. Jagged rock sliced into her clenched hand and fingers. Her forearm and shoulder trembled against the weight of her dangling body. Warm blood trickled down her arm, and she felt herself slip a few inches. The end was close now.

"Sage!" A voice echoed through the darkness. "Sage, are you in here? I'm coming for you." A faint bobbing light illuminated the cavern above her head, and she heard Gus's angry barking.

"Where are you?" The voice called.

"Here," Sage answered weakly.

Gus's barking grew louder, the light in the cavern swelled, and suddenly a headlamp shined down on her from the ledge above.

"Holy--Gus, shut up!" The dog quieted. "Can you reach my hand?"

"No, something's wrong with my arm. I've got my other hand wedged in a crack."

"Let me find something to tie myself to." The male voice sounded vaguely familiar.

Minutes later loose earth and pebbles peppered her face, then a pair of rough hands clasped her forearm and tugged.

"I've got you. Unclench your fist, and I'll pull you up."

"I don't know if I can."

"Just do it!"

Forcing her mind to focus on the fingers of her numb fist, Sage finally felt her hand relax. She slipped down the rock face for an instant before the strong arms jerked her roughly up the incline, then encircled her.

"Hang on just a second." The arms shifted, pulling her against a warm, sweat dampened shoulder. She heard the rustle and clink of climbing gear as he unclasped himself. Sage tried to catch a glimpse of her rescuer's face, but the headlamp blinded her. One of her trembling legs gave way, and the arms lifted her up. She was carried hurriedly from darkness into the dim light at the mouth of the mineshaft.

"Come on, Gus!" He called, his voice angry, worried. "Come on. Get out of there!"

They crashed through the remaining boards into bright, blinding sunlight. Sage blinked, trying to regain her vision. After being gently released to the ground, something soft was placed under her head. A wet nose and tongue drenched her face.

"Back," he ordered. "Give her space."

The blur above her gradually re-arranged itself into someone she knew. Her mind scrambled, and then came recognition.

"Mr. Tim?" She rasped, "What the hell are you doing here?"

"You're welcome." He swiped a fist across his sweaty forehead. "But why don't we go with just Tim?"

CHAPTER FIVE

"Fine, *just* Tim. How did you ... Where did ..." She struggled to sit up but he gently pushed her back.

"Let's get a look at these injuries before we get into details," he said.

Incoherent words stumbled from Sage's mouth as she tried to argue, but Gus bounded next to her shoulder and snuffled her face. He forced her mouth shut with his relentless face washing and nuzzling. In too much pain to fight both Tim and Gus, Sage wearily closed her eyes. Her mind still reeling, she decided to allow herself a few minutes of recovery.

Tim's firm hands probed the bleeding bite marks that crisscrossed her shins and the numerous cuts on her hands and arms. Nothing too serious, Sage concluded as he moved from one injury to another. But when he touched the wound in her shoulder, red hot pain arced a trail of agony through her body. Sage felt herself hover on the edge of consciousness. After a few moments of semi-awareness, she blinked away the haze and found Tim crouched next to her with a canteen. He was pouring water over her shoulder and using a balled up shirt to wipe away blood.

"The ones on your arms and legs don't look too bad, but this one on your shoulder is strange. I think there's something in here. It's stuck." Sage gasped as his fingers grazed against the place that burned like liquid fire.

Tim moved away, and Sage saw him rummage around in his pack. A battered first aid kit emerged, and Tim pulled out a pair of tweezers and a small bottle of antiseptic. Sage watched as he poured it over the tool and then her shoulder. She allowed herself one groan as the antiseptic did its cleansing work.

"So a teacher and a doctor?" She spoke between clenched teeth. "How did that happen?"

"I did a couple of years of medical school before I decided it wasn't for me. I know enough to do stuff like this. Not enough for open-heart surgery."

"That's too—" She bellowed as Tim dug into her shoulder with the tweezers and found the place of pain again. When he tugged, she felt like her shoulder was being ripped from her body. Finally, there was a release. Tim fell back in the dust, holding the tweezers high.

"Man, that did not want to come out," he said, perspiration and blood streaking his white undershirt. Through the slowly receding waves of agony, Sage saw him study the small object for a moment, before setting the tweezers on a rock. She wondered what it was but couldn't muster the strength to ask, especially once Tim poured antiseptic over the wound. She bit her cheek to keep from crying out when he patted the area dry and covered it with a large bandage.

"Looks like the bleeding is starting to slow." He helped Sage sit up then carefully slipped his zippered hoodie around her shoulders before lowering her back to the ground. "I think we made a good start, but you'll need to have a doctor go over these injuries soon. You might need a few stitches. Probably some rabies shots."

It took several minutes of Gus's comforting licks and Sage's shuddering, deep breaths before she could speak again. "Where's that thing you pulled out of my shoulder?"

Tim reached over and picked up the tweezers. "It's smaller than I expected. A tooth, I guess."

Sage took the tweezers with her good arm. Her mind raced to find another explanation, but inescapable dread enveloped her at the sight of the small, bloody ball. "Not a tooth."

"How can you tell?"

"For one thing, it's not shaped like one. Coyote teeth aren't round."

"Then what else could it be?" Tim asked, taking it back from Sage. Gus leaned against Tim and smelled the object. Rearing back, he barked and retreated behind Sage.

"I think it's some kind of a projectile, probably made out of bone." Sage closed her eyes with resignation.

An 'adagąsh, or cursed object, here, miles away from any Navajo towns? If that's what it truly was, Sage knew she was incredibly lucky Tim had located and removed it before it disappeared into her body forever. Even with her healing abilities, she probably couldn't have survived its deadly corruption. Memories flitted into her mind, ceremonies she had attended with Grandfather Benally when he had been asked to perform a Sing. Sage shuddered. Only a witch would have access to an object this powerful and dangerous, but what was a witch doing in a boarded mine shaft miles away from Navajo land?

"It's made out of bone?" Tim's gaze traveled between the tweezers and her. "But I thought you were attacked by a pack of coyotes. How'd you get shot with this bone thing?"

"Where's your canteen? I need a drink." She wished he had something stronger than water.

"It's empty," Tim shook the canteen. "But I've got a fresh one in here." He rummaged again through his backpack.

After he handed it to her, Sage took a sip. "What else you got in there, Boy Scout?"

"Everything I need. Some climbing equipment, a change of clothes, rain poncho, night vision goggles. You know, the typical." He grinned at her.

Sage almost smiled too, but then the reality of last hour came rushing back. She shuddered. "I could have used the night vision goggles a few minutes ago."

Tim's eyes hardened. "To see the coyotes?"

"I'm not sure," Sage said. "It was so dark, but I sensed ... It was almost like—" She fell silent.

"What?" Tim leaned in.

The deeply tanned skin of Tim's forehead creased in concern. Sage noticed a few stray strands of silvery white that speckled the rest of his jet black hair. Incongruous with the rest of his young face, he looked to be not much older than her, probably in his mid-20s. He radiated a stillness that tempted Sage to let her guard down, but she still didn't trust the guy. The images the Wind had revealed to her earlier compelled Sage to come look for Shaun and Tabitha, but Tim wasn't part of the plan. Wasn't it a little too convenient that he happened to be here the moment she needed him? The sooner she got rid of this guy, the better.

A breeze touched her shoulder and a soft whisper sounded in her ear. *You cannot fight this battle alone, Broken One.* Sage shook away the words as soon as she heard them.

She wasn't thinking straight. It was time to regain control of the situation.

"So, thanks for the help. I'm fine now. You can head on out," Sage braced herself on a nearby rock and shakily rose to her knees.

"Excuse me?" Tim dropped his backpack and reached out for Sage. She swatted his hand away and stood.

"What do you think you are doing?" He asked rising with her, trying to steady her again, but Sage took a wobbly step back. "You need to get to a doctor."

Sage slowly unzipped his hoodie and tossed it at him before limping over to her own backpack. She rummaged around its contents until she found her small battery-powered lantern and flicked it on. Sage shook it to see if there were any loose connections. It worked just fine now, but so had the flashlight before she went into the mine.

Frustration at Tim's presence and dread at what she suspected was waiting for her in the dark tunnels of the mountain surged through her. She dropped the remains of her tattered flannel shirt and pulled on a fresh sweatshirt from her pack, ignoring the pain in her shoulder and the torn skin on her arms.

She felt his presence hovering behind her. "I found something in there." Sage said. "I *need* to get back inside the mine and check it out. I think it might be ... might have something to do with Shaun and Tabitha."

"Shaun and Tabitha?"

"Those two kids missing from Black Mills."

"I know who they are." Tim's voice came sharply from behind her. "That's why I'm here. I couldn't get them off my mind today, so I canceled my appointments and decided to help look around."

Sage turned to study him. *What a coincidence.*

Tim continued, "I hiked a couple of trails in the area, looking for something, a clue, I guess, then heard barking. I followed the sound and saw a dog chasing a bunch of coyotes out of the mine. I thought I recognized Gus and told him to find you. We ran down the shaft and found ..."

He shook his head and Sage's stomach clenched. She knew what Tim *would* have found if he'd arrived only a few moments later.

Sage sighed. "Well, I'm going back in there." She took a few more steps to test her legs. Almost back to normal. "You can come with me or not. I don't really care."

Tim shook his head. "Look, you're probably in shock. First, let's get you to a doctor, then I'll go contact the authorities and bring them back here. You should not be on your feet." He planted himself in front of her and crossed his arms.

Sage considered her options. Even as the image of punching him in the face flickered through her mind, she knew she wasn't yet healed enough to force her way past Tim. Besides, she was still curious about his presence. Was it really only by chance he was in the same remote area as her? Probably not. Observing him a bit longer might help her decide what really lay behind his Boy Scout facade.

"If there's any chance of us saving those kids," she said, hoping his sense of duty would override his apparent concern for her, "I think we should go back in there. Don't you? A few more minutes isn't going to affect me one way or the other."

Tim took a deep breath. "I don't think it's wise for *you* to go back in there, but yes, I guess Shaun and Tabitha trump that. I'll come with you if you insist on staying."

Sage nodded and walked back to the mine's opening.

"Hold on a minute, will you? Let me grab my flashlight

... and a big stick," Tim muttered from behind her. She heard him rustling through his bag.

"I don't think a stick's going to do a whole lot of good with what I encountered in there." Sage shone her lantern into the opening of the shaft. "Let's get this over with."

Gus leaned against her, and she buried her hand in the furry warmth of his shoulder. The dog nosed his head under her hand. When Sage glanced down, she found Gus's eyes trained on her. He whined softly and gave her a reassuring wag of his tail.

Sage smiled at him, then glanced over her shoulder. "Ready, Boy Scout?"

"I am. Let's go."

CHAPTER SIX

Tim pulled away the last of the rotten planks, and Sage searched the oppressive darkness for any sign of movement, animal or otherwise.

"Follow me," Sage said and led them through the entrance tunnel, down the shaft, and into the yawning cavern. "Over there." She gestured with the light. "That's where the coyotes were when I first came in." She started forward.

"Now, just hold on." Tim grabbed her arm and pulled her back.

Sage swore in pain as his fingers clamped around one of the gashes on her arm. "Let me go!" She tried to jerk away, but Tim held her wrist tight.

His gaze, illuminated by her lantern, darted around wildly. "We don't even know what's in here—coyotes or some other wild animal. Let's not rush in and get ourselves killed."

Sage jerked again and pulled free from his grasp. "You need to calm down, Tim. There's nothing in here." She glanced down at Gus to confirm and saw the faint movement of his tail wagging.

Along with the many unnatural abilities her dog had exhibited since the night of her family's death, a perception of danger, even more sensitive than hers, was one of his most valuable assets. Gus almost always noticed things before she did.

Tim ignored her and hung back at the mouth of the cavern. Sage sighed. Even though Gus didn't seem to feel anything, she closed her eyes and forced herself to listen. Awareness burrowed its way into her mind with a quicksilver sting. Images appeared, staggering in their clarity. Snapshots of life burned into her inner eye.

All the coyotes were gone. Besides them, the only living things in the cave were a few bugs and a snake sleeping behind a boulder.

"We're safe, Tim. It's empty," Sage said, knowing her assurance sounded trite despite its validity.

"Well, I'm not taking that for granted until we do a sweep to make sure."

"Fine. Do your *sweep*. But I promise you we're alone," Sage sighed. What had happened to the tough guy that had rescued her less than an hour ago? She watched as Tim crept cautiously to the left, down the tunnel into which the coyotes had driven her. Gus whined, and Sage gestured for him to follow Tim down the tunnel. Maybe the dog could help calm Tim down. He seemed ready to jump at his own shadow.

"What a weirdo," Sage muttered and turned to study the various openings around her. To her left, the mine entrance, where Gus and Tim had just disappeared, was in bad shape. Water dripped from the ceiling and trickled down dark, slimy walls to the small icy stream she had stumbled through while trying to escape the coyotes. Sage eyed the decrepit support beams and cross sections installed by miners nearly a century ago and wondered how much longer until the rotted wood gave way and the entire mine disappeared into rock and dust.

When she swung her beam to the right, it illuminated a large cave that hadn't been engineered by human hands; however, the ancient smoke stains that darkened the ochre-gray walls and ceiling suggested human habitation in the past. Pictographs, now faint under the discoloration, decorated the cave's walls.

Sage approached the spidery drawings and studied them. Rather than the hunting scenes that she usually saw in ancient rock art, these appeared to show a battle between two groups of humans. She recognized both horses and guns which meant the pictograph wasn't as old as she'd first thought. Sage's gaze traveled to the large, dark figure that overshadowed the warriors on the left side of the battlefield. Wolf-like from the chest up, the creature stood on its hind legs with its claws stretched over the whole scene. Sage took a step back, disquieted by the eeriness of the image.

She turned just as Tim and Gus came back through the tunnel. They waded through the small stream and joined her in the large cavern.

"We didn't go too far, but I think you're right. The coyotes are gone. Gus must have scared them all away."

They stood in the deepening silence for several moments before Tim took a deep breath. "It's time to show me what you discovered."

Her feet felt lead weighted as Sage led them around the rock undulation that hid a part of the cave from view. Gus trailed behind them. The smell of decay grew as they continued. Sage jerked to a halt when she finally recognized objects in the horrifying chaos. Bones, flesh, hair, and clothes tangled themselves in a bloody heap. Gus whined and settled at her feet.

"Dear God, no," Tim whispered. He sank to his knees and dropped his light.

Sage rescued it from the ground and used it with her lantern to light the remains and tracks around them. The kill was fresh, only a day or two old, she could tell, but the coyotes had been thorough in their work. It was impossible to definitively tell who or what lay in the sad desecration before them, but in her heart she knew.

"This can't be them, can it? Coyotes did this?" Tim looked up at her with a tear streaked face.

"Yes," Sage answered, quietly. "It's Shaun and Tabitha."

Tim turned back, and Sage saw him cross himself. The gesture punched her in the gut, and after setting his light next to him, she walked away.

Tim's words, prayers she guessed, echoed around the chamber, hypnotic in their repetition. Their sound retreated into the background when Sage approached the edge of the cave. A breeze came from the direction of the open shaft, and she caught the hint of another scent, one that had been obscured by the stench of death.

Sage dropped down on all fours and brought her nose to the ground, hoping she would be able to follow the faint scent to its source. Along the edge of the rock walls, underneath the petroglyphs, the cavern narrowed into another small tunnel. Here the ceiling was only a few feet above the ground, and Sage had to army crawl through the last section.

When she came to the end of the small opening, she set the lantern down, its beam aimed against the mica flecked wall. The scent ended here, and she began to dig; the loose, sandy gravel easily gave way to her strong fingers. Before long, she detected a foreign object, something hard and cold. Sage picked it up, and the jagged edge sliced her finger. She swore and dropped it back in the sand.

Sage wiped the bloodied finger on her shirt and popped it into her mouth. The faint taste of chemicals burned across her tongue. With her uninjured hand, she cautiously picked up the object again. It appeared to be a broken tube of glass, almost like a vial. Written on the side, she could barely make out the faint letters L O Z A. Sage brought it to her nose and smelled before reeling back and nearly smacking her head against the low ceiling. It was definitely the scent she'd detected near the bodies.

"Sage, where'd you go?" Tim's voice echoed down the tunnel until it found her.

"Here." Sage called and, after a moment of hesitation, placed the glass fragment, jagged side out, in her shirt pocket. Removing this clue from this soon-to-be crime scene was probably against the law, but she felt compelled to take it. Sage then inched backward until the space finally opened up enough for her to turn and crawl out.

"We need to call the police. Do you have a cell phone?" Tim said when she reappeared.

"Nope. Besides, you don't call the police if it's outside city limits. You call the Sheriff," Sage said. A fact that she wished she'd never had to learn.

"Well, either way. My battery's dead. I guess we have to drive back into town. We'll tell whoever we need to and let them deal with all of this."

Sage considered his words. "Just how much confidence do you have in the law around here?"

"I haven't ever considered that before." Tim answered. "I think most of them are good people."

"That's not what I'm asking, although it's nice to know you think they're *good people*. But I've seen *good people* do irreversible harm despite their very best intentions."

"I'm not following you."

"Does anyone in Black Mills's middle-of-nowhere Sheriff's or Coroner's Office have any forensic training? Resources to analyze the evidence?" She gestured to the grisly remains at the other end of the cave.

"Probably not," Tim admitted. "But why would they need to? Isn't this just a simple animal attack?" He glanced over his shoulder and rubbed his eyes for a moment before continuing. "Two kids wandered too far, ran into some possibly rabid coyotes, and were killed?"

Sage just stared at him, and Tim finally looked away. Letting out a sigh of disappointment, she returned to the remains.

Could he be right? It was weird behavior for coyotes, but ... Sage pressed her aching temples. Would the Wind really have sent her out here for a coyote attack, one that had already come to a tragic end? And what about the vial she'd found? And the dark presence that had tried to send her tumbling to her death?

Suddenly, all she wanted was a breath of clean air. "Come on. We can talk outside," Sage said and jogged out into the sunlight where she filled her lungs with deep gulps of pine-sweetened air. She glanced at the sky above her; it was late afternoon and evening was rapidly approaching. Decision time.

Whatever they decided needed to be done quickly.

There wasn't a snowball's chance in hell she was spending the night here. Not with whatever had shot her in the mine lurking somewhere in the forest. Although faint, she could still detect its presence. Was it waiting for dark to fall?

Tim tapped her on the shoulder.

Sage jumped. "What?"

"Maybe there's more to this than an animal attack." Tim said. After a pause, he straightened and looked into her eyes. Sage returned his fierce gaze. Here, once again, was the forceful guy who'd pulled her from the mine shaft.

"There was ... something in there when I found you." Tim crossed his arms. "I don't know what it was, but I didn't imagine it. I know I didn't."

"What did you see?" She asked.

"I'm not sure, but it wasn't a coyote. For one thing it was taller. Just bigger." His brow furrowed, and he shook his head.

"What do you mean? Was it a human?"

"No. I don't know." He ran a hand through his sweat and dust dulled hair. "It was dark and chaotic. I heard screams, yours, I think, and growling coyotes. Gus was barking as we ran, and I knew I needed to find you fast." He looked down at the ground then back at her, confusion written across his face . "Whatever it was, I only caught a quick glance out of the corner of my eye when it ran past me. I don't think it wanted to be seen."

Sage studied the dense forest that surrounded them. Tim cleared his throat and stepped away.

"You must think I'm crazy."

Sage glanced over her shoulder at him and shook her head. "No, I don't." She wished she could write off Tim's impressions as the wild imaginings of a panicked mind. But the growing conviction that she knew this thing, that it wasn't her imagination or Tim's, made her want to run back to the Jeep and race for home.

After several moments of silence, Tim interrupted her thoughts. "What about you? Did you see anything when you were in there?"

Sage sighed. "You got a camera?"

"What?" Tim asked.

"A camera. I know your cell's dead, but--

"I've got my SLR digital camera. In my pack."

"Of course you do. Next to the night vision goggles?" Sage shook her head. "I think we need to get in there and take a few pictures before we report this to anyone. Just in case."

"I guess, but we've got to hurry. It'll be dark soon, and I don't have my overnight gear. Not that I'd stay here." He shuddered and walked over to his backpack.

Sage watched him sort through his pack's contents, her mind hijacked by the remains in the cave. Revulsion gnawed at her stomach. Her suggestion to photograph the evidence in the mine was a Hail Mary pass. No matter what Sage did, no matter what plan she came up with, two young lives had been snuffed out. Nothing she could do would change that. A deep sadness overwhelmed her, and Sage gasped as it constricted her lungs.

Get ahold of yourself! She forced herself to take several deep breaths. Whatever had happened in that cave, she needed to give it her full attention, without any emotions splitting her focus. Sage closed her eyes and forced herself to picture a closet in an endless, sterile hallway. After opening the door, Sage shoved everything she was feeling, the pain, the fear, the anger, onto the shelves of the dark room. The door of the mental storage closet clicked shut, and Sage saw herself flip the lock.

She opened her eyes and listened to the chattering of two chipmunks wrestling in the branches above her while Tim removed his camera from its case and cleaned the lens. A small whisper of relief threaded through her now desensitized mind. At least she didn't have to go back into the mine alone.

CHAPTER SEVEN

Tim and Sage spent a hurried half-hour photographing anything they thought could be a clue: the remains and the perimeter around them, blood stains on the cave floor, the new nails on the boards used to cover the cave entrance, even the pictographs on the cave wall. Tim's digital SLR camera had a great flash and amazing resolution. He assured Sage that they'd be able to examine everything in detail, even magnified, after he downloaded the pictures onto his computer.

"Magnified, great," Sage echoed. Glancing down at the gnawed, bloody heap of bones, Sage forced the rising bile back down her throat. She took several more shots then returned the camera to Tim.

As Tim moved to take a few more pictures, Sage glanced over her shoulder to the tunnel the coyote creature had forced her down. The dark, gaping passage called to her. She had avoided it since they had re-entered the mineshaft, yet she felt inexorably drawn to it. Shining her light into its shadows, Sage gathered her courage and forced herself back down the tunnel. The icy water enveloped her legs again, but finding footing was much easier with the help of her lantern. The water disappeared from where it came, back under the mountain about a 100 feet down the constricting tunnel. On the bank of the small stream, Sage knelt to study the dusty ground. A distinct set of paw prints marked the dirt, much larger than normal coyote impressions.

"Tim," she hollered. "Come take a picture of this."

"Coming." His flashlight bounced and water splashed as he descended into the bowels of the mountain.

"Gus, sit," Sage ordered, not wanting the dog to disturb what she'd discovered. "That paw print." She pointed as Tim knelt next to her. "See how one pad is shorter and sticks out at a strange angle from the others? I think it must be broken or deformed. Can you get a picture of it?"

"Good idea." Tim snapped several photos from different angles. "A park ranger might be able to identify it. Plus if there's a pack of infected coyotes, they need to either put them down or treat them."

"So we're back to the coyote story?"

"Regardless of what else may or may not have been in this cave, we both agree there were coyotes, right?" Tim glanced up at her.

"Yes."

"And they were incredibly aggressive toward you. That alone merits a report to Parks and Wildlife."

"I guess." Sage rose and followed the tracks another twenty yards. "Good thing you came when you did." She gestured with her lantern when Tim and Gus approached. He shined his beam down into darkness, and they peered into the jagged opening that Sage had dangled from earlier.

"Looks pretty deep," he said, his voice distorted by an echo. "I wonder how far it goes."

Sage picked up a rock and dropped it down the chasm. "One one thousand, two one thousand ..." She got to *seven one thousand* before they heard an audible plunk. "About eight hundred feet, I'd guess, give or take." Her words faded away and deep silence surrounded them, interrupted only by the irregular plink of dripping water.

"So it forced you down here?" Tim asked.

"Yep."

"It's almost like it knew what it was doing." His voice dropped to a whisper.

"Almost." A shiver raced across her shoulders, and Sage wanted nothing more than to feel sunlight on her face again. "Let's get out of here. I think we got everything."

Not caring if Tim followed, she turned and jogged back up the mineshaft. The jog turned into a sprint, and she stumbled over the rotten planks of wood they'd left near the opening. Sage barely made it to the edge of the clearing before she fell to the ground and vomited. Over and over, she heaved, even when nothing remained in her trembling body. She heard Gus whine and felt him settle against her back.

"It's all right, Sage." Tim's voice came from behind her. After a moment, she felt the weight of his hand on her bowed head. "Everything's all right."

Sage jerked away and wiped her mouth with a shaking hand. "How can you say that?" she croaked. "Did you not see what happened to those two?"

"They're at peace." Tim crouched next to her. "They aren't suffering anymore."

Sage shook her head, but a soft breath of air brushed her damp forehead. "He's right, Broken One," the Wind whispered in her ear. "They're at peace now. Their journey with suffering is at an end."

"Let me get you something to drink."

"Thanks," she croaked when he handed the canteen to her.

"You rest. I'm going to try and put the boards back on the entrance. To keep it safe until the authorities get here."

Sage nodded and leaned against an aspen trunk while Gus licked at the gashes on her legs. The gentle breeze soothed her throbbing head. Sage closed her eyes, trying to regain her earlier attitude of detachment, but the vision she'd had earlier flashed again into her mind.

Why did it keep interrupting her thoughts? None of the details matched the reality that surrounded her. The vision showed a cave with a pool in front of it; torn clothes strewn about the edge of the pond and turbulent pockets of mud and snow; jagged screams and terror; blood, everywhere blood.

Sage opened her eyes and studied the dusty depression where Tim's pack lay next to her own. Dry as a bone. No snow, no torn clothes, no screams. And there was no cave; just the dilapidated entrance to an old mine. Nothing matched, yet in her gut she *knew* it was the same place as her vision.

Tim shouldered both packs and turned to her. "Ready to head out?"

"Yes." Sage sighed as she rose. The answer was here, she just needed more time to make the connections. But it was late, and she wanted to get far away from this place before nightfall.

"Wait," Tim said when they reached the edge of the clearing. He turned back. "I forgot my tweezers and that tooth ... bone thing. Whatever it was."

Sage shuddered and followed him. "Don't touch it. Do you have a bag you could put it in?"

Tim knelt before the tweezers and hesitated.

"What?" Sage asked.

"Well, the tweezers are here, but the bone thing's gone." He sifted through the dirt and pebbles surrounding the rock while Gus diligently followed with his nose. Finally Tim stood and shrugged. "It's not here."

The sun disappeared behind a cloud and Sage's gaze darted around the clearing. Now it seemed almost as sinister as the mine. "We should have bagged it sooner."

"Maybe the breeze blew it away?" Tim slipped his tweezers into his pocket.

"Maybe. Probably not," Sage said. Thunderheads scuttled above them and plunged the woods into shadowy darkness.

"Let's go," Sage whispered and in silent agreement the three of them raced along the trail.

"Where's your car?" She asked, out of breath, once they were back at the Jeep.

"Didn't drive. I hiked." Tim hitched the backpack on his hips and secured the waist belt.

"All the way from town?"

"No, outside of town some retired guy pulled over and asked me if I wanted a ride. He dropped me off a few miles away from here."

"That's convenient." The words left Sage's mouth before she could stop them.

"What do you mean?" Tim looked up.

She opened the tailgate, and Gus hopped in. "This place is off the beaten path. It's pretty *convenient* that you happened to arrive here minutes after I was attacked."

"I don't understand," Tim said, his eyes hardening. "Are you accusing me of something?"

Sage leaned against the Jeep; she watched him but remained silent.

Tim glared at her, his cheeks flushed. After a few moments, Sage turned and studied Gus. The dog offered her a panting grin but nothing else. Suddenly drained of all energy, Sage sighed and walked around to the driver's side.

"Get in the car," she said. "I'll give you a ride back into town. You can't rely on mysterious drivers all the time. They tend not to follow through when you need them the most."

"Thanks," Tim said getting in. He remained silent for the rest of the trip.

Sage shot him an occasional glance, but her focus on navigating the rough road conditions soon eclipsed the many questions that still clawed at the edge of her mind.

CHAPTER EIGHT

Darkness blanketed Black Mills by the time Sage and Tim pulled into town.

"You want me to drop you off at your house?" Sage asked.

Tim considered for a minute. "The police department is closer than my house. Why don't we go there, and dispatch will probably put us through to whoever we need to talk to?"

"The police department?" Sage dropped her foot off the clutch, and the Jeep nearly stalled.

"Is that a problem?"

"No, it's fine," Sage answered weakly. She gunned her engine back to life and turned toward the small police station on Main Street while trying to calm her racing heart. "I'm just ready for this to be over with."

"Me too."

Sage coasted into a parking spot on the nearly deserted street and killed the engine. She opened her door, but Tim hesitated.

"What is it?" She asked.

"I'm thinking about Shaun and Tabitha's families. In a very short time they're going to learn their worst fears are true."

Sage leaned back against her seat. "Well, at least they'll know instead of wondering what happened to the people they loved. Knowing is better than ..." Her voice cracked, and she took a deep shuddering breath. "It's better than spending your life searching for a truth you can't find."

Tim turned to her. "Did you--"

"Come on." Sage swung herself from the car and opened the door for Gus. "Let's get this over with."

Tim stopped to get his backpack and followed Sage to the glass door. They entered and looked around, but the small reception area was completely deserted.

"Hello?" Sage hollered. "Anyone here?"

"It looks like everyone's gone for the night." Tim pulled a dirty brown phone across the counter and picked up the handset. "Hello, Dispatch? This is Tim Burgney, and I think I have some important information. Our discovery concerns Shaun Coulter and Tabitha Smalley. We think we found their ... remains."

Sage watched Tim's expression mutate into a scowl.

"Well, can you patch me through to the Sheriff?"

Another silence and then Tim snapped, "This is my official report. I need to speak to someone because I'm certainly not waiting until tomorrow." He fell silent and listened to the phone while Sage tried to hide her growing agitation. Past visits to police stations replayed through her mind with disturbing clarity. They weren't fond memories.

Tim finally replaced the handset in the cradle.

"What going on?" Sage asked.

"They said they'd send someone over, but it might take a while. Evidently *all* the officers and deputies in the county are tied up. Someone shot some fireworks off on 8th Street, and a shed caught on fire."

Sage snorted. "Small town drama. Well, whatever. I'm out of here." She snapped her fingers, and Gus rose from the floor and trotted to her side.

"You can't leave. We have to report what we saw up there."

"You stay if you want, Tim, but I'm not going to wait around all night."

"But what about the kids' parents?" He asked.

"I don't know them."

"Who cares? It's your responsibility to report this. How can you be so callous?"

Sage closed her eyes. She saw another room, similar to one where she'd locked away her emotions after that day's grisly discovery. But this was the room she rarely opened the door to. She watched the handle rattle and knew it was time to leave.

"Look, Tim, it's not going to take two of us to report what we found. Besides, you're a teacher, right? I'm sure you know all the authorities, the parents, everyone who needs to know."

"You're just going to bail on me?" Tim took a step toward her. Disbelief enhanced the fine lines around his eyes.

Sage looked away. The poor kids were already dead. She couldn't do anything to help them now. She still didn't even understand why the Wind had dragged her into this tragedy.

Gus nosed her hand, and she looked down at him. *What are we even doing here, boy?* The dog gazed at her unblinkingly. Sage knew that look; it oozed with self-righteousness.

She nudged Gus with her foot. *Maybe you should have stayed in the car.*

Gus chuffed, then, tail wagging, walked over to Tim and sat at his feet.

"Excuse me," a voice interrupted. Sage and Tim jumped.

They turned and saw an officer with a laptop standing behind the wooden desk. "I understand you think you may have some information about the Coulter-Smalley disappearance."

"Where the hell did you come from?" Sage snapped. "Did you not hear us before?"

"Yes, officer." Tim hurriedly stepped in front of Sage. "We're ready to talk if you are."

"Follow me, please." The officer turned and led them through several desks.

"Hey, you need to calm down a little," Tim whispered, as they walked. "You don't want to antagonize the guy."

"I couldn't care less about antagonizing him. This is his *job*."

"Just let me do the talking until you cool down. You still need to get to the hospital tonight, and I'd rather we wrap this up as quickly as possible."

"The hospital?" Sage stopped short. "Why?"

Tim stopped and shook his head. "You may have forgotten, but a coyote pack attacked you a few hours ago." He gestured to her legs, now hidden by a fresh set of pants from her camping gear. "You might still need stitches, and probably a rabies shot. You have to be in pain, right?"

"Right. Guess I ... got so focused on this that I blocked it out," Sage said, knowing most of the wounds were already gone, except the one in her shoulder. It still stung.

The man stood beside an open door and gestured for them to enter.

"Now why don't you two tell me what you think you saw," the officer instructed once they all sat.

"Why do you keep saying *think* like we're trying to report some elaborate story we made up?" Sage snapped.

Tim put a restraining hand on her forearm. "What's your name, sir?"

"Olson," the man answered without looking up from his computer.

"Officer Olson, I'm Tim Burgney. My friend Sage and I've seen some pretty horrific things today, and we are both a little shaken up."

Olson finally raised his eyes from the screen. "Just tell me what you saw."

Tim quickly launched into their discovery in the mine, probably to keep her quiet. As she listened, however, Sage relaxed. Tim was both articulate and detailed but wisely left out some of the more unbelievable details, like the coyotes forcing Sage down the mine shaft and the disappearing projectile. She appreciated his discretion and kept silent except to agree the few times Tim checked with her for confirmation.

When Tim finished, Olson glanced up from his computer. "I'm going to re-read through the details of your statement and check to make sure I got everything right. That okay with you?"

"Yes." Sage nodded. Maybe the guy was finally taking them seriously.

Unfortunately over the next hour of grilling, Sage and eventually even Tim seemed to realize that Olson had no interest in their findings; only in discrediting them.

"So you say the coyotes ran at you when you first

entered the mine?" He asked Sage for what seemed like the hundredth time. Tim squeezed her arm and excused himself to the bathroom.

"Yes," she answered dully, not sure how much more she could take of this.

"I find that hard to believe, Miss ..."

"Sage's fine."

"Coyotes don't usually attack grown adults."

She crossed her arms. "Guess these ones didn't read their instruction manual."

Olson's face grew red. "If you were attacked as violently as you claim, how were you even able to walk in here? Where is the evidence of your injuries?"

Not this again, Sage's stomach clenched. Olson's smirk brought back too many memories of similar meetings, with social workers, police, teachers; all with demands for evidence her body wouldn't let her provide. Moments of fear and confusion from her childhood paraded through her mind like a macabre play.

She remembered the time Uncle Brian beat her so badly that even the meth heads from the trailer next door had noticed and called the police. By the time the cops had arrived, loaded her into the ambulance, and got her to the hospital, her injuries were already almost gone. From behind the curtain that enclosed her hospital bed, she had heard the doctors and police whispering. They agreed that the meth heads had exaggerated the situation. Besides, without evidence, their hands were tied. The kid was weird, but not seriously injured.

Gus nuzzled her leg, rescuing her from the unwanted memory, and Sage shook herself. Enough of this. She had to get away from this idiot and back outside. It was impossible to focus in here. She needed the Wind and its clarity; nothing about this day made sense.

"Well, I'm done." Sage stood and shoved the chair behind her. "I've given you my info, and grilling me with more dumbass questions isn't going to change anything."

"Excuse me?" Glaring at her from across the table, Olson snapped the computer shut.

"I said—"

"Wait a second," Tim said from where he'd stood, unnoticed, at the door. "I think we're all a little on edge. Our town's lost two young people. Even if the remains turn out not to be theirs, Sage and I discovered something terrible. It's been a long day. Surely you understand we're exhausted, and Sage should be getting some medical attention as soon as possible."

Olson narrowed his eyes. "Listen, buddy, I don't like the way—"

"There seems to be a communication problem between you and us, Officer, so I took the liberty of contacting the Sheriff's Office." Tim moved to stand over Olson, his voice no longer friendly. "It sounds like they're sending someone over. My guess is they should be here any minute. Why don't Sage and I stretch our legs while we wait?"

Olson's chair squealed, and he rose to face Tim. After a brief glaring contest, Olson grabbed his computer and stormed from the interview room.

Sage stood and let out a sharp laugh. "How did you do that? I thought your phone was dead."

"Yeah, it was." Tim smiled. "I wasn't going to the bathroom. I ran out to the Jeep, grabbed my phone and charger and found an outlet in an empty office."

"I'm impressed," Sage said. And she was. Tim gave off a

follow-the-rules, good guy vibe. She hadn't expected him to think outside of the box.

Still, she couldn't wait to get out of here and hopefully never cross paths with the guy again. What did she really know about Tim, anyway? They'd been thrown together in a way that bypassed her typical protective barriers. Besides Liddy and Gus, Sage purposefully kept her world small and safe. She didn't want this ripple-effect of new acquaintances and contacts. Things needed to return to normal as quickly as possible.

Footsteps sounded in the hallway, followed by raised voices. Sheriff Davis burst into the room, followed by a loudly protesting Olson.

The next twenty minutes were drastically different than the ones that preceded them. While Olson had stalled and tried to find flaws in both Sage and Tim's accounts, the sheriff listened, tight-lipped, with few interruptions. Sage even found herself responding to a few of Sheriff Davis's perceptive questions toward the end of their interview. Once finished, Davis barked a series of orders into his phone, directives meant to send much of the law enforcement of the town and county into action.

"So what was that guy's problem anyway?" Tim asked as the sheriff walked them to Sage's car.

"Olson? I have no idea," Davis said. "Thought he'd been kind of a bump on a log in this department, according to the local gossip. Maybe you rubbed him the wrong way."

Tim nodded.

"I know I did," Sage said.

A brief grin split the sheriff's tense face. "I know you did too. You can bet your boots he won't like either of you by the time I finish reaming his Police Chief. Now if you'll excuse me, I got a couple of rough hours ahead of me." He glanced down at his chirping phone and swore softly. "Looks like some campers from Texas have gone AWOL too. Guess this isn't the only missing persons case in the valley anymore." He glanced at Tim and Sage. "Thank you, both of you, for all your patience," he said, then hurried off to his truck.

"Where do you want me to drop you?" Sage asked once they were in the car.

Tim slammed the car door. "We're not headed to my place. We need to get you to the hospital. I'm worried you might be in shock. You don't seem to be in pain at all, and that's not normal." He reached toward Sage's forehead.

Sage jerked away from his hand. *Not normal?* The story of her life. "You need to stop worrying about me. I can take care of myself."

"But what if they keep you overnight? I could watch Gus. Or drop him off somewhere."

"Just tell me where you live, Tim. I want this day to be over."

"Listen, you've *got* to get those wounds looked at. The sooner you get a rabies shot, the better. It's not something to mess around with."

Sage weighed her options. Concern creased Tim's forehead, but his jaw was clenched in determination. This guy was almost as stubborn as her. "Okay, Boy Scout. If you let me drop you off, I promise I'll get the care I need."

"Really? But I think we should—"

"Really. And I don't usually make promises. This is the best you're going to get."

Tim sighed and gave her a short nod. "I live in the yellow apartment building on 4th, just down the street and to the right. Do you know it?"

Sage jerked the car into gear and drove. As with most

places in the small mountain town, it only took her a few minutes to get there. The second Tim's feet hit the pavement, her Jeep peeled away.

On the drive home, Sage's usually quick mind felt like it was struggling through a morass of bewildering details. The house was dark and deserted when she pulled up. Liddy must be with friends or staying at one of her cabins. Sage was thankful for the solitude. Pausing only to remove her shoes, she flung herself on the bed where Gus had already burrowed under the covers.

She spooned her body around the dog and considered how differently this day would have gone if Tim hadn't joined her. Would she be dead, or worse yet, stranded at the bottom of a cavern with no way of escape? Or, what if by some miracle, she'd escaped the madness in the mine shaft and then decided to go to the police on her own? With Olson's strangely antagonistic behavior, would she have spent the night in a jail cell?

Sage chewed on her lip until she tasted blood. Tim's presence wove through this day like the bright red threads of the rug next to her.

She shoved the dirty clothes away and traced the Navajo rug's rough weave, remembering when Grandfather Benally had given it to her.

"It is a *Ye'i* rug" he explained to her. "It was woven by my mother, but the elders of her clan did not like it. They ordered her to bury it because it was wrong to make images of the Holy People."

"But she didn't listen?" Sage asked from where she sat on the dirt floor, cross-legged. Even in the dim interior of the hogan she could see their forms clearly. She traced their strange faces with her fingertips.

"No." Grandfather Benally chuckled. "My mother

knew that she didn't need to fear the Holy People, only respect them, so she finished weaving this rug. She had the spirit of a rebel in her heart. You remind me of her very much.

"This is why I gave you her name, Sage. Sagebrush is impossible to destroy. Fire, drought, snow, wind; none of these can kill it. Sage survives, no matter what. My mother survived many hard things, and you have too.

"That is also why I want you to have this rug. Take it with you when the government people come to get you. It will help you to remember me and your *Diné* family. It will help you remember that you belong to a people who survive."

Sage grimaced. Social services came later that day to remove her from Grandfather Benally's ranch and large, tangled family. She pleaded with the case worker to let her remain, but an underage runaway's words didn't hold much sway. This dusty Navajo sheep farm in the middle of the New Mexican desert had been the first place Sage felt loved or safe in the five long years since her family's annihilation. But even with Grandfather's promises of protection, the State felt Sage would be better off if she was removed from New Mexico and placed in an entirely different foster system, one that would make it harder for Uncle Brian to find her.

Tears fell as Sage continued to stroke the rough woolen images. She felt Grandfather's hand on the back of her head. "You have learned many things while you lived here. Do not forget them, Sage. The world is full of darkness, but there is much light too. Do not be blind to either."

"I wish you could go with me," Sage choked through her silent sobs.

"So do I." Grandfather's voice cracked. After a moment

of silence he continued. "But you do not go alone. The Holy Ones are always there. The Wind will not leave you."

Sage took a deep breath and shook away the painful memory. Giving the rug one last gentle stroke, she turned on her back and pulled the blankets up to her chin.

"You were right, Grandfather," she whispered into the silence of her room. "The Wind hasn't left me. But I still wish you were here. Especially now, with that 'adagąsh--"

Her shoulder flared with pain, and Sage rubbed the tender spot where she'd been hit with the bone bead. Alarm joined the sadness that had settled over her. Sage's gaze darted through the darkness of her small room, and her ears searched the heaves and sighs of the old Victorian home for something more sinister.

It had been a long time since she'd encountered Navajo witchery, but it was just as disturbing now as when she'd first learned about it. The dull ache in her shoulder continued to thrum, and Sage knew sleep would not come easily tonight

CHAPTER NINE

Pine needles tore at Sage's face, but she couldn't slow down. Screams and frantic barking sounded in the distance, but she stumbled on through the forest shadows, unable to find the source of either. *Save them, save them,* a voice in her mind chanted. It was her job to protect, but the dim light made it impossible to see. Every time she tried to veer to the right, in the direction of the screams, a dark shape with red eyes blocked her path. It felt both familiar and frightening. She must keep away from it, no matter what.

A pounding noise joined the screams. The red eyes drew closer, and she could see teeth, a thousand little needles waiting to destroy her. There was no escape. The pounding sound and Gus's barking grew louder.

"Sage? Sage, are you in there?"

She sat up in her bed and frantically searched the darkness of the room. The light on her nightstand read 3:00 am. It was only a dream, she assured herself. Sage lay back down, but let out a shriek when Gus barked and jumped on her chest.

"Get off me!" She bellowed and shoved Gus off the side

of the bed. Crouched against the ground, the dog crawled under the bed until only the faint outline of his mottled white tail was visible.

"Sage, if you're in there, open up! I need to talk to you." A frantic male voice came from downstairs.

So not a dream after all. Sage rose from bed and crept down the stairs without turning on a light. She pushed the blinds on the window aside for a moment before recognition came. After flicking on the outside light, she jerked open the door.

"It's three in the morning, Tim! What's so important you couldn't wait until tomorrow?"

"We're in trouble, Sage." He shoved himself into the room, tossed a duffle bag on the floor, and closed the door. Quickly, he turned the lights back off, and jerked Sage to the ground with him.

"What in the--?"

"Shhhh!" Tim's hand shot out and clenched her forearm. "Be quiet."

"You were the one pounding on my door and screaming my name a minute ago." Sage shook him off.

"You're right. That was stupid, but I had to find you. Grab your stuff because we've got to get out of here. NOW!" He whispered and dread crept into Sage's heart.

"Why?"

Tim grabbed her shoulders. "You barely know me, but I need you to trust me. We've got to get out of here before they find us."

Sage didn't pull away this time.

"Who?"

"Whoever killed those kids. And Ron Davis."

"What?" The words came out as if she'd been punched. First Shaun and Tabitha and now the Sheriff?

Fear, then fiery adrenaline rushed through her, but Sage forced herself to take a deep breath and close her eyes.

Was Tim even telling the truth? *Yes,* her intuition whispered. Then a needle-like tingling zipped through her limbs and her heart thundered in her ears. Danger was coming for her. Fast.

"Sage, I'll explain in the car. But first, grab clothes and some food."

"No need. I didn't unpack." Shoving on her shoes, she grabbed her keys and whistled for Gus. "Come on, boy. Jeep."

Gus shot from the door and raced toward the garage. Crouched at the opening in the door, Sage carefully watched the dog for signs of distraction or alarm, but there were none.

"Let's move," Sage whispered as Gus disappeared through his dog door into the detached building. Adrenaline coursing through her, Sage ran across the yard in a crouched spring. Her senses screamed with desperate alarm. They had to escape now.

"Grab those gas canisters on the floor," she ordered once they were in the garage. "They should both be full." Tim loaded them into the car along with Gus, while Sage manually raised the door.

"Don't turn on your headlights," Tim warned as he buckled his seatbelt.

"Don't worry." The moon picked up the glint of her smile as she jammed the car into first gear. "This isn't my first getaway."

Headlights off, the Jeep charged through her back alley and then across the street in mere seconds. Tim swiveled around, but Sage watched from the rear-view mirror. As they turned the corner, red and blue flashing lights erupted from the darkness at the other side of the alley. The cars pulled up to the garage the Jeep had just vacated.

"The police," Tim said, his voice full of resignation.

"Any of them following us?" She negotiated around the trash cans, utility poles, and potholes.

"I don't think so."

Sirens, from what she imagined was the entire police force of Black Mills blared through the warm night air. Despite the maze of Sage's back alley route, they continued to catch glimpses of emergency vehicles that seemed to materialize from nowhere.

"It looks like they're all headed toward your house," Tim said.

"Liddy!" Sage gasped but then remembered her foster mother hadn't been in the house when she got home that night. Whatever Liddy was up to, Sage hoped it would keep her away from their home for several days.

Tim leaned back into his seat. "That was close. One minute more ..."

"Yeah, you seem to have a knack for arriving in the nick of time," Sage said, trying to put Liddy out of her mind as she steered onto an old gravel road. "First the coyotes, now the police. I hope there's not a third time coming."

"I guess. I don't ..."

In the dim moonlight she glanced over and saw Tim's clenched hands on the dashboard bar. The rush of adrenaline that fueled their escape began to evaporate. "Are you okay?"

"No," he gasped, his voice ragged with pain.

"So Sheriff Davis is ... dead."

"Yes. Dead."

Because of what they'd discovered in the mine? Sage's stomach recoiled. *This was always what happens when authorities get involved*, she inwardly raged. You thought you were fixing something by reporting it, but everything ended up even worse. Why hadn't she listened for the Wind's directions before she barged into a police station like an idiot? Sure, Tim had insisted, but normally she'd never let—

A groan interrupted Sage's internal tirade. Startled, she glanced at Tim and saw him cover his eyes with his hand. The guy looked like he was about to vomit. Sage wracked her brain for something comforting to say.

"Are you ...? I'm so ... sorry, Tim."

"Ron was a good man. A very good man. I worked with him and some of the kids at the church when they got into trouble and he had to step in. I saw how he handled things. The bad things. He had integrity, and he didn't put up with anything less. I really admired him." His voice cracked.

Sage, not knowing what else to do, reached out to touch his arm. Tim grasped for her hand and squeezed, his grip so tight it hurt. After a moment, she tried to pull away, but he wouldn't let go. They rode in silence for several miles before she turned on her headlights.

"Your hand is like ice." He released her suddenly, seeming to come back to the present.

She jerked away. "It's always like ice," Sage mumbled, and Gus whined from behind her. "It's okay, buddy," Sage murmured to the dog. Both of them knew observations about her usually led to unanswerable questions.

Fortunately Tim was too preoccupied to notice. His voice broke the silence awhile later, and Sage could tell he'd been crying. "I didn't even ask. Where are we going?"

"To a safe place," Sage said. "Somewhere nobody'll be able to find us."

"You said this wasn't your first getaway?" Tim asked.

"Unfortunately, no."

"Good. Then you know what to do."

"I know how to get us off the radar," Sage corrected. "But after that? You're going to have to tell me everything."

Tim nodded, but from the white-knuckled fists that lay clenched in his lap, Sage knew it wouldn't be a pleasant conversation.

CHAPTER TEN

They rolled to a stop at one of Sage's most secluded mountain hideouts. The nighttime shadows made it even more challenging than normal to navigate the logging road's hairpin turns and gaping holes before finally arriving at the remote location. Communication had been nearly impossible over the sound of the Jeep's rattling battle with the rough terrain.

The engine ticked as it cooled. Sage looked at Tim. He'd been so silent during the drive she wondered if he'd fallen asleep, but now she saw he was wide awake. Eyes open, but also unfocused, he stared straight ahead, his body radiating tension. He looked almost catatonic.

Sage wasn't sure what to do, but decided action, any type of action, was better than this strange torpor. "Well, we're here. You ready to talk or should we set up the tent? The sun's going to be up soon, but it might be a good idea to get some rest."

Tim blinked, but didn't respond.

"Tim, can you hear me? What do you want to do?"

He took a deep breath and looked around. "We need to

scan the perimeter and determine if this area's safe. Are you sure we weren't followed? Until we know this place is secure, I'd rather you not get out."

"Were you in the car with me the last hour, Tim?" Sage's exhaustion and confusion overflowed into anger. "We're in the middle of nowhere. No one followed us. And you don't tell me to stay in the car. I'm the one who brought us here." She jumped out of the Jeep. "My secret hideout, not yours."

Tim's sluggishness vanished; he exited and slammed the door so hard the Jeep shook. "I didn't realize this was your show. You get to call all the shots, and I'm supposed to shut-up and do whatever you tell me?"

"Sounds good to me." Sage held her ground as he approached. Gus, still in the car, began to bark wildly. "I never asked you to be a part of this, but you keep turning up like some kind of bad penny. Everywhere I go, you're there, shoving your way into *my* business!"

"Your business? I guess I should have left you to *your business* in the mine earlier today."

Sage banged a clenched fist on the hood of the car. "I would have figured something out. I've been taking care of myself for almost 20 years. I don't need your help or anyone else's!"

"This isn't some survival game, Sage. Do you have any idea what happened to Ron?"

"No, because you haven't told me! You showed up at my house like a lunatic and demanded we run."

"I'm just trying to keep everyone—" Tim's voice broke, but then he continued, louder. "There was blood everywhere, Sage! Hacked pieces of him were up in the center aisle, just like Sudan. Smears of blood, bits of entrails, splintered bone. I tried not to step in it, but I couldn't help it."

He grabbed Sage's shoulders in a vice grip. "The same as Sudan ... Even up at the altar." Tim's eyes grew wild. "How could it be the exact same? I never thought I'd have to see—" Tim turned and heaved into the tree next to him.

Gus's frantic barking drowned out the noise, and Sage's mind raced. Another violent death, just like Shaun and Tabitha's? Was there a serial killer loose in the area? It seemed unlikely; things like that didn't happen in small mountain towns. Everyone was too much in each other's business for aberrant behaviors to go unnoticed by friends, family, or authorities. Garbage usually got dealt with before it had a chance to rot.

Then again, evil always seemed to find a way. Sage swallowed. She knew that firsthand.

She watched as Tim finished heaving and wiped at his mouth with a shaky hand. After a moment's hesitation, she patted him awkwardly on the back. "I'm so sorry ... That must have been terrible to see."

Tim straightened and nodded, but kept his back toward her. For all his worry about shock earlier, Sage knew Tim was probably in the full throes of it himself and needed to be comforted. She made eye contact with Gus who had his head pressed against the Jeep's windshield. She pointed at him through the window, and his barking stopped. He jumped onto the passenger seat.

Sage opened the Jeep's door and buried her face into the silky fur on his forehead. "Quiet now. Tim needs you. Go do your thing."

Gus nuzzled her face and trotted toward Tim, now crouched at the edge of the clearing. The dog circled him three times before leaning against Tim's right side and gave his cheek a reassuring lick. Gus glanced back at Sage.

Nodding to him, she began to unpack her gear. As she

wrestled with the tent poles, Sage's mind screamed for answers. Who had killed the sheriff, and why had the police tried to capture her and Tim? Even more importantly, why did Tim happen to show up every time someone died, and was it even safe to be here with him?

Despite all the questions, her weary body insisted it was time for rest. She glanced over at Tim. He shuddered and collapsed against a tree. The guy seemed too traumatized to be a threat to anyone right now. Besides, Gus would alert her if Tim were to prove a danger.

As if sensing her thoughts, Gus looked toward her and wagged his tail. For the moment, Sage knew she was safe. She needed to rest. Tomorrow was going to be one hell of a day.

Sage awoke to the irregular tap of a woodpecker hunting for bugs in a nearby tree. Under the slippery weight of her sleeping bag, her hand clenched at the sheathed game knife that rested between her breasts. Anxiety clawed her stomach as her mind struggled to remember where she was. She rolled over and studied the deserted tent. *Tim!* Her mind screamed. *Where was Tim?* Everything from the day before came roaring back.

Knowing Gus would have alerted her to any danger, Sage figured Tim must be nearby, and her panic ticked down a notch. Still, she hurried to pull on a clean shirt and pants.

She crawled from the tent and blinked in the morning light illuminating the landscape around her with vivid contrast. Pines whispered above and the aspen leaves fluttered in the breeze. Thick drops of dew hung on wildflower petals with glistening brilliance. The sharp, cold air made it seem as though the world had been created anew while she slept. The chuckle of an overhead bird saluted her with a joy that made her skin tingle. She wished this moment, this peaceful dawn, would last forever.

Shielding her eyes from the sun's radiance, she turned in a slow circle. Where were Tim and Gus?

Sage let out a short, sharp whistle and saw the flash of Gus's gray and white coat a few hundred yards down the mountainside. As she started down, Sage spied Tim sitting on a log, head bowed, and Gus now resting at his feet. The dog watched as she approached and wagged his tail, but remained with Tim.

"What's going on?"

"Nothing," Tim said. Sage saw he had a book on his lap.

"Did you get any sleep last night?"

"Not much. Nightmares." Tim didn't elaborate, and Gus licked at his hand.

Sage sat on the log next to him. "What are you reading?"

"The Bible, of course," he said with a short laugh.

"Why of course?"

"That's what all good priests do." He held it out for her to examine.

Sage hesitated before accepting it. She flipped through a few pages before letting it fall back open to the one he'd bookmarked with an aspen leaf. "Priest? I thought you were a teacher."

"Actually, I'm a handyman and a janitor these days. I only help out at the church from time to time with the teenagers. That's the group that nobody wants."

"I don't understand," Sage handed the book back to him and studied his face. Dark shadows encircled his eyes and as she watched his mouth twitch, Sage realized he was barely keeping his emotions under control. She had to get this guy to calm down. "Why don't you read me something?"

He smoothed the page with the leaf and read,

Never again will they hunger;
never again will they thirst.
The sun will not beat down on them,
nor any scorching heat.
For the Lamb at the center of the throne
will be their shepherd;
he will lead them to springs of living water.
And God will wipe away every tear from their eyes.

His voice faded into the still mountain silence.

"That's beautiful," Sage said. "Who is it talking about?"

Tim looked down at the page again. *"These are they who have come out of the great tribulation."*

"Great tribulation? Like Sheriff Davis?" She asked, and Tim's face turned white. He shut the book with a loud snap.

"Yes. Worse than the others."

"I need you to talk about it." Sage said. "And why we had to get away from town so quickly."

"I can't! It was ... I can't do it, all right?," he snarled and the words echoed down the hillside.

"You're going to have to calm--" Sage began, but Gus shoved his nose against her knees, his eyes pleading. Sage swallowed the sharp words on her tongue and continued more softly, "I know we're both rattled right now. I keep asking myself how we could have prevented this. What we should have done different." Listened to the Wind more closely? Sage wondered. Waited until morning when there were more people around? Would that have prevented the sheriff's murder?

"It's not just that," Tim said. "I'm ... I guess I'm not completely sure what I saw. It was terrible, I know that at least. But sometimes, I see things. It's been awhile, but--"

"What do you mean, *see things*?" The glade suddenly plunged into darkness. Sage looked above her and saw a dark thunderhead race across the sky.

"Like, flashbacks." Tim picked up a pine cone and threw it at a distant tree. "I worked in Sudan before I came to Black Mills. Back in my priest days. I was there during the civil war." His hands clenched on his lap.

"I thought you mentioned Sudan last night. So you were in the middle of the fighting?" Sage asked.

Tim nodded. "I had just been ordained. They sent me to this tiny village in the middle of the Nuba Mountains. My congregation was made up mainly of poor farmers who were completely unprepared for war. The genocide happened so quickly. When the killing started, a lot of people came to hide in the church, hoping they'd be safe. We stayed together for a few days before one of the militia groups found us. They didn't kill me, because I was an American, but everyone else ... I tried to stop them, but I got knocked out." He fingered a scar Sage hadn't noticed before running the length of the hairline on his forehead.

"When I woke up, everyone was dead. All over the church. All of them. Even the—" Tim's voice broke. "The children." He stood and walked over to an aspen tree. His fingers found cracks in the trunk, and Tim absently peeled off chunks of the white bark and tossed them to the ground.

"I was sent home by my diocese and immediately hospitalized. With PTSD. For a long time."

"PTSD? The thing soldiers have when they come back?"

He gave her a terse nod. "Post Traumatic Stress Disorder. Eventually it became manageable. I moved to Black Mills. I've been doing better, but last night ... I couldn't be sure of what I saw, what was happening. It was almost like whoever did it tried to make it look like what happened in Sudan."

Sage met Gus's gaze again and mulled over Tim's words. *So anything this guy tells us is suspect?*

The dog cocked his head.

Can I trust him? Is he crazy?

Gus walked over to Tim and curled up next to him. He rested his head on Tim's feet and stared at Sage.

"Why don't you tell me what you think you saw, and we'll wade through it. Together," Sage said.

Tim scratched the stubble on his chin and turned to her, his eyes weary. "But it might all be lies. Something my mind's made up. Or maybe I've completely lost it. If I keep showing up at all these murder scenes maybe I'm the one—" Tim groaned, clenching his fists across his chest. "I feel like I'm going crazy, Sage." He turned from the aspen abruptly. "We should head back to town. I need to check in with a doctor."

"Just tell me what you saw." Sage stood. "Remember those cop cars last night? Remember what we discovered in the mine? I saw those things too. You're not crazy."

Tim leaned his head against the stark white aspen trunk. He glanced at Sage with bloodshot eyes. "I can only tell you what I think I saw," he whispered. "But--"

"That's all I want to hear," Sage said.

CHAPTER ELEVEN

Tim tried to speak several times, but seemed unable to find the words. He leaned against the tree and slid down until he was crouched by the trunk.

Sage kneeled next to him. "So you said you were at the church?"

Tim nodded.

"Why were you in the church and not your apartment?"

"I started out at my apartment. I was exhausted when you dropped me off, so I plugged my camera into my laptop to download those pictures and went straight to bed. I woke up when my cell rang. It said Ron Davis, so I answered it. I thought he might have another question."

Tim shook his head and swallowed. Sage willed him to continue.

"What I heard was terrible. Screaming. Swearing. I think it was Ron's voice, but I'm not sure." He swallowed. Gus moved to rest his head on Tim's knee, and Tim buried his fingers in the soft fur around the dog's neck. "I didn't know what to do. I kept asking if he needed help, to tell me where he was, but he never answered me. Should I hang up, call the police? But I didn't even know where he was or if it was really Ron. Finally the ... noises stopped."

"And then?" Sage asked.

"And then this other ... *thing* came on the line. Its voice; I could barely understand. It was distorted. Weird. Growling and ... I can't even describe it."

"What did it say?" Sage asked, dread creeping across her shoulders.

"Weird stuff like, 'You dare to enter this battle? This is what happens to those who would stand against me.' It sounds crazy, I know."

"What happened next?"

"Well, I think I yelled at it. Demanded to know who it was and what had happened to Ron. All I got was laughter. I kept yelling, but it didn't answer.

"I almost hung up, but then finally it said, 'Your friend was not so brave as he pretended. He begged me to stop at the end. You will too. But come, find what is left of him. He awaits you at your church.'

"That's just down the block from my house, so I ran. I have a key, you know, with the janitor work. I unlocked the back door. The killer was already gone. But Ron ... wasn't."

"Body parts strewn down the aisle, right?"

"And on the altar, just like in ... just like ..." Tim gasped and began to rock gently back and forth, reminding Sage of how he'd been the night before.

"Got it," Sage said and scooted as close to him as she could, their bodies touching. "Don't get stuck, Tim. What happened next?"

"I wasn't thinking straight at that point," Tim snapped. Gus nuzzled Tim's hand. Absently, Tim began to stroke the dog again. "I was about to call the police but then heard sirens. I was so confused. Had I already called them and forgotten?"

Sage shook her head. "Maybe."

"Well, I ran to the church office to look through the window and saw flashing police cars pull up to the front of the church. Olson got out of the first car and other officers followed him to the front door. It was still locked since I'd gone in the back entrance. Olson sent the other officers around the building. Those church windows are old, single-paned, so I could hear everything.

"Why didn't you let them in? Call out?"

"I almost did," Tim nodded. "But something stopped me. Then Olson made a call on his phone, so I decided to listen instead. He said, 'We're at the church. Anders saw Burgney go in, so we should have him in custody in a matter of minutes.'"

"What?" Sage barked.

Tim nodded. "Then Olson says something like, 'Yeah, we're headed to her house next. Anders has some eyes there too, so it should be pretty easy. We'll book them tonight and have the story in tomorrow morning's paper. Sooner than planned, but the best we could do.'"

"What the hell?" Sage jumped up, trembling. "They were trying to pin Davis's murder on *us*?"

Tim looked up at her. "I could hear the police coming in by then, yelling, discovering ... Ron. After a few minutes Olson starts screaming my name, and yelling stuff like, 'I know you did this Burgney! You might as well give yourself up!'

"After the way he treated us at the police department last night, I decided to get out of there. I climbed through the window and snuck back to my apartment. I grabbed my computer, camera, and a few things and ran straight to your house.

"Right away, I spied the *eyes* Olson was talking about. There was a police car parked in front of your house. I looped around the block and came through your alley. I didn't have a plan or anything, just knew I had to warn you. And that we needed to escape."

A familiar feeling of helplessness built in Sage's stomach, quickly followed by rage. She thought she'd escaped this type of bullshit back when she'd officially aged out from the foster system at age eighteen. Since that time, she'd worked to make herself nearly undetectable to any governmental agency or anyone else for that matter. Resignation competed with fury as the full ramifications of Tim's story sank in. She was back on their radar.

"I wonder if I should have stayed in Black Mills," Tim said. "It doesn't look good that I bolted. Maybe I should have turned myself in. But I wasn't even thinking straight at that point. I went into survival mode and ran. I guess I reverted back to..."

"Your Post Traumatic thing," Sage finished.

"Yeah. Again." Tim shook his head. "I panicked. I ran like a coward. Just like before."

Sage shook her head. "I wouldn't call self-preservation cowardly. Only an idiot would have turned himself into Olson."

Tim leaned his forehead against his arms, obviously spent. "Guess I'm not an idiot then."

"No, you're not," Sage said after studying Tim for several moments. "And I don't think you're imagining this."

"Are you kidding?" Tim's head shot up. "The way he died? It's crazy. This kind of thing doesn't happen in Black Mills."

"That's what I thought at first, too, but just because Black Mills was safe in the past, that doesn't mean it's going to stay that way. Besides, if you were making up something, or having a flashback, wouldn't your brain remember what you already saw? You said in Sudan the church was full of people, but this time it was just Ron, right?"

Tim considered her words. "I don't know. I still have nightmares, but I haven't experienced hallucinations for almost twelve years."

"This wasn't a hallucination," Sage said. "Those were real cop cars chasing us out of town."

"Well, what do we do now?" Tim asked, his voice sharp. "Assuming the deaths are connected. Assuming Officer Olson has it in for us."

"I'm going to make another couple of assumptions, based on all that's happened," Sage said, *And not just the parts you know about,* she added silently. "This is bigger than three murders. There's something going on in the Oriel Valley, and it's beginning to leak into Black Mills. Maybe even further."

"So what do we do?" Tim asked.

"It's time to go look at your pictures," Sage said and stood. She held a hand out to Tim and helped pull him up.

He squeezed her hand briefly. "Thanks."

"For what?" Sage asked as they walked up the hill.

"For not letting me lose myself." He shook his head. "I felt like I was sliding back into the darkest parts of my mind. And I never wanted to go there again."

Sage nodded grimly. He had too many memories of his worst moment, and she had none. What a strange combination they made.

CHAPTER TWELVE

After they returned to the campsite, Sage insisted they move her tent under the cover of the trees. They pulled her Jeep as far into the forest as possible and then hid the rest of it with underbrush. The two spent the rest of the morning studying the mine pictures Tim had downloaded to his computer before chaos had taken over the night before.

"Make sure nobody can track us with your signals," Sage warned him again. "I want this place to stay secret."

"Everything that can be tracked is off, I promise."

They examined each image meticulously, Tim magnifying and then zooming out. The feature came in especially handy with the pictographs. Sage had Tim zoom into the images and tweak them with different color filters.

"Huh," Sage said after studying one for several minutes.

"Find something?" Tim asked.

"I don't know. Probably not. There's just a figure in the pictograph I didn't see before." Sage pointed to one of the images near the edge of the battle scene. "I guess the filter on the computer makes it easier to see."

"What is it? An eagle?" Tim asked.

"Maybe. Or it could be a thunderbird." Sage traced the upraised wings with her fingertips.

"Thunderbird? Is that like a phoenix?"

"I'm not sure." Sage shook her head. "But I think it's more a symbol of rain. Or lightning and thunderstorms."

"I don't think that helps us."

"You're right," Sage sighed. "We should go back to the series that shows the coyotes' kill area." She pulled the computer onto her lap and scanned through the pictures one by one. There were two that drew her attention: the close up she'd taken of the bottle she'd found with the letters LOZA on it, and the area where the coyotes had gathered around the remains. Sage observed them with a hardening conviction that something was off.

Sage handed Tim the computer then stood and stretched.

"What are you doing?" Tim asked.

"I've got to run. Or swim. Or do something to let my mind process this without thinking about it," she said.

"Okay," Tim said, closing the computer. "Guess I could handle a walk."

"Alone," Sage spoke without hesitation. "This is the most time I've spent with another human in years. No offense, Tim, but I need some space."

"None taken." Tim turned quickly, and Sage wondered if she'd hurt him. If so, it was his own fault. She wasn't his babysitter, and she needed a break.

"Look, I'm just not used to all this talking," Sage said.

"It's fine. I was just surprised. You take a little ... getting used to," Tim shrugged then reopened his computer.

Used to? Sage watched Tim click through the images again. What was that supposed to mean? If this guy was imagining some sort of long-term relationship evolving out of this nightmare scenario, he'd be very disappointed.

Gus rose to follow her as she jerked the zipper of the tent, but Sage shook her head and pointed at Tim. She still wasn't entirely sure she trusted him; at the very least, he was a flight risk, but Gus would make sure Tim stayed put.

Sage trotted to the edge of their camp and broke into a run toward the valley. She pushed herself down the hill, dodging tree branches and leaping over roots and rocks. The Wind rushed through her hair, whipping it about her shoulders. She ran faster, wishing she could fly away.

When she came within sight of the stream, Sage pulled off her clothes and, climbing onto an outcropping, jumped into a deep pool. Its snow-melt frigidity took her breath away, and she forced her body down, down to the bottom. Her limbs brushed against the water-smoothed boulders where the large trout hid, feeding on insect larvae in the summer and hibernating in the winter. Their slippery fins brushed against her arms, legs, and body as she swam next to them, letting the current drag her slowly toward the end of the basin.

Even though she'd swam in this pool so often she could have done it with her eyes closed, Sage opened them in the dark depths, relishing the water's cold touch on every part of her body. Once she reached the edge, Sage pushed off the rocky bottom and swam toward the sunlight. Breaking the surface with a gasp, she erupted in an explosion of water droplets that scattered like diamonds through the air.

Usually Gus followed her into the water, but this time Sage was thankful for the solitude as she stroked laps back and forth across the pool. So much had happened in the last few days: three murders of striking brutality, Tim thrown into her life, and now the police attempting to frame the two of them for at least one of the murders. She shoved details, feelings, conclusions, and similarities into different corners of her mind.

Exhausted by her icy laps, she flipped onto her back and let herself float in the soft rippling currents. Sage silenced her thoughts, and when she had finally found the center of herself in the empty stillness, the Wind came. It skipped over the pond and whispered in her ear.

"Where is your dog, Broken One? Usually he makes so much noise I cannot speak to you here."

"With the Priest. As if you didn't know."

"Yes, the Priest," the voice hummed. "He is part of this story now too, isn't he?"

"It looks that way," Sage said, "although I don't know if he'll be strong enough to handle all this."

The Wind chuckled, "He is much stronger than you think. Do not confuse his emotion with weakness. He feels the suffering of others with every part of his being. He does not allow himself to ignore their stories. That is not weakness. It is a great pain that he does not hide from."

"You're implying that I hide away from pain?" Sage kicked and the water churned.

"I say only that you are different people. That he embraces pain, and you fight against it. Not everyone walks their path in the same way."

"That's helpful," Sage sighed and swam to the sandy beach. She climbed out and lay on a large granite rock, allowing the sun to dry her skin and hair.

The breeze stroked her forehead and danced through her hair, helping it dry and lulling her almost to sleep. After a while it gently nudged her back to consciousness.

"It's time for you to go."

"And do what?" Sage asked. "We can't go back into

town because the police are looking for us. We've looked at all the pictures on Tim's computer, and there's no answers there. Plus the guy is seriously messed up. And I'm no babysitter."

"Continue to search for what is hidden. You have many gifts. I know you sense the source of this evil, even if your mind has not yet recognized it." The breeze grew louder, and Sage lunged to grab her clothes before they blew away. A cloud passed over the sun. The temperature dropped. Goosebumps pricked her skin, and Sage dressed hurriedly.

"But beware the creature that stalks you. For now its power is limited to the boundaries of Oriel Valley, but not for much longer."

"Wonderful," Sage said. She pulled her shirt over her head and ran her fingers through dry but tangled hair.

"I will be back," the Wind spoke as it danced away in the trees. "But this evil is tangled into many threads. You must find more of what is hidden before we speak again."

CHAPTER THIRTEEN

Cloudy skies moved in over the western peaks, and Sage shivered as she hiked back to the campsite. She scanned the area for Tim but didn't see him anywhere. When she called his name, a whine sounded from inside the tent.

Sage unzipped the rain fly and found Tim sound asleep on his side. Gus watched over him from where he lay curled at the back of Tim's knees. The dog looked up and thumped his tail but didn't move. Sage nodded then zipped the tent closed once more.

Perched on a rotting log next to the tent, Sage tried to ignore the irritation that ricocheted through her. Waiting was not something she enjoyed. She picked at a hole in her cargo pants while the Wind's words reverberated through her mind: *continue to search for what is hidden.*

She let out an annoyed puff. Just once she'd love it if the Wind came out and told her exactly what to do. But if history was any guide, the Wind could not be forced to operate in any way other than its own ambiguous M.O.

Nervous energy buzzed through her, and she pushed up from her perch on the log. It was time to go, but she would let Tim sleep. From what the Wind had hinted at, they'd need all the strength they could get, and Gus would do his best to keep nightmares and anything else at bay.

Sage quietly opened the Jeep, pulled a notepad from the glove compartment, and scribbled a message.

Tim,

Going to hike around for a bit and see if I find anything. Wait here and rest. I'll be back in time for dinner. Stay with Gus.

Sage

Sage rolled up the note and shoved it through the zipper opening of the tent. The sun peeked around the clouds while she considered which direction to go. If she took the path to her swimming hole and continued on over the peaks in front of her, she'd eventually come to the Oriel Valley. The path cut through a forest and then into a clearing a few miles past the now notorious *Coyote* Mine as she'd come to think of it, a place she never wanted to go near again. However, with what the Wind had said, creepy places were exactly where she'd discover something.

After nearly two hours of brisk hiking, Sage came to the last ridge that separated her from the Oriel Valley. Climbing cautiously onto a promontory, Sage surveyed the vista.

Picture-perfect cabins lay scattered across the valley floor. What was it about this place that put her so on edge? The Orielites were fanatics about keeping their natural surrounding rustic and untouched, something Sage strove for herself. But instead of the harmony this shared philosophy should have inspired, she felt disturbed by whatever lurked beneath the beautiful surface.

Her gaze traveled down the length of the lowland then back up the hillside. A few hundred yards away stood the last ramshackle evidence of the valley's early mining history: Old Hank's cabin.

Feeling a tug toward the dilapidated building, Sage set off toward it, but made sure to stay well hidden behind the treeline. Although most of the buildings of the Oriel Biological Research Station lay far below her on the valley floor, she didn't want to take any chance that she'd be spotted by the marmot-obsessed scientists.

Sage had nearly forgotten that Hank lived in this valley. Back when she first arrived in Black Mills, the two regularly saw each other on the mountain trails in the surrounding area. These encounters had become rare in recent years. Sage searched her memory and realized the last time she'd seen Hank was at the opening day celebration for the ski resort last November. Normally she would have avoided such a gathering, but Liddy had begged Sage to accompany her to the party.

The ski resort, in its never-ending quest for catchy advertising, had created a new logo with Hank as a grizzled mountain man on skis with the words *Black Mills Original* underneath.

He was the oldest living resident of the Oriel/Black Mills area and at the unveiling of the logo, the announcer asked. "Maybe you'd like to let us in on how old you actually are, Hank?"

"Not too old to enjoy all these pretty ski bunnies!" He yelled, squeezing the bikini clad girls next to him as the crowd cheered. Liquor flowed, and he'd become wilder and wilder. His behavior surprised Sage because he seemed so quiet and withdrawn when she met him in her mountain wanderings.

His great-grandfather had been one of the original miners who'd discovered the first silver vein in Oriel Valley. Rumors of unbelievable riches circulated and lured thousands of hopeful adventurers to the surrounding area, but the vein was a small one and quickly dried up. A while later uranium had also been discovered, and despite the dangers of its extraction, this radioactive ore had been the true source of Hank's wealth. For all his family's prosperity and prestige, Hank had always seemed to prefer a reclusive life. At least until this ski party.

Sage shook away the memories and crept out from the trees that skirted the graying log cabin. A tingling burst of energy shot through her limbs, and Sage whirled around, sure that something was trailing her. The woods creaked eerily in the gentle breeze, but her sharp eyes detected no movement other than the sway of pine branches and ripple of grass.

The jittery anxiety that flowed through her did not diminish as she navigated the overgrown weeds and underbrush covering the gravel driveway and path. A rusty green bike leaned against the cabin's front wall.

Sage tapped on the front door and called out. "Hank, are you in there? It's Sage."

No answer. She knocked again and the door moved. Sage saw that the lock wasn't engaged and nudged the door open a few more inches.

"Hank?" Sage called into the dim, musty room. Her eyes took a minute to adjust to the darkness. The Wind rustled behind her then pushed the door wide open.

Feathers and bird droppings littered the floor and kicked up into miniature whirlwinds. Water stains trailed down from beneath broken window panes. Sage's gaze traveled to the ceiling, and she saw bird nests lining the rafters.

Ramshackle furniture lay scattered around the room, torn and ravaged by burrowing rodents and other small animals. In the last stages of its lonely decomposition, the room reeked of the decay and waste, and Sage forced herself to breathe through her mouth.

The floor groaned like an old man when Sage crept across the rotting floorboards, around a dusty table, and toward the small kitchen. Scattered cans and pots lay on the counter and stove, as if someone had left abruptly in the middle of preparing a meal. A thick layer of dust coated everything, and Sage shivered. Something terrible had happened here.

"Find it and get out," the Wind said. "You must hurry!"

Suddenly, the air turned electric, and the space around her felt charged, like it did before a lightning strike during a thunderstorm. Sage froze, trying to sense the source of the sudden change in atmosphere. Her intuition screamed at her to flee but not through the front door. Something was approaching from that direction. Rapidly.

She scanned the walls of the cabin, but couldn't find any other exit besides the dilapidated windows. Then she spied the cabin's loft, accessed by a sturdy ladder and a wave of relief surged through her. Sage climbed the slanted rungs two at a time and hid in the shadows of the cabin's loft.

Another gust of Wind shoved her from her hiding place and down the hall. Sage stumbled against a door and fell into a small bathroom. Heart pounding in her ears, she opened the drawers of the old vanity, but found nothing more interesting than a hair brush and Q-tips. She dropped to her knees and dug through the clutter under the sink. Underneath some wadded up towels lay hundreds of small vials. As she grabbed a glass tube, the sunlight beaming through the small bathroom window vanished, darkening the small space. Sage squinted, trying to read the tiny label, but couldn't make it out.

The front door creaked open then slammed shut with a violence that shook the entire cabin. Trembling, Sage shoved a handful of containers in her vest pocket and silently rose to her feet. A dark, grating laugh rose from the room below.

"I am here, Broken One. Did you think you could come into my valley, and I would not sense your presence?"

The floorboards creaked from below and a terrible stench, one that overwhelmed even the cabin's decay, filled the air. Sage shuddered in recognition. It was the same vile odor that had filled the Coyote Mine.

She crept from the bathroom and looked over the railing. A massive black figure weaved its way through the shadows, looking into a closet, and then peering under the couch. With horror, Sage realized it was following the exact path she had just walked through the downstairs. Suddenly it stilled, as if sensing her gaze and wheeled around.

She gripped the railing as her mind struggled to classify the creature's dimly-lit features. Covered in patchy, dark gray fur, it stood upright, taller than a man. A lupine muzzle contorted into an almost human-like smile. Red eyes flashed in the weak light, and with one movement it leapt with awful grace onto the loft's ladder.

Sage ran back to the bathroom and locked the door only a second before the creature's weight battered against it. Her hands shook as she ripped the towel rack from the wall and wedged it between the handle and floor; it would not hold long. Snarls faded into laughter, which Sage found even more terrifying.

"Do you imagine you can escape from me? I have

stalked ones greater than you and never once failed to devour my prey." Sage choked back a sob as singe marks in the shape of claws began to bleed through the wood.

Panic rushed through Sage's mind, but she forced it down into the pit of her stomach. Suddenly a ray of sunlight touched her cheek, and Sage pulled the moldy shower curtain aside. Above the bathtub, light streamed through an octagonal window. She grabbed the first object she spotted, a mug full of shaving gear, and sent it crashing through the glass. Sage climbed atop the tub edge and knocked out most of the broken glass with her elbow. Although the opening was tiny, she pulled herself up and wedged her shoulders through it. Jagged glass sliced her hands, torso, and shoulders.

An angry roar thundered from behind her, and she swore as sharp claws ripped the length of her dangling leg. Sage forced herself the rest of the way through the opening and launched herself off the window frame onto whatever lay below.

Crashing into the slanted granite hillside, Sage heard a pop from her knee. Her right arm was pinned beneath her, and she felt a searing pain in her wrist, but Sage forced herself to her feet. The slathering rage of the creature sounded from above, and she prayed it was too large to follow her through the window.

The Wind urged her forward with gale-force strength into the forest above Hank's cabin. Pine trees tore at her face, hair, and clothes as she sprinted, hindering her escape as if in league with her pursuer. Her torn legs were clumsy, and she stumbled as she ran. There was no way she'd be able to outpace the creature.

A loud crash resounded from only a few feet behind, and Sage knew the thing was gaining on her. Her lungs burned as she sprinted to the pinnacle of the valley, and her heart hammered in her ears.

The Wind surged, its pressure on her back almost like a hand. "You are almost there," It urged. "Make it over the hilltop."

As the ridge's rocky crest appeared in front of her, she heard the creature's roar and felt its claws tear at the back of her shirt. In a desperate burst of strength, Sage vaulted over the top of the jagged rocks. Their craggy edges tore through her pants and her shins before she tumbled to the ground. Curling her battered body into a tensed cocoon, she waited for the thing to pounce, but nothing happened.

Cautiously, she sat up and took stock of her injuries. Her right wrist flopped uselessly, and her scalp and face stung with hundreds of cuts from the vindictive branches. Tattered clothes hid numerous painful gashes from the rocks and creature's claws. Her fingers traced the bulge at the side of her knee. This at least she could fix. Sage shoved the dislocated kneecap back into place, and it settled into its groove with a pop.

Trembling, Sage struggled to stand but stumbled backwards with a sharp cry. Less than two feet away, the beast crouched behind the rocks that separated them. When its eyes met Sage's, the creature leapt. Sage stumbled back, with a shuddering sob, tensing herself against its attack. But nothing happened. The creature jerked and contorted against the space above the boulders as if an invisible barrier held it back.

A relieved, shuddering breath escaped her. "The boundary of Oriel Valley," the Wind whispered in her ear.

The creature snarled and despite her terror, Sage couldn't help but admire it with a horrified awe. She'd thought the thing large in Hank's cabin, but with it only feet away, she saw it was at least seven feet tall. Even though it was slightly hunched over, the creature appeared to be equally agile on either two feet or four as it threw itself against the invisible barrier with increasing rage. Massive shoulders tapered down into sharp, jagged claws that would have killed Sage in an instant if they'd had a chance to truly connect with her body on the chase. She shuddered at the revelation of its awful power.

The creature suddenly paused, something like a smile appearing on its massive snarled maw. Its cruel, red eyes, too human in their perception for a true wolf, narrowed in calculation. Almost as if it could hear her thoughts.

Shock rippled through her; the thing was actually relishing her fear. Rage overrode all other emotions, and Sage took a small step toward it, forcing out a defiant chuckle. "Guess I outran you," she said. Momentarily overcoming the pain of her trembling, damaged limbs, she offered the creature a mock bow.

It slathered a guttural stream of grunts and unintelligible words so hideous, Sage wished she could cover her ears. Instead she stood up straighter, ignoring the spasms of pain from nearly every inch of her body.

"Maybe I'll see you later," she said and made herself walk away without looking over her shoulder. When she reached a thick patch of trees, Sage fell against them and pulled her body into their shadows.

Concealed behind a boxy spruce, she watched as the creature paced the invisible border, its snarls and wails reverberating through the woods. Suddenly it stopped and cocked its head as if hearing a signal. The creature dropped to all fours, writhing and shuddering in obvious pain. Sage gasped as its cries transformed into a howl and the form shifted from the wolf-like creature to a large, but common coyote. Metamorphosis complete, the animal stopped its contortions and sniffed the air. After a moment it let out another howl which was quickly returned by others from around the surrounding hills. The coyote sniffed the air once more before disappearing back down into the valley.

Tim! Gus! The peaceful image of the tent flitted into her adrenaline flooded brain. In a limping jog, Sage raced back in the direction of the campsite where she prayed the dog and the ex-priest still slept peacefully. Although her body screamed with pain, her mind reeled. What if Tim and Gus had followed her into the Oriel Valley?

CHAPTER FOURTEEN

The sun approached the edge of the mountains, and Sage knew she only had a short time before complete darkness fell. If Gus and Tim were missing, she'd have almost no daylight to find them. After what seemed like an eternity, she stumbled into the campsite.

"Tim, Gus!" she screamed. "Where are you?"

Gus's bark sounded, and the dog appeared from behind the tent. Tail wagging, he bounded toward her, and Sage flinched as she prepared for his painful welcoming leap. Instead, Gus halted and with a whine, began to lick her bloody knees and shins.

Her jagged breath slowly returned to normal. With pain-stiffened awkwardness, she leaned down to scratch his neck. "Hey, buddy, did you miss me? Where's Tim?"

The dog ignored her question and continued to lick her injuries. "Tim?" Sage called. "Tim, where are you?"

"I'm here," Tim's voice came from the woods behind her.

Sage straightened painfully and saw Tim's form appear from behind a dense thicket of trees.

"What happened? Where were you?" The annoyance in his eyes transformed into shock as he came closer and registered her injuries. "Are you hurt? *Again*? You're covered in blood!" Gus's excited barks drowned out the rest of his words.

Why hadn't she taken a moment to clean herself up and investigate the campsite before bellowing her presence like a hysterical toddler? She wasn't used to sharing her pain with anyone other than Gus; embarrassment and annoyance overwhelmed her. Tim had already tended her injuries once before, and she didn't like the idea of him doing it again. She just wanted to curl up in her sleeping bag and heal alone like she usually did.

"You should see the other guy." Sage leaned against the nearest tree, attempting to appear casual. Her injured knee buckled, and she collapsed. This catapulted Tim into frantic action.

Using himself as a crutch, he eased his shoulder under Sage's and walked her toward the tent.

"I just ran a couple of miles, Tim. I'm fine." Sage tried to pull away, but the arm around her waist tightened, and Tim held her fast to his side.

"You shouldn't have gone off on your own. It's not safe," he said angrily. "You're probably in shock again."

"You're obsessed with shock. I'm not in shock!"

"You might be!"

"Just leave me alone, Tim. I can take care of this myself."

He ignored her and held Sage against him all the way to the tent. "Wait here for a second."

Sage tried to limp away, but Tim quickly returned with a sleeping bag and first aid kit. He circled in front of her, throwing the bag to the ground at her side. When he reached out, she jerked away.

"You've got to lay down, Sage! You look like you're about to fall over. And what's the matter with your arm? Your wrist is flopping all over the place." He gestured to her useless hand while Gus paced nervously between them.

Sage pulled the offending limb behind her. "You don't have to play doctor, Tim. I told you, it's not that big of a deal."

"For the love of ..." Tim sank to his knees next to the bag. He jerked his hands through his hair until it stood wildly on end. "You're completely delusional, Sage. Would you please, *please,* lay down and just let me splint your wrist?"

"*You're* the one freaking out, Tim. Stop ordering me around like some--"

"Hey!" Tim barked but then took a deep breath and continued in a soft, almost hypnotic voice. "I'm sure you're right. Everything's fine. I'm overreacting. But to humor me, let me take a quick look at your wrist. It's good practice for me. In case I ever meet someone who's *actually* hurt."

Sage glared at him, but the energy it would have taken to continue the argument escaped her. The adrenaline from the encounter at Hank's cabin had played out, and she found herself at an utter loss for words. She just wanted a few minutes of quiet to rest and figure out what to do next.

Clumsily, Sage lowered herself to the sleeping bag and sighed as the silky fabric cocooned her battered and broken body. She closed her eyes and after a moment Tim began to probe the wounds on her arm.

It took a while for Tim to set and splint her wrist, tend to her numerous gashes, and clean the scratches on her face, hands, and legs. All of Sage's remaining energy was spent in fighting the unremitting pain of Tim's aid. When she registered that he was finally done, Sage opened her eyes. Tim crouched next to her, studying her arm, his face unreadable.

After a moment his gaze travelled from her arm to Sage's eyes. "You realize you need to see a real doctor don't you? Your wrist was dislocated. And it's probably broken."

"It'll be fine." Sage sat up and stretched. The sun had dipped below the mountain peaks, and the trees' evening shadows stretched long and thin.

"You see, normally I'd argue with that, but look at this," he commanded and grazed his hand down the jagged remains of her pants and brushed her shins. Sage shivered away from his touch.

"What?"

"Gone. All the claw and teeth marks from yesterday? Completely gone." His voice grew sharp, with fear or anger she couldn't tell, but he abruptly moved away. "At first I thought I must be confused. That I was just missing the injuries from yesterday. That they were hidden by these new ones. But aside from the broken, dislocated wrist and torn up knees from today, the marks from yesterday are gone. Vanished."

He stood above her, his form backlit by the last rays of sunlight. "And there," he gestured toward her shoulder, "where I pulled that bone thing out of you? That was a really serious injury. But there's barely a mark. Just a small scab and some bruising."

"What can I say?" Sage struggled to stand and caught her breath against a nearby tree. "I heal fast," she said, staring at him defiantly.

"Right, like superhero fast."

"Come on, Tim. Superheroes are for kids," Sage said and closed her eyes.

"I'm serious." He angled his neck to study her face more closely. "What's going on here? Are you even ..." She watched as he took several steps back. "Human?"

Sage's mind scrambled for an explanation. "Do I look like some kind of alien to you?"

"Not an alien." His voice came faintly after a minute. "But not human either."

"So, neither alien nor human." She forced out a hollow laugh. "Maybe I'm a hybrid? Or a zombie? Just waiting for a chance to eat your brains?"

Tim sighed and knelt to clean up the dirty gauze and discarded wrappers. "You could trust me, you know," he finally said.

"I don't know what you're talking about." Sage turned away and forced the tremor from her hands. "Can you please drop this? We've got bigger things to worry about." Her skin crawled as she remembered the creature from Hank's cabin. What on earth did the Wind want her to do about that ... *thing*?

"Look, it's part of my job description, my old job anyway, to have faith in the unseen, the unexplainable. That kind of thing doesn't phase me like it would some people," Tim said, his voice gentler now. "There's something going on here that's outside the realm of normal." He paused then continued reluctantly, "That seems to include you as well, and I want to understand."

"So you're scared of me now?" Sage snapped. "I'm not some monster."

"I didn't say you were. But you're more than what you're pretending."

"Look, I'm not the thing you should be worrying about," Sage snapped. "You have no idea what I encountered on the other side of that mountain, in Oriel Valley." She shuddered.

Tim was silent, obviously torn between his interrogation of Sage and this new piece of information. "We're not done talking about this," he insisted, "but fine. Tell me what you saw."

Sage moved to a stump at the edge of the trees and sank down. Tim and Gus followed her. Suddenly she realized how exhausted she was and wished for nothing more than the tattered but homey warmth of her bedroom at Liddy's. Instead, she closed her eyes and the details of her adventure in Oriel Valley and Old Hank's cabin spilled out, like water from a broken dam.

When she finished, by telling Tim of the creature's transformation to a coyote, only Gus's gentle snores broke the taunt silence. Finally she couldn't stand it anymore. "So, what do you think? Should we look at those pictures on your computer and see if we can find some sort of a link between all this? Or do you want to just go to sleep and wait until morning?"

Tim jumped up as if electrocuted. "You've got to be kidding me. Are you actually considering staying here another night?" He pulled the sleeping bag off the ground and rolled it into a ball. "After what happened today? No way, Sage. We can't take that chance." He ran to the tent. "As soon as we get packed up, we're out of here. Give me a hand with these stakes."

Sage bristled. "First off, that's *my* car and *my* gear. You don't tell me what to--."

"I understand but—"

"Second, we're not in danger here. I promise."

"How on *Earth* can you promise that?" He demanded, his voice rising. "Look at you!" He pulled a backpack from the tent. Sage bolted after him, wincing as every muscle in her body screamed in protest.

"We are NOT leaving!" she said as he flung the backpack into the back of the Jeep. Her voice echoed around the empty space. A breeze rustled through the trees, scattering moonlit aspen leaves between them.

"There's no way we're spending the night here with that *thing* running around in the dark," Tim said, trudging back past her. "You're already hurt." He called over his shoulder. "I don't care how fast you heal. You can't handle another attack."

Tim went into the tent again. After a few moments he reappeared with the two sleeping bags. He dropped them on the ground and began to break down the tent.

"It's ... complicated, but I promise you I know. We're safer here than anywhere else. For tonight, anyway." Her hair whipped across her face.

"No, it's too risky." Tim wadded her tent, the sleeping bags, and the last of the camping supplies into a makeshift bag and dragged them back to the Jeep. "I don't care if you kick and scream the whole way. I'm not letting you risk your life out here when you can barely stand to defend yourself." He started pulling the branches off the Jeep's hood.

"Stop it!" Sage demanded, but he ignored her. Sage knew, deep in her bones, they should not leave this place. Not tonight. Desperately, she jogged to where Tim was tossing the last of the brush off the Jeep and shoved him away. He tripped over a root and fell to the ground.

"What is the matter with you?" Tim eyed her with disbelief from the forest floor. He stumbled toward Sage, grabbed her shoulders, and shook her. "Do you want to die like Shaun and Tabitha did? Like Ron Davis?"

Sage swore and jerked away. "I told you, we're fine," she

shouted, but another gust blew the words from her mouth. Tim glanced at the whipping trees before turning back to Sage. He reached for her arm and tried to guide her to the Jeep's door, but Sage punched him in the gut with her good arm.

He let out an *oof* of pain but gritted his teeth and reached for her again. Sage smacked at his hands, her color-fully worded protests drowned out by wind tearing at the branches above them. Gus ran circles around the protesting pair and howled frantically.

"*SILENCE.*" Like a clap of thunder, the Wind's demand exploded into the clearing; the gusts immediately ceased, causing cascades of leaves to flutter to the ground around them. The two froze mid-struggle as an electrical current permeated the air around them. Sage felt like her limbs were on fire.

"What ... who was that?" Tim whispered.

"You heard it too?" Sage asked, shocked.

"Of course I heard it. I'm not deaf!" Tim jerked his head toward her, the emotions of the last minutes still playing across his face.

"Must you turn upon each other like quarreling chil-dren?" The voice boomed. "Will you tear each other apart before the true enemy even arrives?"

Sage and Tim clapped their hands over their ears, Sage flinching at the pain in her wrist. "Your bickering must cease," it continued, now gentle enough for the two to lower their hands. Gus leapt and frisked in front of them, as if he was playing a game of tug with an invisible master.

"Who—?" Tim croaked. He cleared his throat and tried again. "Who are you?"

"We are not strangers." The breeze rippled his hair.

"The other Holy Ones and I have watched you wander in the lonely places of these hills and valleys."

"You have?" Sage gasped. The Wind moved to her and looped around her body.

"Surely you did not think you were my only charge, Broken One?"

Curiosity bubbled within Sage as she looked at Tim. "I guess I did." So far she'd considered him a liability, or at best, someone good at first aid. Maybe there was more to Tim than met the eye.

"There are many who struggle to see beyond the illusions of this world. Some, like you, Broken One, have suffered much, but been given much. Others would leave it a better place before they depart, no matter how small their gift. If not for them ..." the Wind left the thought unfinished.

"*Kyrie eleison*. Lord, have mercy," Tim whispered in a trembling voice.

"That is my hope," the Wind agreed.

The moment radiated a stillness so beautiful, so peaceful, Sage felt she could touch it. But then Gus licked one of her wounds and snapped Sage's mind back to the problems at hand. "Hey, we need to move past introduction time and figure out what to do next."

Tim gasped and stared at her with a look of disbelief. The Wind shook the campsite once more, so hard that the ground beneath them seemed to move. Sage tensed until she realized it was laughing.

"Oh, Broken One," it finally sighed in her ear, its voice tinged with sadness. "You have been a warrior-heart since birth. It is woven into your very soul."

"Warrior-heart?" Sage grew still when the Wind caressed her and found her wounds. Flinching as It probed them, she tried to hold still. Even though it hurt, she knew the Wind's touch would help them heal faster.

"We must do battle together against this dark creature before he destroys any more lives." The Wind, finished with Sage's injuries, cooled her sweat-dampened forehead with a soft breeze. "The evil he perpetrates grows greater by the day."

"Is it ... it can't be. Can it?" Sage stuttered.

"Yes," the Wind agreed, its voice mournful.

"But a *yee naaldlooshii*, here?" She remembered the creature changing into a coyote on the mountain ridge and shuddered. "I've never heard of the *'Ánt'įįhnii* or their ways here." Witchery was one of the few things she hadn't missed when social services relocated her from New Mexico to the middle of nowhere, Colorado.

"Evil disguises itself in many forms, but they are all facades of destruction. If allowed to continue, it will cripple countless lives."

"Tell me what to do." Sage sighed. "I'll need your help; it's tried to kill me twice now, and I don't see how I'll be able to destroy it. The thing shot me with an *'adagąsh* in the cave."

"Help is already here." The Wind pushed her now mostly healed body toward Tim.

"Him?" She glanced at Tim. He looked as surprised as she felt. "How can *he* help? He's not like me, is he?"

"Not at all, and that is why he can help you. His heart longs ever after peace and reconciliation."

"Peace." Sage spat out the word. "How can you talk about peace when that creature and other ones like it are on the loose?"

"Others?" Tim asked. "Are there more?"

"Evil, destruction," the Wind said, "they tear at the

fabric of our earth and ever have since the beginning of this world and all its many ages."

"But why?" Sage asked the question that always rattled in the broken places of her heart. "Why can't *you* just destroy it? You're obviously powerful enough to."

"Can you begin to imagine the battles I have fought? And am already fighting?" The voice boomed, loud and harsh once more. "Do you not believe I and the others are doing all within our power to overcome?" The voice dropped to a whisper. "You were saved for this very moment." The Wind cupped her cheek. "You have spent your whole life preparing for this battle, even though you did not know it. And you two have been chosen to destroy this evil that poisons all it touches. For long years it has slept in these valleys and lulled many into thinking it was gone."

The Wind laced its way between their two hunched forms. "Broken One, a warrior must be tried and tested. Must prove to both herself and those around her that she is ready to be strong. Trust the priest will see some things more clearly than you. He has spent his life trying to listen, trying to understand how the vices of your kind weave themselves into the ordinary, becoming monsters most fail to recognize. He can see weakness and not despise it. You must fight the *yee naaldlooshii* together; otherwise, it will prevail and many will suffer as you have both suffered."

Sage considered the words.

Tim's voice broke the thick silence. "I ... I still don't understand exactly what's happening. Or what you want from me or Sage." He raised his hands in supplication.

"Listen and you will," the Wind soothed as it began to retreat. "You know that answer better than anyone, priest. Listen." It disappeared, and the trembling aspen leaves fell silent.

Sage let out a deep sigh and rubbed her eyes. She felt Tim shift next to her and turned to look his way. He was already walking toward the perimeter of the clearing.

"Where are you going?" She demanded.

"Gotta be alone for a bit," he shot back without turning around.

"Don't go far," she shouted after him.

He gave no indication he'd heard her.

"Better go with him, Gus." The dog trotted from his customary sentry position next to her. "Make sure he doesn't go far." She watched Gus follow Tim and suddenly felt very alone.

Sage paced back and forth until she knew she had to do something or go crazy. Time to unpack the Jeep once more.

CHAPTER FIFTEEN

Several hours later, Sage woke to the sound of the rain-fly being unzipped. She flicked on her tiny camp light as Tim and Gus entered. Tim climbed into his sleeping bag, and Gus curled into a ball at Sage's feet.

"I hope we can be honest with each other now." He finally spoke. "And by *we,* I mean you."

"I'm sure you have some secrets you haven't shared with me," Sage said.

"Yes, but the difference is, if you asked, I'd tell you," he said. "I can't remember you giving me a straight answer since we met. Who are you? What are you?"

"Why it is so important for you to understand?" Sage flicked off the light. The sudden darkness pushed down on her like a suffocating weight. "Can't we just move forward?"

"No." Tim's voice was soft yet strong as granite. "If it's our job to destroy some evil creature, you have to tell me what's going on."

A voice inside Sage screamed in protest. She knew she couldn't open all the doors of her past. She wouldn't do that for herself, let alone a stranger. Besides, no one else believed her the few times she'd even hinted at the truth, except Grandfather Benally, and he was like no one else on earth. But the Wind's revelation that Tim was now part of this terrible drama played through her mind, and Sage knew she'd have to tell him something.

"Fine. Ask away." She sighed. "I'll consider answering."

"How long have you been talking to that angel?" he asked.

"Angel? What angel?"

"The one we were talking to!" His voice rose with irritation.

"That wasn't some kind of mythical creature, Tim," she barked at him. "That was the Wind. The Wind who lives Beyond-the-Sky."

"Wind?!" His voice was incredulous. "Did you not see that thing?"

"See it?" She echoed. "There wasn't anything to see."

"You're serious?" He flicked the camp light back on and studied her face for a moment. "You *are* serious."

She nodded. "Of course I am. I don't see anything, but I hear it. And of course I feel it. The Wind's been talking to me since ... since I was a child," she finished lamely. "But no one else has ever heard it except me." Not the foster parents who'd made brief appearances in her life, certainly not Uncle Brian, and not even Grandfather Benally. But somehow this random guy could hear and evidently even see the Wind, a revelation that both excited and annoyed her.

"Is it the Wind that heals you? Or does that happen on its own?" Sage felt Tim scoot closer to her sleeping bag. She glanced over and saw him studying her in in the lantern's dim glow.

How could she formulate an answer that would satisfy

him? "I had an accident as a child. It was terrible." *And I couldn't tell you much more than that if I wanted to,* she almost snapped. Frustration and anger threaded through her as they always did when she tried to conjure the details of that night. Why couldn't she remember what happened? Ambiguous explanations from her social workers and the brief write-up she'd found in an old newspaper were all she had. That and the nightmares.

"When I first woke up in the hospital, I couldn't see, but I could hear. The doctors and nurses left me alone most of the time. I'm pretty sure they thought I was a goner. They barely even came to check on me, but the Wind did. It would sneak into my room, through a window, I think. It took care of me, healing my wounds." *At least the ones on the outside.* Sage quickly silenced the thought.

"It took a while, but I got better. Ever since then, my body heals itself quickly. And the Wind's been there ever since too, no matter where I am. But I hear it better if I'm alone."

"And the sensing thing?" Tim prompted when she didn't continue.

"That came after the accident too. I could sense things: smell them, feel them. It's usually with animals." Sage lay on her back and closed her eyes against Tim's probing gaze. "Like right now, there's a raccoon circling the Jeep with two kits. She just climbed into the back and is trying to open the food bin. But she can't manage the lock." Sage paused for a moment and waited. "Now she's going to lead the kits to the stream down the hill and hunt for fish."

She opened her eyes and glanced over at Tim. His face reflected disbelief and awe.

"That's why I know the creature isn't close by," Sage continued. "I also know it can't come over the ridge of this mountain. Yet." She added, remembering the Wind's words. "We're safe here tonight. But we'll need to move tomorrow."

She pulled the sleeping bag up to her chin, now annoyed with how much she'd shared, but also strangely relieved.

When Tim continued to stare at her, Sage added, "I've only told a few other people about this. My foster mother doesn't even know. It's hard for me to put in words." She let out a deep sigh as a bone-weary exhaustion settled over her.

Tim nodded. "I guess that's enough for now, but you need to remember a couple of things."

"What?"

"Obviously, I'm more vulnerable than you. I wasn't raised by the ... Wind. I don't have super healing abilities. I can't sense animals. I can't smell evil creatures. Should I go on?" His voice suddenly sounded rough, angry. "I'm just a normal guy. The more you hide from me, the more at risk I am in all this. I'm not afraid to die, but I'd prefer not to. It would break my mom's heart. Ever since I came back to America, Thanksgiving and Christmas mean the world to her. I think she's as scarred by my Sudan experience as I am."

Sage tried to picture his mom. *I bet she was with him while he was being treated for his PTSD.* A longing that pierced her heart with sudden swiftness. Gus crawled from his place at her feet and shoved his head against her chest.

"For some reason, we've been thrown together in this situation," Tim continued. "I don't know why, my brain still refuses to accept all that's happened in the past 48 hours, but I'm here. I'm willing to try and stop this ... *thing* before it kills anyone else, but the more honest you are with me, the better."

"I'll try," Sage said. But long years of careful secrecy would not have let her share everything even if she'd wanted to. And she didn't.

Tim turned off the lantern and let out a huff of frustration as he fell back against his pillow. A tense silence filled the tent.

"Gus's special too." She finally broke the quiet. "He's twenty-two years old but doesn't act like it. And sometimes we can talk without words."

"Great." Tim rolled over. "That's exactly the kind of detail that will help keep us alive."

CHAPTER SIXTEEN

With unspoken agreement, the two skirted any more talk of the Wind, Sage's abilities, or the creature and fell into a taut silence.

Sage's head ached as she considered the magnitude of their situation. Just as she knew their campsite was safe for tonight, she also knew that come morning, they would need to pack up and leave. *But where?* Her mind demanded. She had no answer.

And how, exactly, did the Wind expect her and Tim to *fight* the Skinwalker, as it had instructed? With their bare hands? Listening for obscure hints? She envisioned the two of them standing before the terrible creature that had chased her from Old Hank's cabin. The only outcome she could conceive of was a complete bloodbath.

Last but not least, a sick feeling of betrayal (or was it jealousy?) tried to sabotage any of the more logical, survival-driven questions that demanded answers. It annoyed her that the Wind had revealed itself to Tim. It annoyed her even more that he not only heard it, but saw it too. *Surely*

you did not think you were my only charge, Broken One?
Yeah. She had.

The tension in her neck and shoulders thrummed. Sage tossed angrily in her sleeping bag, dislodging Gus who moved to the edge of the tent with an irritated grunt.

"I can't sleep either." Tim's voice broke into her thoughts. "What the heck are we going to do?"

Sage threw her hands up in the air then smacked them down on the bag. "Die, probably."

"Don't say that," Tim said, his voice suddenly sad. "It's not something to joke about."

"I'm not joking," Sage muttered.

Tim didn't respond but sat up and dug around in the backpack at his feet.

"What are you doing?" Sage asked.

"The only productive thing I can think of," Tim said and pulled out his computer. He set the backpack behind him and leaned against it. "I'm going to look over those pictures I downloaded from where we found Shaun and Tabitha. Maybe there's something that will help us."

Sage didn't respond. Suddenly shame joined confusion and jealousy in the parade of emotions that marched through her. *But I wasn't joking,* she wanted to explain to Tim. *You don't understand the thing we're up against, but I do. And I see no other pathway than death! I wish I did, but it's hopeless.*

Sage eyed Tim and the whisper of an idea flitted through her mind. What if she left him? She and Gus could sneak away after Tim had fallen asleep and drive far, far away. They could escape from all this chaos and drama. But then the Wind's words filled her mind once more: *You must fight the yee naaldlooshii together; otherwise it will prevail and many will suffer as you have both suffered.* Sage took a shaky breath. She wouldn't wish her childhood on her worst enemy.

"Hey, here's the cave drawing you had me take a picture of," Tim said and shifted the computer toward her. "Why don't you explain to me why it caught your attention."

Sage hesitated for a moment before sitting up and leaning closer to Tim. "Pictographs usually show hunts or battles, but see the horses and guns in this one? That means it can't be very old. And look at that thing on the left."

"Is that what the thing at Hank's cabin looked like?"

Sage nodded.

"Huh. So maybe that monster isn't the first one to live in the Oriel Valley."

"Maybe not," Sage agreed, and Tim clicked to the next picture.

As she studied the images with Tim, she was drawn back to the terrifying experience at the mine. But now she was able to analyze the memories and their implications without the distraction of fear.

"See the way that the bones and flesh are all piled into that huge heap?" She pointed at one of the close up shots. "Coyotes would never do that. The Alpha gets the first pick of the remains, since they often scavenge from stronger, more skilled predators. Next, the other coyotes in the pack, the dominant females and the up and coming juvenile males, take their pick of the kill. Each of them will move away from each other to feed because none of them trust each other. As scavengers themselves, they're always waiting for someone to steal from them. They'd never keep their share of the kill together like that."

"Was the way they ganged up on you normal behavior?" Tim asked as he scrolled through the images.

"No. If they were desperate, like in the middle of winter, and starving, maybe. Or if I was smaller, the size of a child, then they might try something like that. But during a normal summer without food or water shortages, coyotes would never attack a full grown human like that. Chase me out of their cave maybe, but never corner and kill me. Especially with Gus nearby."

Sage leaned forward and wrapped her arms around her knees. The barrier of secrecy that protected her unique abilities had not been breached since her days with Grandfather Benally. To be so unguarded with her words felt strange and uncomfortable, like life returning to a limb that had gone numb.

"The weirdest thing was, I couldn't make a connection with them. I've come across predators before, but I've always been able to convince them to leave me alone. I speak to their thoughts, like I do with Gus, and then they accept it when I tell them to move on. But this time, something was blocking our communication. I think ..." Sage fell silent.

Tim glanced at her, his face illuminated by the computer screen. After a moment he looked down again. "What about this?" He pointed to the large paw print with the deformed foot. "That's not a coyote paw print, is it?."

Sage shuddered. "No, it's not. I think it belongs to the same thing that chased me from Hank's cabin."

"You seemed to know what it was when you talked to the Wind. You called it something ... yee nada... I didn't recognize the words."

"*Yee naaldlooshii*. It's a Navajo word."

"How do you know that?" Tim asked.

In an instant, Sage was transported back to an Enemy Way ceremony Grandfather Benally had performed. Sage had watched, wide-eyed and silent as an unconscious young woman tossed and turned in a feverish stupor. Her mother slumped next to Grandfather, sobbing, and told him of how her daughter had been witched while out collecting prickly pear fruits.

The girl had stumbled home in the middle of the night raving about a *yee naaldlooshii*. How it had appeared in the middle of the desert and chased her for hours. The mother gave Grandfather Benally the few details she could piece together from her daughter's fevered ravings: the girl had hidden in a small canyon and finally an intense afternoon rainstorm had driven the *yee naaldlooshii* away. The girl waited as long as possible before the stream rose and flushed her from the flooded canyon. Somehow she had found her way back home.

As a holy man *Hataɫii* or Singer, Grandfather had performed a healing ceremony. Although it lasted for over a week, the poor girl had not seemed entirely recovered.

"Sage?" Tim interrupted her memories. "I asked how you knew about the Navajo word."

"I lived with a Navajo family for a while," Sage answered and swallowed down her sorrow. Memories of Grandfather Benally still punched her in the gut.

"And what's that other word you and the Wind mentioned?" Tim asked.

Ánt'įįhnii, Sage thought but didn't say it aloud. "There's not really a direct translation to English, but it's the term for a powerful witch, one who has skills in shapeshifting. It can take both human and animal forms, often a coyote, wolf, or owl. Most Navajo won't even speak of them because they're terrified by the witches' power over death, curses, and destruction."

"And now one's after us?" Tim asked.

Sage hesitated then, nodded.

"But why? Just because we discovered Shaun and Tabitha? And now Sheriff Davis? Their deaths are already going to create a storm of questions, without ours being added to the headcount. I'd expect some evil mastermind to be more subtle." He hesitated. "Besides, could it even kill you if it wanted to? With your healing powers?"

Sage shifted away from him and pulled the sleeping bag tight around her neck. "I'm not invincible, Tim. My powers are nothing compared to this thing."

Tim chuckled, and Sage looked up. "What?" She asked, sharply.

"Nothing? I think your powers are pretty incredible. You probably take them for granted at this point, but think of all you've gone through these last couple of days. And you still had the strength to almost knock me out when I was loading up the Jeep."

Sage gave him a reluctant smile. "I guess. I mean, he did shoot me with that cursed bead, an 'adagqsh. Those are usually deadly. Even though the wound isn't completely healed like the others from that day, I'm still alive."

"Exactly," Tim agreed. "Plus, we've got Gus."

Sage glanced back at the computer. It had automatically started a slideshow of Tim's pictures. An image of Shaun and Tabitha's remains quickly extinguished the brief burst of optimism. Sage looked away. "Every time I see that creature, this primal fear takes over. It is the hunter, and I'm the prey." She looked up into his eyes. "It *would* kill me, Tim, and it would enjoy every moment of it."

Tim shifted the computer on his lap and gently rested his hand on top of Sage's head. "Don't. Don't let your mind go there. This is not hopeless. I don't believe that."

Sage nodded and tried to ignore the unfamiliar warmth

that spread through her at his words and touch. She glanced at the computer and saw the shadowy picture of the glass tube she'd found in the mine.

"The vials!" Sage exclaimed and sat up.

"What?" Tim asked.

"See that vial from the mine? I found some more in Hank's cabin, but I forgot all about them." She patted her vest pocket and felt a crunch. "I think they're mostly broken." Her fingers gingerly probed the crumbled shards before finding one larger intact piece. She held it out to Tim

"It looks like a prescription vial," he said, studying it in the light of the computer screen. "I can't quite make out the letters."

He handed it to Sage, and she squinted at the tiny, fractured letters. "Cloza ... Clozapi ... that's all I can read. The rest of the letters are cracked."

"Could they be an *N* and an *E*?" Tim asked.

Sage squinted. "I think so. I definitely see the *E*."

Tim let out a whistle. "Clozapine. That's a serious antipsychotic. The kind they use when nothing else is working and all that's left is a drug that might kill you."

Sage wondered if he spoke from experience. "It matches the vial in the cave," Sage said. "It had the letters *L O Z A* on it. I bet it was Clozapine too."

"Maybe." Tim pulled a tissue from his pocket and wrapped it around the shard. "How many vials were there in Old Hank's cabin?"

Sage pictured the contents under the sink. "At least 40 or 50."

"That's scary," Tim shook his head. "I didn't know Hank very well. Did he seem like he had mental issues? Schizophrenia or maybe bipolar disorder?"

"Definitely not." Sage shook her head. "He and I ran

into each other plenty of times. Not as often lately, but a lot when I first moved here. He seemed like a loner, a mountain man. Nice enough but really bored. And maybe a little depressed."

"Bored?" Tim asked.

Sage considered his question. "Yeah, whenever we happened to meet up in the backcountry, it seemed like he was looking for something to fill his time. The rumor was, he became insanely rich after he sold his land to the Oriel scientists. I don't think he knew what to do with himself once he got all that money."

"When did all that Oriel buyout stuff happen?" Tim asked.

"Back in the early '70s, I think. Maybe earlier."

Tim yawned and returned the computer to his backpack. "You know the thing I don't get about him? How old is he, really? I mean he goes by *Old* Hank, for Pete's sake. I've seen newspaper clippings of him at the Oriel guest center. He even looked ancient in those, the ones that show him signing the deed for his land to Terrance Storm."

"That's true." Sage nodded. "Now that I think about it, people talk about him like he's been around forever."

"Is there another *old timer* resident in Black Mills we could ask about Hank?" Tim settled down into his sleeping bag. "Since the Skinwalker came to his cabin, I think we have to find out more about him."

Suddenly an idea flitted into Sage's mind. "I need to talk to Liddy."

"But we can't go back into town. The police are probably still looking for us." Tim's voice slurred with sleep.

Sage shifted as Gus wormed his way between her and Tim. "No matter what, we can't stay here," Sage murmured. That part wasn't negotiable.

A snore sounded from her right, and Sage knew it wasn't Gus's. She rolled over and listened to the gentle breeze that danced through the evergreens surrounding the tent. Her mind strained after the details of a newly imagined plan, but sleep blurred and finally silenced them.

CHAPTER SEVENTEEN

Before dawn, Sage shook Tim awake and the two of them packed most of the camping gear into the Jeep. After replacing the shrubs and branches to camouflage it, they grabbed their backpacks and entered the forest just as the sun came up over sparkling snowcapped peaks.

"So where are we headed?" Tim asked between mouthfuls of energy bar.

"Another place I know. Also safe. It's a cabin about 15 miles from here." Sage led him and Gus down the hillside adjacent to the one she'd gone down the day before. She didn't have the stomach to even consider going back to Oriel.

"Is it a secret lair?" Tim asked. "I could really see you with a secret underground lair. Like Batman."

"What are you talking about?"

"You're the closest thing I've met to a superhero."

Sage let out a bark of laughter. "I'd need a lot more spandex to qualify."

"Well, who knows what you're hiding under that flannel shirt and jeans?"

Sage stopped and turned to Tim. "Excuse me?"

Tim's grin disappeared. "I mean, like a secret identity. Like when Clark Kent goes into the phone booth and pulls off his clothes--" Tim stumbled over a rock and nearly lost his balance. "I didn't mean ... I'm not *thinking* about what's under--"

"Tim, I got it. Relax." Sage turned away and continued her steady march down the hill.

She glanced down at Gus. "You spend one night in a tent with a guy ..." Gus wagged his tail and barked. "But I know you'll keep an eye on him for me." The dog nipped playfully at her before darting away to race after a squirrel that startled across their path.

Sage heard the crack of underbrush and felt Tim catch up to her. She glanced up but he carefully avoided her gaze.

They hiked on for several hours in companionable silence. When the sun was reaching its zenith, she stopped at a fallen pine tree and set down her pack. "We're over halfway there now, but I've got to stop and eat. I'm starving."

"So you think it's safe for us to go into Black Mills?" Tim munched on a handful of nuts.

"Not really, no," Sage answered between bites of her fruit leather. "We're going to need some help. My guess is that Officer Olson has been busy while we've been up here. Everyone is going to be on the lookout for you and *Crazy Sage*. Some of the people in town call me that, if you hadn't heard."

"Well, I had, actually."

"What?" Sage stopped chewing. "We only met last week."

"Yeah, but you were all the catechism kids could talk about during the parade."

"Huh." Sage folded up the fruit leather and put it in her pocket. "Hear anything good?"

"I'm not sure *good* is the right word. I found out that the only person you really talk to is Liddy, but since she's well liked, people put up with your ... reclusiveness. Also, you only come into town every once in a while, and nobody knows where you go the rest of the time."

"And," Sage prompted, knowing this was a very bland version of what he must have heard. "They all think I'm crazy."

"Pretty much. The kids in town are scared of you. Some of them told me you're a vampire."

Sage opened her canteen and took a drink. "Well, at least it keeps them away."

"Guess that's one way to look at it," Tim said.

Sage stood and flung her backpack over her shoulder. "I'm sure this is a shocker, Tim, but slumber parties and town bingo night aren't exactly the best way to keep supernatural abilities secret."

"That's not what I meant." Tim reached toward her, but she stepped back.

"It's fine. I learned a long time ago that letting people write you off as a weirdo is a whole lot easier than the alternative." Sage took a moment to find her bearings, then continued up the hill. She struck a brisk pace, hoping that it would keep Tim too winded for any more conversation.

"What are all these trails?" Tim asked after they had paused for water a couple of hours later.

"They're old Indian trails," Sage answered. "Mostly the Ute's."

"Aren't you worried we'll run into someone?"

"Who?" Sage turned a sharp eye on Tim. "The Utes and other Indians have all been exiled to reservations. Tourists and day hikers don't walk them. They aren't scenic enough and aren't monitored by forest rangers in case someone wanders off the trail. Wildlife only uses them now." Sage looked around and sighed. "They're from a different age, a different way of life. Pretty soon, animals or not, they'll probably disappear. The forest will consume them."

"So how do you know about them?" Tim asked as they shouldered their packs once more.

"The Wind showed them to me," Sage answered shortly. A breeze rustled through the air as if to acknowledge her statement, and suddenly Sage realized she hadn't even hesitated to tell Tim this detail. One she would never have dreamed of uttering to another human a week ago. The revelation made her stomach tighten.

A short while later, Sage paused near the rim of another valley. A few hundred feet below, the forest thinned out and a dilapidated, solitary cabin slumped in the middle of the meadow flush with yellow and white wildflowers.

"Who lives there?" Tim whispered.

"No one. It's one of my foster mom's rental cabins," Sage replied. "I'm hoping it's vacant at the moment. You stay here with Gus, and I'll go scout it out and make sure it's empty. If I signal you, grab my pack and come quickly."

Tim nodded and crouched next to Gus. "What happens if there's someone in there?"

"Run," Sage said without hesitation.

"I'm not leaving you here," Tim's whisper rose a few levels. "The Wind said we had to do this together."

"It's just a precaution, Tim," Sage snapped, too tired

from their long hike to have this conversation. "I don't sense anyone there. Just shut up and let me check it out."

"I'm getting tired of everything having to be your way or the highway," Tim stood up and took a step toward her. Sage had to tip her head to keep eye contact with him. "Like it or not we're a team, and I get to have an opinion too without you going into rage mode every time I say something."

Sage balled her fists, but Gus whined and they both looked down. The dog wagged his tail frantically.

"Fine, if there's someone in there, do whatever you want, but I'm not going to waste time brainstorming a *Plan B* with you."

"Maybe I'll—" Tim swallowed and crossed his arms. "Just be careful."

Sage blinked, then nodded. She stole to the very edge of the clearing and smelled the air. Crouched down, she darted half the distance toward the cabin. Her eyes scanned the woods around the cabin for any movement. Seeing none, she dashed the rest of the way to the back of the building. Sage crawled along the side until she was under a window. Carefully, she rose to peer through the dusty panes. It was impossible to make out anything through the grime, so Sage wiped the window with the edge of her sleeve. Again, she strained to detect any movement, but saw none. She closed her eyes and checked once more for any presence on this hillside besides Tim, Gus, and her. Nothing.

Rising from her crouched position, Sage beckoned to Tim and Gus. They bounded toward her from the cover of the forest and followed her to the front porch. Sage felt for the key behind the kerosene lantern that hung next to the front door. She let out a sigh of relief when her fingers touched the rough, cold metal.

She unlocked the door and in one swift movement, ushered Tim and Gus inside. Before closing the door, she grabbed the lantern off its hook and set it on the railing on the front porch.

"What did you do that for?" Tim asked once she was back inside.

"To let Liddy know I need her," Sage answered and took her pack from Tim's hands. "The lantern on the porch is my signal to let her know I'm here."

"How will she see it?" Tim peered out the dusty window. "We're in the middle of nowhere."

"We are, but Liddy can find us," Sage answered. "She has rental cabins all over this area, although she hardly does anything with this one anymore. It's falling apart." Sage gestured to the missing slats in the wall and floor, covered by unsightly plywood. Even with Sage's creative handyman skills, it would take a large chunk of money for Liddy to fix all the problems with this cabin, something Sage knew her foster mom didn't have.

Sage dropped her pack by the lumpy, threadbare couch and collapsed into it.

"But how will she know to look for you?" Tim settled into an oversized chair next to her.

"Liddy worries when I've been gone from town too long, so we settled on this cabin as a check-in location; it's the only way I can keep her off my back. If the weather's bad, I sometimes stay here for a few days. Or leave her a note," Sage answered, tucking her knees up to the side to make space for Gus at the end of the couch. "She always keeps tabs on me."

Tim turned and punched the lumpy cushion behind him. "So you don't mind it when *she* does it?"

"No." Sage closed her eyes. "But she doesn't butt into my business."

"Well, now it's my business too," Tim said.

"Be quiet." Sage pulled a blanket off the back of the couch. "I want to sleep."

"You're the one still talking."

Gus sighed with contentment and soon all three of them were sound asleep.

CHAPTER EIGHTEEN

A rumble of distant thunder woke Sage to the dim shadows of twilight. She tensed and lay still for a moment, eyes on the ceiling, trying to remember where she was. Gus and Tim's gentle snores broke the silence, and her shoulders relaxed. She settled back into the embracing cushions. Liddy's cabin. She was safe. At least for the moment.

Gus raised his head and the two made eye contact. The dog jumped off the couch and nosed the front door. "Gotta go out, buddy?" Sage followed him and peered through the front window down the dirt road. A plume of dust rose from a distant vehicle.

"What's up?" Tim asked in a sleepy voice. "Everything OK?"

"I hope so." Sage took a step sideways, to the edge of the glass. "Someone's headed up here."

Tim came and stood behind her.

Sage squinted through the dirty panes and studied the pair of distant headlights as they meandered up the road. "I think that's Liddy's truck. Hard to tell, though, since it's almost dark. Let's go upstairs just in case." She whistled to Gus and led the three of them up the steep stairs into the loft. Once there, she gestured to the back window. "That's an emergency escape. We can go out that way if the truck doesn't belong to her. It's not too far of a drop."

Gus wiggled next to Sage and Tim's crouched position against the sloped roof line. Memories of her encounter with the Skinwalker at Hank's cabin replayed through Sage's mind on an inescapable loop. Heart racing, she tried to still the anxiety that thrummed through her. Tim murmured something soft and indistinct.

A loud crunch of gravel sounded as the truck pulled in front of the house, then the engine went silent.

"It's her." Sage let out a ragged sigh. "We're safe." She moved to crawl from their hiding place, but Tim quickly pulled her back.

"Wait. How do you know?"

"It's fine, Tim." Sage said, firmly grasping his hand and pushing it away. "Look at Gus."

Tail wagging, Gus pranced across the loft. He then hopped down the stairs and bounded away with a happy yip. "He wouldn't do that if it was ... if the person was dangerous."

Following Gus, Sage scrambled down the stairs. She opened the door right as Liddy approached with a load of bags.

"Sage, honey, I'm so glad you're here," Liddy said. Dropping her load to the ground, she pulled Sage into a tight hug. "I've been worried sick about you. The police are on some kind of rampage. They have pictures of you up around town and in the newspapers."

"I'm sorry. I couldn't think of a safe way to contact you," Sage said. Gus slipped past her legs and frisked around

Liddy before heading to do his business in the trees next to the truck.

"Now just what the heck have you gotten yourself into this time?" Liddy pulled back and cupped Sage's face.

"Well, Tim and I—"

"Tim?" Liddy took a step back and peered around Sage. Tim stood in the shadows behind her.

"Hello," he said, and stepped forward with an extended hand. Liddy eyed it but didn't move, so Tim let it drop after a moment. "I'm Tim Burgney. I don't believe we've met."

"I know who you are." Liddy said, shortly. "Both your pictures are splashed everywhere. Whatever the two of you have done, you've created a hornet's nest of trouble with the local authorities." Her face blanched, and she pointed at Tim. "They're saying that you're the reason the sheriff—"

"Was murdered?" Tim asked, his voice jagged.

"Yes, that, and a whole bunch of other things, sonny." Liddy gestured to the groceries still on the front step, and Tim moved to pick up the bags.

"Who's accusing him?" Sage said and helped Tim with bags. They followed Liddy into the small kitchenette.

"Officer Olson, the acting Sheriff. According to him, Tim Burgney here is actually some sort of disgraced priest— a serial killer, Satanist in disguise. Which is why he murdered the poor Sheriff in such a terrible way. Documented all this evidence of grisly crimes that happened at some church he worked at. In Africa, I think. Got witnesses to say that he was creepy. Evil. That sort of thing."

Sage looked at Tim. He placed his bag on the counter and wearily leaned against it. "They'd have their pick of terrible stories from Sudan. Wouldn't be hard to substitute me into the role of villain." He clenched his fists and walked away.

Sage felt a surge of rage. "And me?"

"That's the really strange thing." Liddy opened a can of soup, poured it into a pot, and placed it on a propane burner. "They're saying you stole all these whatchamacallit fancy things from the laboratory in Oriel."

"Oriel? What does any of this have to do with the labs at Oriel?" Sage said. Tim returned and stood behind her.

"I don't know, but that's what the head scientist over at the Research Station said. That Terrance Storm fella. I guess it's expensive stuff because they keep saying 'you're wanted for questioning.'" She stirred the soup and gave it a taste.

"Also, Tim, you're suspected in the kidnapping of Old Hank," Liddy said and shook her head.

Sage glanced at Tim. "I was up at his cabin, Liddy. It was trashed. It didn't look like anyone had been there in a long time. And there were medication bottles all over his bathroom. Antipsychotics."

"Anti-what?" Liddy turned the burner to low and set the spoon down.

"Antipsychotics," Tim answered. "The medication doctors give people when they're not doing well. Mentally."

"Like going crazy?" Liddy shook her head.

Tim looked down. "Well, crazy probably isn't the right word, but--"

"I've known Old Hank for near on 60 years. Heck, he was here, living in that awful cabin all by himself, back when my folks moved her in '55. He was a recluse, all right, but I wouldn't call him crazy." Liddy paused and tapped her lip. "But he has become more wild in these last few years, since the Oriel scientists bought his land. I just figured it was all that money. Who wouldn't get a little wild if a million dollars suddenly fell on his lap?"

"Maybe he took his money and left." Sage shrugged. "And they're just trying to find more things to pin on Tim."

"Well, like I said, everything's a mess. In fact, the whole thing sounds like a bunch of hooey to me. And most of the townspeople too." She turned to Tim. "By the way, everyone that knows you says it can't be true."

"That's refreshing," Tim said.

"What we need is a way to be invisible," Sage said. "To get back into Black Mills or Oriel and find out what's really happening."

Liddy eyed the two for a moment. "Well, the Honey Festival starts tomorrow. Guess you could disguise yourselves as tourists and sneak around some during the shindig. I've got a box or two in the crawl space full of forgotten clothes from old guests. You're welcome to use anything you find."

"Thanks," Sage smiled. "We'll do that."

"Well, disguise or no, you two better be careful," Liddy said as she walked back to the door. "Like I said, your pictures are splashed everywhere. Flyers, newspaper, TV. Better make sure no one sees an ex-priest and a mountain girl, or you'll be arrested faster than you can blink. Even though that Officer Olson is as shady as the day is long, he seems determined to make some of these crazy charges stick."

"Don't worry about us," Sage said, following Liddy to the front door.

"I will worry about you, sweetie," the older woman said and pulled Sage into another tight hug. "I always do. And you too preacher man," she turned to Tim and stuck out her hand. "Guess if Sage trusts you then I do too."

"Thanks," Tim said as he shook her hand. "I'll do my best."

"You do that, sonny. I'd better get going. I'm pretty sure Olson is having me followed. Dodged a guy down by the bridge, but I don't want to take any chances of leading them in your direction."

Sage followed her to the truck and allowed herself to be enveloped in one more comforting hug.

"Put that lantern outside again if you need anything," Liddy whispered into her hair. "Don't have this cabin reserved for the rest of the summer so you're safe here for now." The older woman pulled back and wiped her eyes. "We'll figure this out, honey. Everyone knows that Olson is a shady character. I'm just praying the two of you get this sorted soon."

Sage nodded, swallowing down the lump in her throat. She waved as the truck pulled away and waited until long after the red tail lights had faded in the distance.

CHAPTER NINETEEN

Back pressed against rough rock, Sage stood under the convex curve of the cliff. It was twilight, but she could just make out a group of women and children that surrounded her. Together, they were all huddled just inside the cave entrance. One of the children cried out, and a woman hushed him urgently, pulling the child to her shoulder and glancing wildly around the clearing.

The women and children were dressed strangely. Most wore long blankets and furs over animal hide clothes and boots. Some of the boys wore dark pants and button up shirts, but many were dressed in skins as well.

Where am I? Sage wondered. Confused thoughts rattled around her brain. Whoever these people were, they seemed terrified.

Sage sniffed the air and caught the acrid scent of ashes and decay. It grew stronger. She peered to her left, past the muddy pond, through the dim forest. Her eyes strained for a glimpse of something in the darkening woods.

There. She caught a movement in the trees opposite them. Another flash of a white shirt and light hair.

A loud shriek erupted from one of the women, and she pointed toward the forest while clasping her child in terror. Other cries joined hers as half a dozen figures crept from the shadows, slinking through the darkness and forming a silent line opposite the women and children.

Collectively, the aggressors turned back toward the woods and the one who was their leader. He gave a sharp, guttural sound, and the group let out an answering shriek. As one, they turned and advanced upon the women and children, slashing at them with hatchets and knives.

Cries of terror and agony rent the air. Sage turned to help the sobbing woman next to her, but suddenly she found her arms were pinned behind her in a vice-like grip. Whimpering, she turned and found herself inches from the wolf-like form of the *yee naaldlooshii*. Its tongue flicked out of its mouth and licked lips curled in pleasure.

Sage tried to wrestle free, but its hold on her was too strong. It pulled her closer, and its coarse hair stung her cheek.

The fetid breath was suffocating as it whispered in her ear, "Watch well the doom I have brought upon these little ones." Sage saw a man with a hatchet first attack a mother and then her weeping child. She tried to close her eyes against the gore, but found her eyelids pulled open.

"Now they will destroy the bodies, Broken One. These ones will find no peace, even in their afterlife. For who could mend such destruction done upon a body?"

Staining the snow like a river of blood, the carnage before Sage was incomprehensible. Once vibrant lives hacked apart on the banks of the muddy pool.

Sage's subconscious railed against the horror surrounding her. This didn't make sense. It *couldn't* be real.

"This is just a dream," she screamed over her shoulder. "You can't kill them! You can't kill me!"

The creature spun her roughly until she faced its hideous, glowing red eyes. "Are you so sure?" It smiled, and rows of razor sharp teeth gleamed at her. The mouth opened wider and wider and then swallowed her whole. Sage screamed as she felt herself being consumed, sinking into darkness.

"Sage!" she heard a voice yell in the distance. "Sage!" It was insistent, but her attention remained focused on the darkness. Brief snatches of light illuminated pale, unseeing faces.

Shaun and Tabitha appeared, along with others she didn't know. Then came a bedraggled face that she struggled to place. Why did he look so familiar?

Recognition finally came. "Hank?" she whispered. There was no reply.

"Sage, Sage! Wake up!"

She reached out to touch Hank, but then something grabbed and shook her. She lost her hold, and Hank's face disappeared.

"Please, Sage, please God. Wake UP!" The voice shouted, forcing her awake. She was back in the cabin in her cot with Tim's hands at her shoulders. His anxious face peered down at her, illuminated by the silvery moonlight.

"What? Where am I?" She choked out, her throat hoarse and painful.

"Are you awake?" he demanded.

"Yes, yes." She tried to pull away from his hands, but he wouldn't let go. "Calm down, I'm fine."

"Calm down? You've been screaming for help for the last ten minutes!"

"Ten minutes?" Sage swallowed, the raw, lacerated ribbons of her larynx suddenly making sense. Gus, on the other side of her cot, whined and leaned up to lick her face.

"Yeah." Tim released her shoulders and ran a trembling hand through his hair. "I couldn't wake you. I didn't know what to do."

"I was back at the ... mine," Sage began, suddenly knowing it was true as the words came, "but it wasn't from our time. It was a cave and with a huge pool in front of it. There were people dressed in animal skins. Women and children. They were terrified." Silent tears streaked down her face.

She continued, not shying away from any detail, no matter how horrific, telling Tim everything she remembered. When she got to the part with the creature pinning her arms and then swallowing her whole, a sob began to build in her throat. Tim wrapped a strong arm around her shoulders, and Sage gulped down the tears before quickly finishing her story.

Tim remained quiet so long, she wondered if he'd fallen asleep, but then his voice broke the silence. "Do you think those were real people? Did that really happen?"

Sage considered the question for a moment. "Yes."

"Wouldn't we know about it?" Tim asked. "Massacres usually grab a lot of attention. Have there been any around here?"

Sage shrugged, her head pounding with emotion and fatigue. "Maybe there weren't any survivors to tell the story."

"What about the men?" Tim argued. "There had to be fathers with all those children. Some of those women had to be wives."

"I don't know." A tear slipped down Sage's cheek, and she brushed it away, but not before Tim saw.

"How are you?" he asked, his voice gentle.

"Fine."

He leaned closer. "Here's the thing, I know about nightmares, Sage." She felt the brush of his fingertip trace the path of the tear down her cheek. "I told you that before, right?"

Sage nodded. "You still get them?"

"Yes." Tim nodded. "And they still feel real, every time."

Sage gulped.

"But you're safe. You're with me, with Gus, and we have the Wind. It's always protected you hasn't it?"

"From some things, yes."

"Gus, hop up here with Sage." He patted the space near her feet, and Sage felt the dog jump and settle there. "Why don't you try to fall back asleep. Gus and I will keep watch for a bit." He shifted his weight from the edge of her cot and settled on the ground next to her.

"You don't need to do that."

"No, I want to. I want to puzzle through that dream a bit more before I fall asleep."

"But I'm fi—," the rest of her reply was cut by an earsplitting yawn.

"Just go to sleep, Sage." Tim's voice dropped to a comforting rumble in the darkness. "And let me think about that dream. Why would they go to the mine? Or cave, or whatever it was? That's a terrible place to go if you think you're going to get attacked. Why not stay in a town. A defensible town? Or hide in the woods?"

She felt herself relaxing, lulled by the soft cadence of Tim's wondering and the warm weight of Gus at her feet. It helped to know Tim was trying to figure out what the dream meant, if anything. Usually post nightmare, she was too keyed up to fall back asleep, but Tim's voice was almost hypnotic, and Gus's presence always comforted her like a warm blanket. Sage forced the last of the nightmare's images away and finally drifted off to sleep.

CHAPTER TWENTY

The next morning Sage awoke to the smell of brewing coffee and the clatter of kitchen tools. She dressed quickly and descended from the loft to find Tim preparing a breakfast from Liddy's supplies. Gus woofed a gentle greeting, and once Sage sat down at the rickety table, the dog extended an upraised paw to her knee. Sage buried her face in the fur around Gus's neck, thankful for his reassuring presence.

"How are you feeling?"

Sage looked up. "Okay, I guess."

Tim had moved away from the eggs he was scrambling. He poured a cup of coffee and handed it to her. "Did you sleep better, after—"

"Yes," Sage stood abruptly and sloshed the coffee over her legs. Flinching, she walked to the window. "Any thoughts on disguises?"

"Disguises?"

"Yeah, so we can go to the Honey Festival. Remember?" She took a gulp of coffee. It burned her raw throat, and she spluttered.

Sage turned around, and Tim offered her the cardboard container of milk. "Do you think it's a good idea come out of hiding while we're still in the dark about everything?"

"I don't know what other option we have." Sage poured some milk into her coffee. She took another sip. Much better.

"But Black Mills isn't hosting the Honey Festival this year. Oriel is. I remember reading about it in the newspaper. The county fairgrounds got destroyed by the spring flood, so they changed the location to a large tract of BLM land that runs up against OBRS. Storm and the gang were not impressed, but the land doesn't belong to them, so the BLM ignored their complaints." Back at the stove, Tim scooped the eggs into a chipped bowl and set it on the rickety table. After the two sat down, he offered some to Sage, but she shook her head.

"Oriel's not a safe area for us, is it?" He asked after several bites.

"No, it's not." Sage drummed her fingers against her cup. "That's where the creature seems to be centered. But I've been thinking, with all the festivities going on, there would be safety in numbers. It's hardly going to attack us in the middle of a crowd. That's not the way they tend to operate.

"Plus, it might be interesting to see what we can discover in Oriel. Evidently Storm has accused me of stealing a bunch of expensive equipment from the Research Laboratory. Why on earth would he do that?" Sage shook her head. "Out of everything Liddy told us, that's the thing that confuses me the most."

"Do you know Storm?"

"I've met him once or twice," Sage answered, remembering the most recent time in the gift shop. "Mostly when he and his students are out studying their marmots or whatever it is they do. Then I get the *you're on Oriel's private property with a dog and need to get off ASAP* speech."

"Oriel, the Shelton Reservoir, that whole valley in fact, has always given me a pretty evil vibe." Tim finished the last of his eggs.

"Vibe? I didn't think priests believed in vibes."

"I say vibe, but what I mean is a presence," Tim said and straightened in his chair. "I noticed from the first time I visited, way before all this started."

Sage let out a deep breath, "I know what you mean. I've never liked it there either. I usually avoid it if I can."

Tim laced his hands behind his head and leaned back. The old chair groaned under his weight. "There's a lot of really good climbs in the Oriel Valley. When I first moved here, I tried few of them, but whenever I was in that valley, I felt like I was being watched. And that it wasn't safe for me to stay." Tim shook his head. "My radar told me to get the heck out of there."

"All paths seem to be leading to it, though," Sage sighed. "I think there's some old mountain bikes in the shed out back. If we use them, we could probably be in Oriel in a couple of hours. Plus, I don't think anyone will expect us to go there."

"But what are we going to do once we get there?" Tim stood and gathered his dishes from the table. "We don't even know what to look for."

"The Wind will show us what to do. It's always shown me before. Plus, it did tell you to *listen*, remember?"

"I remember," Tim nodded. He set the dishes in a basin and filled it with hot water from the kettle. He walked over to the window and leaned against the pane. "And believe me, I've been trying. Before you woke up this morning, I sat out behind the cabin, listening. For over an hour. But all I get are a jumble of words and images. A red bird. A sign with the word *Rand.* A woman crying in front of a computer."

"What does that mean?" Sage asked.

"That's the point!" Tim smacked his hand against the counter. "I don't know what any of it means. Everything's moving so fast. But listening takes time. And quiet."

"I guess you'll have to listen while we're on the bikes," Sage said. "If we want to get to the Honey Festival, we have to find some disguises. Now."

A short while later Tim stood before her, now bald, courtesy of Sage and a razor she'd found in the bathroom; however, she left the three day's scruffy growth on his chin. Tim had changed into his jeans, dusty from their time at camp, a white T-shirt, and dark boots. Black marker tattoos, which didn't look too bad from a distance, covered his upper arms. Most of the cast-offs from Liddy's crawl space were moldy and unusable, but Sage had found Tim a pair of wrap-around sunglasses and a rugged denim vest to complete his scruffy look.

"I don't suppose we could quickly pierce your ear," Sage said as she walked around Tim, surveying the overall effect.

"No, we couldn't," he said.

"Everyone will recognize your type but none of them will look too closely at the details."

For her transformation, Sage had cut a pair of her own pants into tiny, ragged shorts. In Liddy's box, she found a black bra that nearly fit and paired it with a sheer white tank top she normally used as a base layer and not a fashion statement. Tim's first aid kit had come in handy yet again; Sage repaired a large pair of broken sunglasses with some athletic tape, which she then colored with the black marker.

She had also rubbed iodine all over her face to copy the look of orangey foundation. A liberal application of shockingly red lipstick she found in the kitchen junk drawer was the final touch.

"I'm not sure about you," Tim shot back, carefully keeping his eyes on her face. "I think your details will attract some serious attention."

"Yeah, but no one will notice my face, Tim. That's the point. The guys will want me, and the girls will judge me. It's the easiest way to make yourself invisible. You're just some forgettable, faceless slut." She walked to the mirror and pulled her hair into a messy bun.

"I'm sorry," he said.

Sage turned from the mirror. "For what?"

"For whatever it is you've gone through." Tim watched her with sad eyes. "Growing up in the foster system, I know that's not easy."

You couldn't imagine, not even in your worst nightmares. The look of compassion in Tim's eyes unlocked something. Dark memories, moments of pain and humiliation rolled through Sage. She bit her cheek until she tasted blood. This had to stop. Now.

"Whatever, Tim." She turned away from him and walked toward Gus. "We need to get going."

Sage knelt beside the dog and pulled him into her arms. His reassuring warmth calmed the panicked beat of her heart. "You're going to have to stay here, buddy." Sage murmured into his ear. "You're just too beautiful to disguise."

Gus whined and pleaded with soulful brown eyes, but Sage forced herself to give him one last squeeze and step away. "It's okay. We'll be back soon," she said, attempting to block the dog from her mind, but she knew Gus wasn't fooled.

The dog tried to bolt out when she opened the door, and Sage had to shove him back in before she could close it. The eerie sound of Gus's crying howl followed them for several hundred yards as they walked the bikes through the woods.

"Is that normal?" Tim finally asked, breaking their tense silence.

"No," Sage answered. It wasn't.

ORIEL MEADOW OPENED UP BEFORE SAGE AND TIM AS they came to the edge of the woods a few hours later. Sage was relieved to see a massive crowd of revelers. The visitors snaked their way through the merchant tents and milled around the large stage that would host several bands later in the day and into the evening.

"You ready?" she asked.

"Ready as I'll ever be." Nervous tension radiated from him.

"You've got to calm down, Tim. Right now, anyone looking for someone suspicious will see you coming from a mile away."

Tim crossed his arms. "I'm sorry, but I've never done anything like this before."

Lucky you, Sage thought. "Don't stand up so straight. You look like a soldier. Or a cop." Tim slouched. "Better. Now look angry. Scary. Like everyone is a threat to your manhood."

Tim let out a muffled groan, and Sage tugged him forward.

"Make sure to be handsy," Sage said leaning in towards him, "like I'm your babe, and you own me."

"Anything else, your highness?" He slipped a tense arm around her shoulders.

Wrapping her arm around his waist, she slipped her hand into his back pocket and squeezed. "I'll let you know."

The smell of sugary sweet treats and gasoline generators enveloped them. The crowd jostled and surged with curious tourists, hyper kids, and a few easy going locals. Sage and Tim wandered through the crowd, as slowly as Sage could make herself go, when all she wanted to do was dash through the tent city toward the research cabins of Oriel. Tim helped steady her, dragging her to different tables and pointing out things for her to study.

"Hey, babe," he barked in a deep voice. "Look at this. You like it?"

"Nah," Sage drawled through her nose, pretending to examine whatever trinket he held before her. "It's kinda tacky."

As Sage had predicted, nobody paid much attention to either her or Tim's faces. While most people shied away from Tim, Sage noticed quite a few of the male revelers eyeing her with the lecherous attention she'd predicted. Tim kept her close to his side, however, so even the brave ones didn't approach her.

Just as the sound of the first band warming up vibrated through the valley, Tim and Sage approached the last of the tents. Before them lay the main cluster of cabins that comprised the Oriel Biological Research Station. Their eyes met, and Sage felt a current of anticipation travel between them. It was time to find some answers.

CHAPTER TWENTY-ONE

Sage and Tim snuck into an outbuilding at the edge of the fairgrounds. It was filled with a small fleet of ATVs and motorcycles, ones that Sage had seen with the scientists on more remote mountain excursions. Of course she'd reached the same locations on foot, but then, tracking marmots was evidently hard work.

Tim followed her to the windowed back door and peered at the buildings that spread up the hillside behind them. An outsider would think they were looking at old miner's shacks and merchant cabins, since Terrance Storm insisted that all the original buildings be repaired to keep their historical appearance. Newer buildings were carefully constructed to look at least 100 years older than they actually were. The effect of the dark, rugged cabins, after the raucous energy of the honey festival, was unsettling. The faux ghost town dotted its way up the side of the mountain like jagged, broken teeth.

Sage shuddered and tore her gaze away. A breeze rippled through the leaves and moved next to her.

"It is time," came a whisper. Sage remained still. But

where to go? There were at least two dozen buildings in her line of sight. The Presence nudged her head a few degrees to the right, and Sage honed in on a one story cabin near the top of the hillside.

"What are we supposed to do?" Tim asked in a strained voice.

"Did you not hear it?" Sage asked.

"Hear what?" Tim asked.

"Come on." She tugged his hand and pulled him into a jog. A prickle of anxiety suddenly shot up her spine. Something was tailing them.

"But which one do we go to?" he hissed as they dodged in and out of the shadows of trees and cabins.

"That one, I think," Sage pointed to building near the top of the hill.

The two sprinted up the hill, dangerously exposed as they left the cover of the more densely populated valley floor. Gasping, they finally arrived at the front of the building. Sage glanced at a bronze plaque that designated it as the Rand Building, but Tim grabbed her arm and jerked her around the corner.

"Did you see, Tim? The Rand Building," Sage gasped out. "The word you got."

"This place is dangerous, Sage." He panted, ignoring her question. "Can you feel it?"

"Yes," Sage answered. She didn't tell him all she felt. The creature was close by, and a sense of overwhelming urgency hammered at her heart. "We've got to get in there. NOW."

"Let me go first," Tim said, but Sage ignored him and the two slipped onto the porch together. When Tim gave the doorknob a tentative twist, it opened with an eerie squeal. Sage looked up at Tim, and he gave her a tight smile before entering the cabin.

Once her eyes adjusted to the dim interior, she glanced around in confusion. It looked like a normal living room, with mismatched furniture positioned in front of a large fire place. Sage walked around the perimeter of the room. Aside from a few bookshelves and a closet there was nothing else.

"I don't understand," she stammered even as her perception of danger grew stronger. "There's nothing here."

"Did you notice a chimney when we were outside?" Tim walked to the large fireplace and felt along the bricks. "I didn't. This should have been along the wall we were just standing next to."

"No, there wasn't one," Sage said.

"It's a false wall." Tim ran his hands over the fireplace surround. "There's got to be a panel or something here."

Bookcases framed the fireplace, and the smell of musty, decaying paper stung Sage's nose. Above the shelves on the right side hung a mounted coyote head. Its beady glass eyes bored into Sage's, and she felt a rush of premonition. "That one." The words burst from her. "That's a door."

Tim jerked at the bookcase frame. "It's bolted to the wall."

"There must be a switch or handle." Sage ripped several books off the shelf and flung them behind her, the hair on her neck nearly dancing with fear.

Tim fiddled with a screw that stuck out along the edge of the shelf. There was a groaning noise, and suddenly, the bookshelf moved revealing a shadowed opening behind it.

As Tim wrenched the hidden door open, they heard a scrabbling of claws across the front porch. Sage snatched an old fireplace poker from the hearth and slammed it across the exposed screw, breaking it off where it met the wood. A shrill howl sounded and an explosion of shattering glass filled the room. Grabbing Tim by the shirt, Sage pulled the two of them behind the bookcase and slammed it shut, fireplace poker still in hand. Darkness engulfed them, and the hidden door shuddered from the impact of the creature on the other side.

Sage let out a shuddering breath.

"That was close," Tim said. Sage felt his hand find hers. "Did you know that was coming?"

"Let's go." She tugged at his hand.

"I can't see."

"I can, just barely." Sage pulled and this time he followed her down a set of stairs.

They both listened for whatever had followed them into the cabin. It was only a matter of time, Sage knew, until it found a way into the bookcase, despite the broken switch.

After a while Tim spoke, "I thought this was going to be a tunnel that lead us somewhere else in Oriel, but it's not. We're going really deep into the mountain."

"I don't know what it is," she whispered. "But hopefully it leads somewhere."

"Guess there's no going back, even if we did choose the wrong door." Tim let out a half-hearted chuckle.

"Well, I'm sure as hell not going back there," Sage said. The minutes ticked by as they continued down stone stairs that grew rougher and more precarious. Finally, they turned a corner, and a strange humming sound invaded the silence. Sage sensed they'd entered a large chamber. When she stopped, Tim bumped into her back.

"Feel for a switch or something," Sage said. "This room is huge. There has to be some sort of light."

They ran their hands over the smooth cold walls for several minutes before Sage discovered a switch and flipped it. There was a rapid *plink, plink* as the overhead florescent lights struggled to life, and Sage gasped at the massive space that stretched before them.

"You could play a football game in here," Tim said taking a few steps forward and turning in an awed circle.

"What is this place?" Sage whispered, her voice barely discernible over the humming din.

Row upon row of desks stretched back into the still, dim recesses of the cavern. On them sat hundreds of computers and other machines filling the air with their electric noise. Aluminum siding lined the windowless walls on both sides. The wall on the left side was full of doors. Some of the doors had windows, and inside them, Sage could see lots of stainless steel equipment and other machines.

"All these desks ..." Tim said. "What are we supposed to do? It would take years to go through all this." He gestured wildly at the massive space before them.

"Not sure we have that long," Sage said as a familiar tingle crept up her spine.

Tim turned and met her eyes. "You mean ..."

She nodded.

Tim sat down in the nearest chair and covered his face with his hands. Sage could hear him mumbling incoherently. Whether he was asking for help or saying his final prayers, she didn't know, but she wasn't going to wait around and find out.

Sage turned to the nearest computer and jerked the mouse around until the monitor slowly glowed to life. A box popped up on the screen requesting a password. She rushed from one computer to the next in the cluster of desks, but they were all the same. As Sage's gaze travelled over the hundreds of computers that stretched through the bunkers, she tried to ignore the fearful foreboding that raced through her.

They were screwed. There was no way the Wind would be able to speak to her in this concrete bunker. Electric fear shot through her limbs. The creature *would* find another way into this ... whatever it was. It was only a matter of when.

"Tim, come on. We've got to get out of here!" Sage shook his shoulder. "Maybe there's another way out."

Tim looked up from his hands, his eyes vacant and unfocused. "I keep getting the same picture in my head. Over and over again."

"I don't care! Are you deaf? That thing is coming for us!" Sage grabbed his arm and tried to pull him from the seat.

"No!" Tim jerked away from her and stood. "There's a desk, toward the back, that we need to find. A woman worked there." Tim closed his eyes again as if trying to remember something. "She was upset by what was on the computer. But she was scared too." His eyes snapped open, and he began to jog toward through the rows of desks, speeding up as he went. "She decided to disable all the security on her computer and hoped that someone would discover it."

"How do you know this?" Sage bellowed as she sprinted behind him.

"I don't know," Tim hollered back. "But we have to find her computer."

CHAPTER TWENTY-TWO

Tim slid to a halt near the back of the building. He paused, then drifted indecisively around several of the desks.

"What are you doing?" Sage snapped after watching him for a moment. "Come on, Tim. You gotta keep me in the loop."

"There's a bird," he muttered, then sprang into frantic action, knocking files, keyboards and pens off the desk beside him. Then he turned to another desk and did the same.

"What the hell are you talking about? Have you gone crazy?"

"In the picture." Tim swept a monitor onto the floor. "The one in my head. The woman's desk had a red bird on it."

"You mean like a birdcage?" Sage scanned the area with a desperate glance.

"No. There was no cage! Just a red bird. We've got to find it."

Sage turned and jogged to another section of desks, her mind still trying to picture the red bird he described. She turned a corner and suddenly a power cord tangled itself around her legs. Sage tripped and slammed into the wall of a large cubicle. The rough fabric scraped her cheek then collapsed beneath her weight. Climbing to her knees, she tried to regain her bearings. Then, from the corner of her eye, Sage saw a flash of red. She crawled toward it and came to a wooden desk surrounded by several other large metal ones.

"Here, Tim! There's a picture of a red bird. It's taped to the edge of the computer."

Tim sprinted toward her, leaping over the collapsed walls and office debris. He sat down and tapped frantically at the keys. They watched as the screen slowly glowed to life, just like the others. Except this time there was no password prompt. Only a screen image of an older woman hugging a small, pale boy close to her side.

"I'm in." Tim whispered and began to click frantically with the mouse. "I can't believe it. I'm in!"

"Hurry." Sage cautioned. The feeling of urgency had abated but not entirely disappeared. Something must have delayed the creature, but she knew there wasn't a snowball's chance in hell that it had been stopped.

"Help me look through these files." Tim grabbed her arm and pulled her up next to him. He scrolled down a page filled with hundreds of document and spreadsheet files, most of them with names that didn't even make sense, just combinations of numbers and letters. Sage's eyes blurred at the sheer number of them.

"It's too much." Sage said. "There's no way we can find what we need in time."

"Let me see what she was working on last." Tim clicked a few keys. A brief email popped up:

Sue,

I understand your concerns about the Meta Project. However, the decision has already been made by the board. I need you to finish compiling the data on the spectral analysis and have it on my desk by Monday morning.

Benson

"The Meta Project," Tim said then typed the word into the computer's finder. A folder popped up and as soon as Tim clicked it, fields full of data began to pop up on the computer.

"No time to read this now," Sage said. "Can you email it to your computer?"

"I doubt it," Tim said, "Even if she disabled the security on her individual computer, there's probably no way she hacked this place's firewalls. But maybe I can download it onto something." He ripped open a desk drawer and dug through it furiously. Finding nothing, he slammed it closed and tried the neighboring desk. "Here! A flash drive."

"Hurry," Sage said. "Time's almost up."

Tim nodded and turned back to the computer.

Nervously, Sage leafed through a stack of papers that had slid from the desk to the floor. While most of them were files with meaningless labels, Sage gasped as she neared the bottom of the pile and found one labelled *Shaun Colter*. She dug through the remaining folders and after a moment found one with *Tabitha Smalley*'s name on it too.

Sage opened the first file and quickly scanned through it. The first few pages gave information typically found in a doctor's chart, from Shaun's birth, up until the present. Confused, she stared at the diagnosis *cystic fibrosis,* indicated at the age of around two years. Sage reread the words several times and shook her head. Shaun was a star athlete. There's no way he had a terrible lung disease.

Suddenly a tingling sensation shot up Sage's spine.

"You about done, Tim?" She ripped a few of the pages out of Tabitha's and Shaun's files, folded them in half and shoved them in the back pocket of her shorts.

"I don't know!" Tim said. "I'm just copying and pasting files. I don't even know if it's the right stuff. And there's thousands of them."

"We're out of time." Sage clutched his shoulder. The tingling traveled past her spine and through her entire body in a giant burst of adrenaline. "We've got to go *now*!"

Tim's finger flew over the keys, "Okay, okay just let me paste—"

A loud crash echoed from the tunnel, followed by a bellow of rage.

"NOW!"

Tim yanked the flash drive from the computer, and the two sprinted toward the back of the massive warehouse. Tim tripped over the feet of an office chair and nearly went down, but Sage grabbed his arm and jerked him back up.

Another crash sounded from behind them, followed by a primal screech that sent shudders up and down Sage's spine. Louder and louder the wails echoed through the air, and it took everything in Sage not to cover her ears and cower.

"There may not be an exit back here," Tim shouted next to her.

"I know," she gasped. "But you can bet your ass I'm going to look for one."

As they neared the end of the warehouse, the walls transitioned to stone as if carved directly into the mountain's rocky surface. Gone were the prefab walls of sheet metal.

They skidded to a stop before the stone face, and Sage glanced over her shoulder. The creature, halfway across the building's expanse, ran toward them with alarming speed.

Now in its coyote form, flecks of foam dripped from its gaping jaws.

"There," Tim shouted pointing up. "There's a hole in the wall, up there next to the roof. Do you see it?"

Sage squinted. The rugged dark wall slanted away from her, but up near the top, she saw several indents. Maybe one of them was deep enough to crawl into. "Yeah, but does it lead anywhere?"

"Who *cares*?" Tim bellowed and shoved her against the wall. "Start climbing."

They inched up the jagged, granite slab with the howls of the creature echoing in their ears. Clattering desks and chairs sounded from below. Sage expected to feel the burning slice of claws in her legs at any second. Tim quickly outpaced Sage, and bits of rock and debris showered down on her face, loosened by his scrambling feet.

"Careful," he hollered from a few yards above her. "It gets really slick up here."

Sage lunged for a hand hold out of her reach and barely caught it. Her sweat-slickened fingers trembled in the small fingerholds she clung to, and her arm muscles burned with fatigue. She took a shuddering breath just as something slammed into the rock beneath her with concussive force.

"Don't look down, Sage. Grab my hand!" Tim shouted.

Sage glanced up and saw him perched on the edge of a small ledge. He leaned over, arm extended. "Just a few more feet."

A groaning sound came from below, and Sage gathered her feet underneath her. Another deafening crash exploded a few feet from her head. Glancing over her shoulder, she saw a contorted desk tumble to the floor next to the creature. Standing erect, now in its Skinwalker form, it snarled at the broken lump of metal and lunged toward another desk a few feet away. Sage forced herself to focus back on Tim and reached for another hold.

"Broken One," the Skinwalker called with soft menace. Deep and guttural, his voice sounded like a tortured gear grinding through a broken clutch. "You cannot escape. The Wind is not here. There are no boundaries to hide behind. You are finally mine."

His voice filled Sage with a debilitating, primal terror. She struggled to understand the sway it held over her, even as the panic it inspired overtook her mind. Her breath came in choking gasps. She felt her grip weakening. A panicked sob escaped her.

Sage glanced back over her shoulder. Slavering beneath her was the *yee naaldlooshii*, massive and hideous. Unbelievably, a desk lay cocked in its extended arm, and a look of triumph glowed in its red eyes. Its malicious laughter sapped the last of her strength. She felt first one finger slip. Then another.

"Sage!" The word broke into her fear hijacked mind, and she looked up. Tim strained toward her, reaching with extended fingers.

Her mind still blurred with the impenetrable haze of horror, Sage struggled to focus. What did Tim want from her? He called to her again, his face red with the effort, the veins in his neck bulging.

"Sage, stop! Stop looking at it!" His voice ricocheted through the cloying shadow of fear like a renegade bullet. Sage's mind snapped back to attention. What was the matter with her? She readjusted her hands on the grip with renewed strength and determination.

A loud clattering sounded beneath her. "Quick, grab my hand!" Tim yelled in a hoarse voice. "Climb up here before that thing gets back up!"

Sage's gaze locked on his, and with a mighty effort, she launched herself up the wall. Tim's hand wrapped around hers with vice grip strength, and with a mighty heave, he dragged her onto the ledge.

A hideous shriek of rage erupted from below.

Tim pulled her against him in the shelter of the narrow opening and rested his chin on the top of her head. "You're safe." His voice and arms trembled. "But we've got to move before it starts tossing desks again." He let go and gently pushed her into the opening in front of them.

CHAPTER TWENTY-THREE

Sage crawled through the dark opening, wincing when its jagged rocks assaulted her pounding head and trembling limbs. She heard Tim's exclamations of pain as they tore at him too.

Finally, the passageway enlarged. Sage straightened up, and Tim stood hunched next to her.

"What are all these tunnels?" Tim asked.

"I think they might be mineshafts," Sage answered. "That's why we can see. The miners would drill air shafts every so often to keep from suffocating. Sometimes light comes in too. Come on. We'd better keep moving." Sage trotted forward.

"It seems like it's going upward," Tim observed as they continued to steadily jog.

Long minutes passed. *What if this goes nowhere?* Sage tried to tamp down the fear, but it would not be ignored. *What if we're just going deeper and deeper into the mountain?* The thought of never seeing the sun again punched her in the gut. She forced back a shudder.

Just as she had convinced herself they should probably turn around, a dim flicker appeared before her.

"Tim, I think I see a light."

"Finally," he said, his relief palpable.

Light gray rocks were now visible, and the tunnel opened up. Sage rounded one last bend and felt a breath of air ruffle her hair.

Bright daylight flooded the chamber and blinded them. Tim and Sage tripped out onto a small overhang that quickly fell away to a steep canyon. A roaring waterfall poured from a ledge to her left and pounded down nearly 40 feet into the granite rocks and pools below.

Tim took a step back. "Whoa, that's a steep drop." He glanced over his shoulder. "Can you tell if it's still coming?"

Sage closed her eyes and considered. "Yes."

"Fast?"

"Yes."

Tim crouched down and studied the rocks around the ledge. "I'm not sure how easy this will be to climb down. The wall is inverted, and I don't see any hand or toe holds."

"There's no time, Tim. It's almost here." Sage gasped and a faint howl sounded from the opening.

Tim rubbed a weary hand across his eyes and stood. "Then I think we're going to have to jump." He studied the river below. "That one there." He pointed to a pool far to their right. "That one looks pretty deep."

Sage swallowed. "What if—"

"You go first," Tim ordered. "I'll jump when you're all clear."

"No, you should—"

A piercing cry echoed up the tunnel. Tim pulled Sage back. "Try to take a running jump." The cry came again, louder. "Go!" he yelled and shoved her.

Sage sprinted a few short steps and vaulted into the air. She felt something crash into her back just as a roar erupted from behind her. It was followed by Tim's agonized cry.

The ground approached, and Sage realized she'd over-jumped. She was too close to the lip of the granite pool. Turning, she tried to shield her body, but her shoulder slammed first into the water and then the unforgiving rock. Her head whiplashed into a scrubby pine tree at the pool's edge. And then all faded into nothing.

As she ran through the woods, Sage could sense twilight rapidly approaching. The air was tinged with the cool scent of evening.

"*Tsx̣įįłgo!*" The words sounded again and again from up ahead. Something crashed into her. A young woman, carrying an infant in one arm and leading a small girl with the other, struggled to keep up with the large group of women and children.

Sage paused and gestured to the girl. "Can I carry her?"

"*Háíshą 'ánít 'į?*" the woman replied.

Sage pointed to the girl and mimed carrying her. The woman nodded. "'Aoo' ."

Sage hefted the girl into her arms, and the two ran in the direction of the other women and children. After a few minutes, she caught up with them. They huddled at the edge of a cave.

Just like her vision before, it also had a partially frozen pool in front of it.

"Oh no." Her mind lurched with the realization that they were about to be slaughtered. "Quick, everyone, we have to get out of here. They're coming. They're going to kill everyone!"

"*Ge'*!" several women whispered.

"*Ha'it'iishq'*?" A child whimpered only to be hushed by his mother.

A baby cried, and Sage felt a sick sense of dread, knowing the attack was mere seconds away. Even if the others wouldn't follow her, she could at least save the child she held. Sage tightened her grip around the girl and tried to run, but found herself frozen to the ground.

She spied movement in the trees just beyond the pond and tried to scream, but her lips felt stiff. A loud shout sounded, and the strained silence was rent with cries of terror as a band of disheveled men advanced upon the group.

The girl in Sage's arms wailed. Now finally able to break free from her paralysis, Sage dropped to the ground and shielded the child with her body. When she glanced up, her gaze was drawn into the dark woods. Through the swaying pine branches, she saw the pulsating eyes of the creature as it laughed, hidden behind the trees.

The stale scent of liquor filled her nose as an attacker paused before Sage and the child. He raised his arm to strike. Suddenly, his eyes glowed red, and his face transformed into the *yee naaldlooshii*.

"There is no escape for you, Broken One." It laughed and traced the curve of her back with the blade of the hatchet. "No escape!"

Sage's hand darted from the trembling child to the knife she somehow knew would be strapped against her thigh. Jerking it loose, she quickly raised her arm and stabbed down hard, pinning the creature's foot to the ground. A terrible howl rent the air as Sage picked up the child and raced through the dark woods.

Just as she was nearing a stand of aspen, a sharp pain cut into her back. Sage tripped, and as her vision went dark, she clutched desperately at the little one against her body. Now she was falling, falling.

Her body jolted awake before the impact.

"Sage!" a ragged voice called. "Can you hear me?"

She cracked her eyelids open, but saw nothing in the thick darkness. The angry roars of the creature still echoed through her mind. A surge of nausea overpowered her, and Sage struggled not to gag. She tried to rub her eyes, but when she moved, a dull throb of pain shifted through her shoulders and upper back. She rotated her arm and heard a loud pop.

"Don't move. Your shoulder ... it's dislocated, I think. Your ankle's bad too--" The voice next to her broke into a hacking cough.

Sage gazed into darkness, but gradually her eyes adjusted to the light. She could barely make out the rocky ceiling several feet above her head. The smell of damp earth and the gentle drip of water overwhelmed her groggy senses.

Where am I? The confused images of Tim in biker gear, a giant underground warehouse, the creature chasing them, and a terrible massacre tried to arrange themselves in her mind. She longed for Gus and his comforting presence. Shifting slightly, Sage tested her body to see the extent of the damage. Her head, shoulder, and ankle throbbed with a steady persistence.

Gingerly, she raised herself up on her good arm. "Tim?" she whispered. "Are you here?"

A groan came from her left. She crawled toward it and collided with a body. "Tim, are you alright?"

"Not really." Sage felt a jolt of shock as she realized *the voice* belonged to Tim. Without its usual deep, smooth timber, she hadn't recognized the raw and painful rasp.

"What's the matter?" she asked, letting her fingers run over his contorted body. His shoulders and chest were covered with sticky warmth. "You're bleeding?"

"That ... thing got me," he whispered, groaning in pain when her fingers probed his wounds. "Scratched my chest, throat, and face up pretty good. Think it did something to my voice."

"Oh, Tim." Sage's fingers traveled to his face where she felt ragged flesh and more blood. Tears stung her eyes. "You should have jumped first." Sage choked on the words.

Tim let out a broken chuckle. "Nah. I know you always have to--" his words dissolved into a painful cough.

Sage took a deep breath and struggled not to panic. Tim needed her logic right now, not her emotions. "What happened? Can you tell me, or does it hurt too much to talk?"

"I'm fine," Tim said, but she noticed he forced his words out as if each one cost him something. "It all happened at once. You jumped. I heard a roar and turned to look into the tunnel. The creature burst through. It's funny how surprised it looked. I don't know. Maybe I imagined it. It attacked me. I thought I was a goner."

"But, but how did you get away? How did I get away?"

"I'm not sure. The angel ... the Wind was there, and I called for help. Then the creature went crazy. It thrashed around, like it was in pain. It knocked me off the cliff and then I seemed to float down to the pool, next to you." Tim coughed and continued, his voice much weaker. "You

weren't awake, but I was pretty sure you were still alive."
He fell silent.

"Tim, stay with me! What else? What else happened?"

"You were laying there. I knew your body heals itself. I
thought if I could get you out of the water ... I think I
dragged you to the far side of the stream, away from the
tunnel. The Oriel side. Maybe the creature can't get us
here?" He coughed. "I found this cave and—" He coughed
again and made a strange gurgling sound.

"Okay, that's enough," Sage ordered, terrified by the
noise. "You need to rest. I'm going to see where we're at and
make sure I don't sense the creature." She had to think.

"OK," Tim whispered his voice barely audible. "But
don't go far. Please."

"I promise." Sage swallowed and squeezed his
cold hand.

CHAPTER TWENTY-FOUR

Sage crawled out of the cave and limped into the clearing. Silvery grass and shrub willow surrounded a rushing creek. Indentations in granite rocks held rainwater that reflected the moon's glow and shimmered when Sage stumbled through them to the banks of the stream. The place would have been magical if not for the debilitating dread that raced through her.

"NO!" She cried in a choked voice and pointed at the night sky with her good arm. "You can't take him."

"He's dying." The Wind whispered from the quivering pines that encircled the glade.

"No, he can't die," she shouted, but remembering that Tim lay only several yards away, forced herself to continue in a strangled whisper. "Not him too."

"He's at peace," the Wind breathed. "He has no fear of death."

She felt rage building up inside her. "What about the other night? You said that we had to defeat this thing *together*. Well, it's not defeated yet. I can't do this alone. I won't."

The Wind was silent.

"Did you hear me? I WON'T fight this thing without Tim. I'll just leave."

"*Won't?*" The Wind tossed her damp hair around on her shoulders. "Do you think you can bargain when the destiny of this valley lies in your hands?"

"Why don't *you* take care of this valley?" Sage shouted into the night, her thin grasp on control snapping. "Why don't *you* destroy that thing if it bothers you so much? It kills everything. Over and over again, it kills!"

The Wind let out a sad sigh. "Over and over again your kind invites its presence back here." The voice died and the pines grew still.

Sage tripped over a rock and clung to a tree with trembling arms. "Fine! Maybe some of them. But Tim sure as hell didn't. He's ... he's so good. Please. Please don't let him die." Her voice broke in a ragged gasp.

Silence.

"Please. I'll do anything," she choked.

Silence and then. "Anything?" The Wind whispered gently. "Even though it may—"

"Anything!" she shouted. "I promise ... just please heal him."

Silence again. Sage resisted the urge to scream.

Finally the Wind spoke again. "You have been heard. Go pour out the depths of your suffering, and he will be healed. It will diminish you, your abilities, but it is the only way."

"What does that mean?!" Sage staggered around the clearing. "What do I have to do?"

"Go to him," the voice rushed past her through the clearing. "Before it's too late."

Sage stumbled back into the cave and was immediately

greeted by the shallow rattle of Tim's breath. She gently placed her hands on his neck, knowing that wound was the most deadly. "Tim?" She whispered. No response.

She replayed the Wind's words: *Pour out the depths of your suffering, and he will be healed.*

What does that mean? Her mind screamed again as the ominous rattles from Tim intensified. She had to do something. Frenzied words rushed from her mouth, muddled and of their own volition.

"So when I was little I had this great family." The long forgotten memories stabbed at her heart, but desperation made her continue. "My dad was a teacher in Gallup. My mom, she was amazing. Every day she met my brother and me at the bus after school. And she loved surprising us. Little things like fresh, hot sopapillas or a set of new pencils for us to do our homework."

Sage shuddered and felt tears begin to trickle down her cheeks. Tim choked, and she leaned closer to him trying to catch a glimpse of his face despite the darkness of the cave.

"My little brother, he was funny. A pest, you know? He loved to tease me, annoy me, but he had the sweetest heart. Whenever the girls at school were mean to me, he'd make funny little drawings and sneak them under my door to try and cheer me up. He'd give me his dessert at dinner and refuse to take it back until I promised I was happy again." A sob caught in her throat, and she fell silent, unable to speak, but then another death rattle in Tim's throat propelled her to talking again.

"After they were gone, I thought I'd died inside. But I was wrong." Her voice broke, and the tears came faster now, streaming down her face and dripping all over Tim. "Even though I was hurting, deep down inside, I was still me. But that only lasted until the court sent me to live with Uncle

Brian. Then I discovered that there are adults that care nothing for the innocence of a child. That it brings them joy to destroy it. Gus and I—"

"Gus was alive back then?" Tim's ragged voice broke into her story.

"Tim!" Sage gasped and cupped his face with her hands. "Can you breathe?"

Tim let out a ragged cough. "It's a little hard. But yes, I think so."

Sage brushed Tim's damp, sticky hair off his forehead. "I thought you were dying. You *were* dying."

"I think I might have been," Tim said his voice stronger. He coughed, and this time it sounded normal. "My breath kept getting stuck in my throat. I felt like I was suffocating."

Sage ran trembling fingers along his cheek, throat, and the tattered remains of his shirt. "I think you've stopped bleeding."

Tim caught her hand in his. She was surprised by the strength of his grip. "You saved me." He sat up, his voice filled with wonder. "The drops on my face, they burned like fire. And your voice. I think it brought me back."

Sage's nerves zinged with electric energy. Had she saved him? Was he truly healed? "Let me get you some water."

Tim nodded. "Thanks. My mouth, it tastes like metal."

Sage's head pounded as she stood, and her left ankle felt weak, ready to give at any moment. Using the cave's wall as a support, she limped from its opening and then to the river once more. Painfully, she extended her arms and filled her hands with sparkling, cold water which she carried it back to cave.

"Here's your water," she said, kneeling next to Tim, but he was silent. Sage dropped the water and leaned her ear against his ribcage. A choked sob escaped her when she heard the strong, steady beat of his heart. She allowed her head to stay against his chest and savored the soothing rise and fall of his deep breaths. Was he really completely healed?

She ran her fingers over this neck and face once more. The tattered, bloody mess was gone. Tim's breathing was deep yet quiet, with none of the ominous rattles or whistles of before.

Confusion danced at the edge of her mind, and a profound weariness joined the terrible ache of her injuries. Whatever had happened, understanding would have to wait until tomorrow. She curled up next to Tim, reassured by the tempo of his breathing. In only a few seconds, Sage felt sleep overtake her aching body with the welcome oblivion of sleep.

CHAPTER TWENTY-FIVE

Something dripped on Sage's cheek, and she emerged from confused dreams to reluctant wakefulness. Her limbs felt leaden and even small movements caused shooting pains throughout her entire body.

She opened her eyes. Faint rays of sunlight illuminated the damp gray rocks above her. When she lifted her hand to rub her crusty eyes, Sage's body protested even more urgently. What on earth had happened to her? It felt like she'd been run over by a semi-truck.

A movement against her back startled her. She tensed in anticipation of attack. Then a soft snore broke the taut silence. Tim.

Suddenly Sage was aware of him, the warmth of his body next to her, the weight of his arm draped across her waist. Wincing, she carefully rolled over and found him inches from her face, mouth open in oblivious slumber.

She moved closer and breathed deeply. The metallic tang of dried blood was muted by the earthy, sharp scent she'd come to associate with him. She placed a gentle finger at his neck and felt his heartbeat there, strong and steady. The rhythmic thrumming calmed her jittery nerves.

Evidence of the Skinwalker's wrath remained as a terrifying reminder of their escape. Tim's shirt was a tattered, bloody mess. Through the ribbons of fabric, fine white scars in the shape of ragged claw marks traced their way along the right side of his face and crisscrossed his neck and chest. They reaffirmed with brutal clarity how close to death Tim must have been. Sage shuddered. No one could have survived these injuries; not without supernatural help.

It was true then. Somehow he'd been healed. Had it been her tears? Her words? With trembling wonder, Sage reached out to trace one of the scars that ran along his throat and collarbone. Her finger hovered a hair's breadth from his skin before she pulled back.

What was she doing? These scars, they weren't the kind of scars an ex-priest looking for peace should have to wear the rest of his life. Especially Tim. He'd already had enough close encounters with death and danger in Sudan. He didn't need Sage dragging him into more of the same. Another casualty in the long line of people she loved dying terrible and premature deaths.

Sage gently disengaged from Tim's sleep-heavy arms. Allowing herself one last glance at his peaceful face, she painfully crept to the front of the cave. With trembling legs, she lurched through its mouth, dizzy from the intensity of her pounding head. Sage eased herself against a large, lichen covered boulder and panted with pain.

When she caught her breath enough to sit up, Sage studied herself in the dawn's weak light. Oozing scratches and dark bruises covered her arms and torso. "What's this? Why are these injuries still here?" she asked, louder this time.

The Wind moaned its way through the trees and settled next to her. "You gave away much of your power last night, Broken One, to heal the priest. Unless I help, you will no longer regenerate as you used to."

"This is permanent?"

"For now."

"I'd almost forgotten what this feels like." Sage rotated her arm and swore. "It hurts."

"Do you regret your decision?"

"Not at all," she snapped and limped to the stream. The icy water quickly numbed her hands as she scrubbed at the crusty blood that covered them. "I can handle some scrapes and bruises."

The Wind let out a sigh. "You can barely walk."

"Fine. If I can't heal myself any more, you do it."

"You can still heal, only more slowly than before. Like the rest of your kind, it will take time.

"I don't have *time!*" Sage snapped. "I have to get back to Liddy's cabin and figure out what those files mean. Then *I* have to destroy that thing."

The Wind tousled her hair and moved to wrap itself around her. Sage grimaced as wisps of air probed painfully. Pain was joined by the tell-tale electric tingle of healing.

"What did you say?" It gently reprimanded. "*Who* will destroy the creature?"

"It seems like it's getting stronger," Sage said, ignoring the question.

"It is."

"Why is that?" Sage asked.

"The evil in these mountains is rallying for its surge. There are many who feed it with their dark deeds, dark appetites. Our enemy knows that soon it will be powerful enough to destroy all who oppose it."

"Not me." Sage jumped up and tested her ankle. It felt strong, and the throbbing pain was nearly gone. Her head had stopped pounding, and the scratches had scabbed over. "Not without a fight, anyway."

The evergreens groaned and creaked as the Wind slashed at them. "You are at a crossroads, Broken One. You believe you have no alternative course of action than the one you have set your mind to. But that is a lie. The priest is your—"

"Enough!" Her voice rang, harsh and sharp through the clearing. "Maybe it is a lie, but this is my life. You don't get to control everything. I will not put Tim in danger again. And I won't allow you to either."

Abruptly, the rustle of the trees ceased and the rocky canyon fell silent.

Eyes stinging with unshed tears, Sage spun at the crunch of gravel behind her. Tim emerged from the cave, hand raised and blinking against the brilliant sunlight.

"Hey, there." Sage bent hurriedly and pretended to adjust her boot laces. She used the dirty hem of her shirt to wipe her eyes and nose. "How are you feeling?"

"Fine, I think. Actually, great."

Sage straightened and walked toward him, swallowing the exclamation of surprise that jumped to her lips. Here in the sunlight, the scars were much more conspicuous than what she'd seen in the cave.

He cocked his head awkwardly, as he studied the same marks on his neck and chest. "It doesn't even hurt, but how is this possible?"

Sage shrugged. "Who knows? But it's time get going. I think this is Quick Draw Creek. Liddy's cabin should be about five miles away, over that ridge."

Tim's attention snapped to Sage, but then his face softened into a familiar grin. "I just got out here. Maybe you could give me—"

"No. Grab a drink, and let's head out."

"Wait. What about what we discovered? And last night." Tim took a step and reached for her hand. "What happened in the cave? I think I was—"

Sage backed away from him. "No time. If we hustle we can get to the cabin before dark. Poor Gus must be dying, locked up in there for so long."

"Oh, right. Gus." Tim paused. "But once we get there—"

"We'll see if that flash drive is completely destroyed. You still have it right?"

Tim patted his pant pocket and nodded, but his eyes betrayed confusion and something else Sage didn't want to identify.

She turned and trotted along the side of the creek. "Try to keep up." She ordered over her shoulder, making sure to avoid Tim's gaze.

AFTER SEVERAL HOURS OF ALTERNATE JOGGING AND hiking, during which Sage had ignored all of Tim's attempts at conversation, they left the stream and the faint footpath that paralleled it. Turning south, Sage led them through a dense conifer forest filled with spruce and ponderosas. Low hanging branches grabbed at her hair as she cut a jagged trail through the pine needle encrusted undergrowth. A massive downed evergreen blocked her way. She climbed over the partially rotted trunk into a meadow and heard Tim follow.

Before them lay a small pond, with faint wisps of

steam rising from it. Trotting to its edge, Sage looked down. Clear turquoise waters and smooth granite rocks beckoned.

"This place is beautiful." Tim crouched next to the pool and dipped his hand in. "A hot spring? It doesn't even smell like sulfur."

"Not much, anyway." Sage sat down on a rock and untied her boots. "I think we both need to get some of this dried blood and grime off. We're close to Liddy's cabin, but all she's got there is an unheated water pump."

"But what about Gus? I thought we were rushing because you were worried about him."

"Oh, right." Sage remembered her excuse. If Gus was desperate enough, Liddy's ramshackle cabin wouldn't prove that much of a challenge. "We don't have to spend hours here, just a few minutes."

Tim didn't answer.

Sage peeled away her socks and then unbuttoned her shorts. Tugging them down her hips, she froze as she looked up and saw Tim's shocked expression.

Unbidden, the image of his body curled up next to her in the cave flashed into her mind. Something tickled in her throat, and she kicked her shorts the rest of the way to the ground before tugging off her stiff tank top.

Once it was off, she glared at the profile of Tim's averted face. "God, Tim, don't be such a prude." Quickly, Sage flung her bra and panties on top of the pile. "It's not that big of a deal." She jumped into the pool.

When she emerged, Sage saw Tim sitting on a rock several feet from the pool. He cleared his throat and kept his gaze fixed on the mountains in the distance. "Why are you doing this?" he said, his voice heavy.

"Doing what?" Sage laughed as she swam from one

granite rocked rim to another. "I'm not trying to seduce you, if that's what you mean."

"I know you aren't," Tim said, his eyes still on the horizon. "You're trying to do the opposite. To push me away."

Sage felt her stomach drop, as if someone had heaved a large stone into her soul. "Push you away?" She tried to force another laugh, but found she couldn't.

"Whether you like it or not, there's a bond between us, Sage. I didn't give up on you when that creature wanted to rip you off the wall, and you didn't give up on me when I lay dying in that cave."

"I don't know about dying," Sage answered. A ripple of air rustled through the leaves. "I guess we were both pretty banged up."

"Don't try to rewrite what happened," Tim said sharply. "I heard some of what you said. About your family. Your uncle." He shook his head. "And your tears. They burned when they fell on me."

"Well, it was pretty chaotic, Tim. I'm sure we both imagined a lot of things."

"Imagined?" Tim's voice held a note of disbelief. He stood and finally looked at her. "I thought you were braver than this, Sage."

The ripple of a breeze turned into a gust, and Sage dunked under the water, staying there as long as her breath would allow. Finally, when her lungs screamed in pain, she surfaced. Seeing no one, she panicked for a moment before she spied Tim among the trees at the edge of the clearing. He sat huddled in the shadows.

A wave of shame enveloped her. Was this the coward's way out? Couldn't she talk to Tim? Convince him that it was too dangerous for him to continue on their treacherous trajectory?

No. He'd never listen. In fact, her arguments would probably make him even more adamant in his commitment to stay. This was the only way.

With grim determination, Sage climbed from the pool and jerked her stiff, filthy clothes back on.

"Liddy's cabin is just over the hill behind you," she yelled in his direction. "I'm done, so take as long as you want."

Tim gave no indication he'd heard her. Sage dashed past him, through the woods in the direction of the cabin as fast as she could, eager to escape the breeze that moaned between the pines.

CHAPTER TWENTY-SIX

Relief flooded through Sage as she came over the hilltop rise and spotted Liddy's cabin in the warm, soft light of late afternoon. It enveloped her in a wave so strong that she staggered against a large boulder next to the trail.

The sound of Gus's frantic barking quickly chased the relief away. Sage raced the last few yards to the cabin. When she jerked the door open, the dog bolted onto the porch and nearly knocked Sage over with a mighty leap. She tripped down the rickety stairs and collapsed into the grass.

Gus raced frantic circles around her legs, occasionally leaping up to lick her face. "Calm down, calm down." She murmured and attempted to hug him, but the dog continued to race circles around her. Surprised at the tears that ran down her cheeks, she finally tackled Gus and pulled him to the ground in a full body embrace. "Just relax, you big baby. I'm fine."

Gus gave one last wiggle then lay still, but after a moment flattened his ears and whined.

"What is it?" Sage asked, sitting up. The dog looked pointedly at her side, behind her, then back at the woods.

"He's fine too. Just taking a little longer at the hot spring."

Gus cocked his head disbelievingly.

"What? He's safe. And I needed a little space." She reached out to scratch Gus's ears, but he pulled away.

"Are you kidding me?" Sage slumped against the rough porch. "I thought you were always supposed to have *my* back."

Gus nosed her hand and yipped, but remained standing.

"I don't know what happened. I mean, we both almost died. Multiple times. And then I think I saved him and lost some of my power in the process. I woke up, and he was lying next to me. It's all a complicated mess and ... and..." Her voice cracked. "I seriously can't handle this interrogation right now, okay?"

Gus crawled onto her lap and licked her chin. He whined again. Sage buried her face in the rough of the dog's neck. Long minutes went by until Gus finally raised his head and licked her tear-salted cheeks. When the rumble of her stomach sounded, Gus leapt back and gave a startled bark.

Sage rose with a half-hearted chuckle. "Let's get some food, buddy."

Gus barked once more and ran to the nearest tree to relieve himself.

"You're a good dog," she called gently as he ran back toward the porch. "A good friend."

Tim arrived at the cabin just as the sun set, and Gus gave him a similar welcome to the one he'd given Sage.

Alerted by the dog's ecstatic yips and howls, Sage left the soup she'd been heating. "I was starting to get worried," she said when Gus's greeting calmed down. "Thought you might have taken off."

"Nope," Tim responded shortly.

Sage leaned against the porch railing and studied her ragged nails. "Well, you can't have been in that hot spring the whole time. You'd smell like a rotten egg."

"I wasn't. I spent some time thinking. Processing all that happened. Praying. And I have to tell you something."

"Oh." Sage took a step back. She wasn't in the mood for a lecture.

Tim climbed onto the porch. He stopped a few inches in front of her and remained silent until she looked up into his honest gaze. "I heard what you said about your family. I wish you could trust me, but I get why you don't. And why your closest friend is Gus. I want you to understand that, Sage. You've gone through more than I can fathom."

Sage nodded and swallowed, tearing her eyes away from his.

She felt hemmed in by the railing. Tim was so close she could feel the warmth of his breath on her forehead. Her body suddenly ached with the desire to be touched by someone other than Gus. Her fingertips tingled with the anticipation. What if she reached out and took his hand? Or traced the rough stubble of his cheek? What then?

Instead she slipped past him and back to the doorway. "The soup's almost ready. There's bread too. Would you like some?"

Tim swallowed, then gave a small nod. "Yes, thanks. I'm starving."

They sat at the table in a thick, strained silence, broken only by the sound of Tim's spoon against the bowl.

Gus sighed in contentment beneath the table. *At least he's happy,* Sage thought, kneading the dog's back with her toes for several minutes. Unable to stand the quiet any longer, Sage retrieved Tim's computer from the loft and set it next to him.

"Want to see if anything on the flash drive is retrievable?"

Tim fished the device out of his pocket. "I'm not hopeful, but we can try."

He plugged it into a computer port and clicked his mouse. After a few minutes his eyebrows shot up in surprise.

"Something?" Sage asked.

"Something." Tim nodded but didn't look up. "But I'm not even sure what I'm looking at. Basically, it's just page after page of medical records." Sage scooted her chair next to Tim and shifted the computer between them.

"Medical records? But—" She scanned through several pages of data. "But why are they so obsessed with townspeople's health charts?"

"I don't know," Tim replied. "It looks like most of the population of Black Mills and from what I can make out, a few of the other nearby mountain towns."

Sage scrolled through pages and pages of information. Tim spoke again. "I don't understand why these records are so valuable to them. Valuable enough to store in an underground bunker. And to possibly kill people for?"

Sage nodded. "They're incredibly detailed. Is that normal?"

"I noticed that too. Like I said, I didn't finish medical school, but they do seem more intense than normal files. "

"There's genetic data on everyone in town. How are they getting this?" Sage tapped the screen. "There's no way all these people are asking for DNA tests." Sage considered the older inhabitants of the town and knew they were mostly the hearty mountain stock type who prided themselves on self-sufficiency.

"Look, here's Liddy." Tim scooted closer to her and clicked to another file.

"Liddy?" Sage laughed. "She *never* goes to the doctor. She barely has enough money to pay her bills, let alone get expensive genetic tests done. And I know she's suspicious of anything new."

"And the Anderson family." Tim pointed to another entry. "I know them, and they only go to a naturopath in Denver. It's one they keep recommending I try out. As far as I can tell, they've never even been to a traditional doctor's office."

"Who are the doctors listed on these files?"

"Only one person. Someone named Benson. I can't think of a doctor by that name. Can you?"

Sage smiled and shrugged her shoulders.

"Oh right." Tim shook his head. "Not that you'd ever need one. Although I noticed there's still some bruising on your forehead and arms. Why is that?"

"There's only one urgent care clinic in town," Sage deflected quickly. "Aren't Dr. Chase and Dr. Stringfellow the ones who run it? And the only doctors in town?"

"That's what I thought too." Tim nodded. "Who is this Benson guy? Does he even live in Black Mills?" He sighed and pushed back the computer. "I wish I could do a search for him."

Sage wracked her brain for anyone named Benson. She turned back to the computer. "Most of these files seem to be about whatever this genetic testing showed, not normal doctor visits for colds or injuries. I keep seeing the words *food and pollen allergy markers*." She jabbed her finger as she read. "Also markers for cancer, autism, congenital heart or lung defects."

Tim scanned through the list. "I know a lot of these people. A few of them have some issues but most of them are healthy and normal as far as I can tell."

"I don't really understand this stuff," Sage said. "If someone has a genetic marker for a disease, does that mean that they only have a chance of developing that disease?"

"Genetics were just emerging when I was in med-school, so I'm no expert on it either." Tim shook his head and took a slice of bread from his plate. "But I think you're right." He chewed for a moment. "What about the stuff you got? Was it destroyed by our escape?"

Sage pointed to the wrinkled, torn pages that lay in a mess on the kitchen counter. "They've been drying out all afternoon."

Tim moved to study them. "The writing is so faint. I don't think I can read them without my reading glasses."

"I can." Sage gently collected some of the papers into a pile. "This is Shaun's medical file. He was diagnosed with cystic fibrosis back in 1988. Which is weird. He's a superstar athlete."

"Huh. Maybe he had good treatment?" Tim asked.

"Well, he got tons of shots. Monthly injections. This records all of them and next to each injection date there's notes." Sage traced the first paragraph with her finger and read: *Yr. 5. Subject very advanced in fine and gross motor skill development. Physically at the level of a 10-12 year old. Muscle mass and development also accelerated. Reflex speed and sensitivity at level of Olympic athlete. Overall physical health and appearance: outstanding.*

"*Negative side effects: Subject's parents report night terrors and erratic sleep patterns typical in schizophrenic personality disorder. EEG analysis of nocturnal brain waves confirms schizophrenic susceptibility. Daytime behavior, however, is considered normal (aside from being physically advanced).*"

"Olympic athlete? That sounds normal," Tim snorted.

"Yeah, and get this. The Negative Side Effects section grows longer each time he gets a shot. And once he turns eleven, guess what he has to start taking?"

Tim paused for a moment but then leaned forward excitedly. "Clozapine? The same as Old Hank?"

"Yes!" Sage tossed the papers down. "Exactly like Old Hank."

"What about Tabitha?" Tim asked.

Sage picked up the other pile of papers. "Evidently Tabitha was diagnosed with something called *Fragile X Syndrome* in 1989, right around the time Shaun was diagnosed."

"I haven't heard of that before," Tim said. "I wonder if it's a lung disorder too."

"I don't know," Sage answered, "but her chart's different than Shaun's. His has all these notes about physical development, but Tabitha's keeps repeating the words *extreme cognitive acceleration.*" Her finger traced the words as she read.

"What about her negative side effects?" Tim leaned over her shoulder and squinted at the writing.

"They increased too, just like Shaun's, but even sooner, starting when she was only nine years old. She's been on Clozapine ever since then."

Tim shook his head. "That's a long time. The poor girl. Poor both of them." His eyes clouded, and he turned away.

Sage set the papers on the counter and eased herself onto the rickety barstool next to it. Her twisted ankle and dislocated shoulder still ached. The Wind's ministrations had helped, but obviously not completed the healing process. She massaged at her shoulder, wincing as her fingers probed the tender area in the front. Sage glanced up and found Tim's gaze on her. She quickly snatched her hand away.

"I think it might be good to let all this information settle in our minds for a while," Tim said, his voice tight.

Sage nodded warily.

"I wondered if you might want ..." Tim paused. "I'd like it if we could talk about what happened in the cave. Sage, I was dying. We both know that. And then you told me those things about your family--"

"Stop. Shut up!" Sage blurted the words, unanticipated and sharp. She wanted to take them back as soon as they were out. Her stomach twisted at the hurt on Tim's face.

"Would you relax?" Tim held his hands up. "I don't understand why we can't--"

"No. I'm not talking about them again." Sage tried to keep her voice completely blank, the way she always did when questions came up about her family. The silence grew, and she bit her cheek until she tasted blood.

Tim took a deep breath and turned away. He began to clear the table. "You should get some sleep."

"What?" Sage asked, studying the droop of his shoulders as he carried the dishes to the small sink.

Tim set them down and turned on the water. "It's been a really long day. I'm sure you're exhausted."

"What about you?" she asked.

Tim turned off the water and returned to the computer. "I need some breathing room. I'll be up soon. Goodnight." He dismissed her without looking up.

Gus gave Tim's hand a lick and then followed Sage to the foot of the loft's stairs. She glanced at Tim once more, but he kept his eyes determinedly on the computer in front of him. She climbed up the stair with Gus, annoyed at the confusion and regret that gnawed at her stomach.

CHAPTER TWENTY-SEVEN

Sage quickly settled into the sleeping bag on her cot, but despite her bone-numbing exhaustion, she jerked awake every time she began to fall asleep. Harrowing images filled her mind. The Skinwalker's terrifying chase through the underground cavern. Tim's bloodied body and near death in the cave. The bizarre massacre dream she kept having over and over, with slightly different details, but the same bloody ending.

Her stomach churned with fear, rage, and confusion. Sage rolled to her back, careful to avoid her aching shoulder. Gus, who had endured her tossing and turning long enough, jumped off the bottom of the cot and disappeared down the loft stairs.

Now she was truly alone. Longingly, she remembered the whiskey Liddy kept in her nightstand drawer. Sage would hide it in some obscure kitchen cabinet when Liddy had drunk too much. But tonight she would have gladly joined her foster mom in drinking herself into oblivion.

After a while, Sage finally heard Tim climb the loft ladder and felt him move across the floor to stand over her.

The intensity of his gaze was almost palpable, but she forced herself to lie still, to pretend to be asleep. It was all she could do not to flinch when she felt his hand settle gently on her head. Snatches of his soft prayer, a plea for protection and peace, enveloped her, and she almost spoke. But she held her tongue, and Tim moved away.

The cot next to hers creaked and groaned. Minutes later she heard his deep, regular breathing, and jealousy engulfed her. How could he fall asleep so easily? Had none of this affected him? Was he made out of stone?

No, he was not made out of stone. He was flesh and blood. *Fragile* flesh and blood. Sage sighed and gave free rein to the plan that had been creeping along the edges of her mind since she awoke in the cave. Sadness threatened to overwhelm her, but Sage knew she couldn't give in. Tim's life depended on her making the right decision in this moment.

She waited for an hour before slipping out of bed. Her night vision still unaffected by the change in the cave, Sage located her clothes without difficulty. Holding them under her arm, she eased herself down the creaky stairs.

From his perch on the couch, Gus's accusing gaze followed Sage as she dressed and gathered some crackers and granola bars from the kitchen. She collected her boots and sat next to him while she slipped them on. Gus let out a low whine and moved his silky muzzle against her thigh.

"I want you to stay here with Tim." She rubbed his nose and scratched behind his ears. "He doesn't sense things the way you and I do. I need you to be his bodyguard."

Gus furrowed his brow and whined again.

"I know you want to come, but you have to stay here with him." Sage looked away from the knowing in Gus's eyes.

She gave his ears a final scratch and leaned down to kiss his muzzle. "Take good care of him, and don't try to follow me." She stood and watched to make sure Gus obeyed. He moaned softly, but lay still.

"Good boy," she whispered and slipped through the front door into the comforting shades of night.

Thankful for the nearly full moon, Sage glided along familiar forest trails. With the Wind's healing last night, she was hopeful she'd have the strength to run most of the way back to Black Mills. It wouldn't take her more than a few hours to get there, and she planned to search for what she needed at the library.

Sage cut off the main trail and headed west, knowing she'd soon intersect with the highway. Ducking under a branch, then leaping over the small trickle of a stream, she tried to direct her mind toward what she and Tim had discovered under the Oriel Research Station buildings.

Sage fixated on the cavernous facility underneath the Rand Building in Oriel. Why was it there? When was it created? At the library, Sage planned to comb through Black Mills' old newspaper clippings. Maybe she would discover a clue of what had happened to turn a tiny mining town into the strange, dangerous place it had become.

She also needed to scour the county records for a Dr. Benson. Why was he collecting genetic information on everyone, and who did he or she work for? The person must live somewhere in the vicinity. The files Tim had shown her represented years of work that couldn't have been collected by an outsider.

Tim. Even his name conjured pain, shame, and other emotions she didn't want to identify. Her eyes stung, and she shook her head angrily.

"Why did you bring Tim into my life?" she asked the

deep silence of the night. "The few things we've discovered, I could have figured out on my own. Now his life's in danger. All he's done is complicate everything."

"Broken One," the Wind whispered softly, dancing along the edges of the moonlit wildflowers in her path. "You have hidden in the darkness of your soul for more than a decade now. Do you really think that a dog should be your only link to the living?"

"I want to go back to the way things were." Sage slowed to a walk. "This feels much too dangerous."

"The *yee naaldlooshii*? *It* feels much too dangerous? You've faced perils in the past, yet never complained of danger."

"All of this feels dangerous!" Sage snapped. "And painful. Before last week, months went by without me thinking about my past. But now I feel like I'm reliving it on a daily basis. I can't stand it!"

"Bringing a dead one back to life involves pain." A gust rattled the trees next to her. "And there must always be a sacrifice."

"A sacrifice? What do you mean? *Who* do you mean?" Sage demanded, but the Wind retreated away, down into the valley. Sage broke into a run and didn't stop until she reached the outskirts of Black Mills.

CHAPTER TWENTY-EIGHT

Sage paused at the edge of Black Mills, near the abandoned bridge where the high school kids hung out after school and got up to the trouble their parents imagined they did. Thankfully it was deserted now. Sage glanced at her watch and saw it was close to 3:00 am. There were still several hours of night to protect her from curious or malicious eyes. She quickly stole through dark alleys and side streets to the Library.

Sage bypassed the front and back doors, knowing they would be locked tight. Elena was fastidious both in her duties as a council member and librarian. Besides, the old stone building had stood through blizzards, gale force winds, and fires; Sage knew it wouldn't be easy to force her way inside. She prowled around the perimeter several times before pausing in front of the fire escape at the back of the building.

Rusty metal stairs crisscrossed the back of the library, leading up to the old belfry, a throwback from the days when the building had done triple duty as the town's church, school, and library. Sage climbed the stairs and pulled herself over the ledge into the old opening where a bell had once hung. Creaking wooden planks covered the three foot wide circle where the bell rope had descended into the building. Sage slipped her finger under several of the planks, hoping for a loose board, but all she got was splinters.

Cursing, she popped her finger into her mouth and stamped on the floor in frustration. The crack of splintering wood echoed in the small enclosure. Sage jumped and heard another groaning crack. Again and again, she jumped until she felt several of the boards give way. Kneeling on the stone lip, Sage pried at the jagged pieces until one came loose. After that, she was able to slip both hands under the boards and the rest of the ancient pieces gave way easily, as if they were tired of fighting.

Sage peered down into the darkness below. Although barely visible, the moonlight illuminated an attic floor many feet beneath her. She sighed. This wasn't going to feel good. She crawled through the opening, holding onto the remaining plank of wood, and hoped it would hold for a moment while she readied herself to drop. It didn't.

Sage's shriek of surprise sounded as the board gave way, and she plunged into the darkness below. She crashed into a pile of tarps, and then through the shelves that held them, before finally landing on the floor. Rising unsteadily to her feet, Sage shuffled across the room until she found the trap-door that led to the level below. Once on the main floor of the building, she leaned against a bookshelf and let out a shaky breath.

The library's musty smell began to work its magic and soothe her jumpy nerves. Sage walked to Elena's desk and found a small flashlight in one of the drawers. Frequent power outages during Black Mills's winter blizzards meant most buildings had a flashlight somewhere, as long as you knew where to look.

The nearly full moon illuminated much of the library through its windows. Despite the familiar surroundings, a nagging sense of danger still danced at the edge of Sage's mind. She pocketed the flashlight and decided to rely on the moonlight as much as she could.

In the silence of the deserted library, her footsteps seemed amplified as she creaked along the scuffed wooden floors toward the reference section. Sage ran her finger across the city and county records until she found the most recent phone book. She pulled it from the shelf and settled at a table near close by.

"Benson ... Benson. Let's see if we can find you." She scanned through the residential section. "A few Bensons but not a single Anders." Next, Sage flipped to the business listings but found no clues there either. She found a Benson's Propane supplier and a Benson's Feed and Ranch Supply, but Sage couldn't link those with the Benson on the medical files.

"What am I even looking for?" She studied the clouds as they scuttled across the moon in the skylight above her. "Who's Benson, and why is he collecting information on everyone's DNA?"

The library windows rattled with a sudden gust of wind. Something scratched and tapped against the door. Sage gently closed the phone book and slipped down into a crouch. Her gaze travelled along the dark caverns created by the endless rows of bookshelves, alert to any sign of movement.

The violent nighttime gusts settled, and the scratching sound, from what she supposed was a tree, ceased. Finally satisfied she was safe, Sage moved back into the seat and flipped the phone book open once more. The pages parted at the city government section, the only part of the book she hadn't scoured. Sage forced herself to scan through the endless departments and services. A name jumped from the page, as if it had been waiting for her to find it.

Anders Benson, Department of Revenue, Department of Local Affairs, Colorado Division of Property Taxation. Sage gently tore the page from its binding and let her mind race through its implications.

Taxes? But the information on the flash drive made it seem like Benson was a doctor. How was he in charge of property tax?

She tapped her fingers against the phone book. Every home and property owner had to pay property taxes. What other department would have such detailed records on the entire population of Black Mills? It didn't reveal how or why this Anders Benson person had DNA records on nearly the entire town, but it did explain his access to information. The Department of Revenue would be able to gather data on every household to determine its property taxes. It probably wouldn't be hard for Benson to also gain access to government and maybe even medical records for all of the residents, especially in a small town where rules were easily bent if you knew the right people.

"I might need to squeeze in a little visit to Benson's office too," Sage murmured and put the book back on its shelf. The building creaked and moaned in another gust of wind. "But first some research on Oriel." The old newspaper microfiche files were in the basement.

At the top of the dark stairs, a shiver trailed down her back. *What's the matter with you?* She chided herself. Why did she feel so jumpy? Was it because Gus wasn't at her side? Fear of the Skinwalker was one thing, but this vague sense of worry was unfamiliar and confusing. Sage gave herself a mental shake and forced her feet down the yawning staircase.

Without windows to let in the moon's gentle gleam, the basement lay in utter darkness except for a few glowing power strips. Sage slipped the flashlight from her pocket and turned it on. The sounds of the storm faded away as she moved through the bookcases to the far corner where the dusty, neglected microfiche machine resided. After collecting a few film reels from the filing cabinet next to it, she inserted one into the machine and eased atop a rickety stool. Scrolling through back issues of the Black Mills Herald, Sage focused on the 1960s and '70s, when Terrance Storm had first purchased Oriel.

World Renowned Scientist to Purchase Crumbling Ghost Town, read a headline from 1973. *Terrance Storm Buys Township of Oriel from Last Remaining Resident For Undisclosed Sum* and *Study of Rare Marmot Species to head Oriel's Scientific Research,* were others.

Sage knew the details she needed weren't only in the big stories; they'd also be found in the notices, blurbs, and obituaries in the backlog of the newspapers, so she forced herself to slow down and read through the minutiae of 1970s life in Black Mills.

Nothing new stood out. Storm had bought the defunct uranium mining town of Oriel from Old Hank, the last remaining resident, for an undisclosed sum of money. He planned to make it one of the premier research centers of North America, while in Disney-like fashion, retain its old ghost town appearance.

Sage sat up from her hunched position and stretched. Flicking on her flashlight, she replaced the microfilm in its box, put it back in the cabinet, then absently retrieved another. The Oriel Research Center must have been an expensive venture. What could have persuaded Storm to pour so much money into a location that was accessible only four or five months a year? Especially back in the '70s, when many of the roads were either one lane or dirt? Why not locate your research area off an interstate? Or at least in a larger city?

Sage used the machine's dim glow to fit the next roll on the spool. After a few moments of confused reading, she realized these newspapers were from the 1930s. Annoyed she'd gone back too many decades, Sage began to remove the film when a headline from a Sunday edition caught her eye:

Healing Uranium Mine Receives National Recognition

The now defunct uranium mine, Dante's First Circle, was converted into a small sanitorium in early 1910. Infirm visitors once came to the area because of claims that the mine and surrounding hot springs cured various ills including arthritis, respiratory disorders, women's disorders, and other health issues. Dante's Sanitorium *is small, housing only 5-10 residents.*

"We don't get that much interest way out here in the middle of nowhere," says Ralph O'Malley, descendant of the founder of the lodge and health spa. "Folks only come up to Oriel if they're really desperate for a cure."

This might be about to change, thanks to Alice Dodd, a Californian socialite whose Rheumatoid arthritis was cured during last summer's visit to the sanitorium. *Friends and acquaintances from her home town of San Francisco were shocked at the change in Dodd's health and word spread like wildfire. The editor of* Life

Magazine, a friend of the Dodd family, decided to run a story on the sanitorium. A writer and photographer will arrive next week to document the serpentine caves of Dante's First Circle.

Owner O'Malley is excited at the prospect of some free publicity, but doesn't think it will lead to more infirm patients making their way to Oriel. "We're just too far off the beaten path," he says. "I think most folks will forget the story as soon as they finish reading it."

The Black Mills Gazette *isn't nearly as skeptical, but we'll keep you updated.*

Sage scanned the immediate issues following the announcement, but concerns over Germany's invasion of Czechoslovakia, Poland, and France began to obliterate all other headlines and soon World War II was in full swing. She found a small notice in a 1943 issue that the sanitorium was closing its doors because it hadn't had a patient in several years and O'Malley's three sons had all enlisted in the US Army's 10th Mountain Division.

"Can't run the place on my own," O'Malley was quoted as saying. "I'm moving to Denver so I can keep up with the news of where my boys are." The short notice went on to say a man named Nicholas Benson was buying the Dante's Sanitorium and had plans to open it under a new name after the war.

Sage leaned back in her chair. A sanitorium? She'd only ever known Oriel as the Research Station. And Nicholas Benson—-he had to be related to Property Tax Officer Anders Benson. But if someone named Benson had bought the sanitorium, why did all the headlines of Oriel's purchase by Terrance Storm say that Old Hank was the last remaining inhabitant of the town?

Reverting to a more recent film reel, she scanned for Hank's name. Nothing. Sage sighed and stood. The search could continue after she took a pitstop at the restroom and found a clock to gauge how much time she had left. Sage flicked the flashlight on again, but after a brief sputter, it died.

"Are you kidding? What is it with me and flashlights?" Sage jiggled it a few more times before giving up. Hopefully, Elena had extra batteries in her desk. Fingers groping, she felt her way through the darkness and forest of bookcases.

As she reached the foot of the stairs, the grating, scratching sound of the storm resumed, louder now and more frantic than before. Sage stopped to listen and her stomach dropped. "That's not a storm," she whispered.

Scrabbling, tearing claws ripped at the door, tore at the windows. An eerie howl rent the air and was joined by several others. Sage dropped her flashlight and bolted back downstairs.

Heart ricocheting a frantic beat in her ears, she raced to the furthest corner of the basement. Crouched next a bookcase, she tried to listen. The books and distance muffled most of the sound, but not all. Another howl sounded, followed by the shattering of glass.

The floorboards directly above her creaked, and Sage choked back a gasp. Something clicked and scraped above her in an irregular beat.

Suddenly, the loud report of a shotgun layered over the top of everything else. Sage fell backwards. Another shot. Then another. Then silence.

Minutes ticked by. Was the thing dead? Sage forced herself to focus but still couldn't get any sense of the presence upstairs. Her power to regenerate and heal was gone;

had her perception abilities disappeared as well? An even deeper terror gripped her as she realized just how blind and helpless she was without her gifts. If something was coming for her, it was only a matter of minutes before she'd be cornered in this basement.

Sage stole through the darkness, guided by the dim power strips. The soft gleam of an ancient *Exit* sign flickered to her left. Sage tried the door, but it was locked. There was nowhere to run.

Even though she couldn't see anyone, Sage knew that meant nothing. Usually prey never saw their predators until it was too late. She forced herself to stand still. Listening. Waiting for her pursuer to strike.

The exit door behind her swung open. Sage spun and crouched on the floor.

"Who's down here?" a voice called, followed by the sound of a pump action shotgun being cocked.

The corona glow of the *Exit* sign lit a small figure. Relief flooded through Sage. "E-Elena?"

"Sage? Is that you?" The woman sputtered. "What on earth are you doing in here?"

"What are *you* doing here?" Sage asked, slowly rising.

"Trying to scare away that pack of damn coyotes." Elena snapped.

"P-pack?" Sage steadied herself against the bookcart next to her.

"Yeah. I woke up because of the windstorm and saw them circling the building. They were acting crazy. Trying to break in through the door and the windows. Thought they'd give up and go away after they saw it was no use, but then a big one tried to jump through the window. Had to scare them off with my gun."

A shudder ran through Sage, and she felt a surge of

pathetic gratitude for the sturdy old building. And Elena too, despite the outrage that radiated from her bedraggled, bathrobe-draped form.

"You didn't answer me. What are you doing here?" Elena demanded shrilly, her shotgun still pointed at Sage's midsection

"I'm just ... just trying to find some answers. That's all."

Elena's features flickered in the wavering green light. "You're a wanted fugitive. Did you know that?"

Sage nodded. "Yes, but I didn't do anything. I promise."

The librarian lowered her gun a few inches and sighed. "Whether or not that's true, you'd better come with me." She gestured to the stairs behind her with the gun.

"I'm not sure it's safe—"

"The coyotes are gone. And I want you to move, so right now, that's your only option."

Sage hesitated. If she rushed Elena, she might be able to overpower her before the gun went off.

Elena sighed. "Look, I'm not going to turn you in. At least not until we've talked."

"But I still need to—"

"My house is next door. And I'm not asking." She raised the shotgun once more and trained it on Sage's head.

Out of arguments, Sage swallowed. She'd better play along for now. Besides, she'd rather be stuck with Elena than the coyotes, the Skinwalker, Olson, or whoever else had it out for her. She eased her way past the gun and up the basement stairs.

CHAPTER TWENTY-NINE

Sage drummed nervous fingers against Elena's kitchen table as she waited for the older woman to finish preparing the tea. Elena had declared that the two of them needed something to calm their nerves and ordered Sage to sit down while the large pot brewed. In Sage's mind, the shotgun Elena kept within hand's reach negated any of the relaxing properties of the herbal tea.

"Honey?" Elena asked after she poured Sage a steaming mug.

"Sure."

"Lemon?"

"I guess. Look, Elena, I'm sure you've—"

"Drink your tea," Elena ordered in a don't-mess-with-me librarian tone. Sage obediently took a sip.

"Now then. I'd like you to tell me what in the hell is going on in this town?"

Sage choked and tea went all over the table. Avoiding the librarian's eyes, she grabbed a napkin from the pile in the center of the table and wiped up her mess. "I'm not sure what you're—"

"Oh, Sage, spare me your wide-eyed innocence." Elena gestured to the shotgun on the table. "We both know things are spiraling out of control. And you and Tim Burgney seem to be mixed up in all of it."

"I haven't killed anyone, if that's what you're suggesting." Sage clenched the damp napkin in her hands.

"I'm not. You've been in this town for nearly five years, and I've kept an eye on you the whole time. You never know how foster kids are going to act. But I was pleasantly surprised by you." Elena looked down at her mug. "And I appreciate how you help Liddy. She needs someone like you."

"Oh. Thanks, I guess."

"And I know Tim. He's the handyman at our church and as harmless as a flea. But someone sure wants to make it look like you two are the Bonny and Clyde of Black Mills."

Sage let out a weary sigh. "You're right. But I don't understand why. It's like Tim and I are stuck in a rabbit hole. The deeper we go, the less we know."

Elena tucked her bristly white hair behind her ears. "Well, lay it on me. Let's see what we can figure out."

"You?"

"Yes, me. I used to be a forensic scientist in Boston before my husband got a job here and dragged me to this God forsaken mountain town 30 years back."

Sage shook her head. "It's probably best if I don't. What if you get pulled into this too?"

Elena took off her bifocals and rubbed them on her shirt. "Looks to me that I already am in the middle of this. Fugitive sitting at my kitchen table and all. Besides, don't worry about me; I know how to take care of myself."

Sage looked at the shotgun and shrugged. "Fine."

Maybe someone who had lived here 30 years would be able to figure out the puzzles she and Tim couldn't.

Haltingly, Sage tried to explain the events of the past week, an exercise in futility since she didn't understand most of them herself. Even though Sage left out the more unbelievable elements, like the Wind and the Skinwalker, the story still sounded ridiculous, even to her. Elena refilled their tea several times through the conversation, asking occasional questions to clarify, but other than that remaining silent.

Sage finished with her findings at the library, her suspicions about Anders Benson, and her discovery of the Uranium Mine turned sanitorium.

"I'd never heard about Dante's Sanitorium. Have you?"

"Oh, yes." Elena stood and retrieved a pad of paper and pencil from a kitchen drawer. "I'm a member of the historical society, and I'm writing a book on the history of Black Mills. Have been for the last 20 years, though." She snorted. "It's one of those ongoing projects."

"But Dante's Sanitorium?" Sage prompted.

"Oh yes. It wasn't well known, not even in its heyday. Mostly just older locals used it, but there were some kids too. Ones with different diseases, illnesses. Seemed like the doctors only sent the terminal cases there for a visit. Of course it was a silver mine back before any of that. In the 1800s." She began to sketch what looked like a map on the piece of paper.

"So the Benson guy that bought it. Why isn't he ever mentioned as a resident of Oriel? You only hear about Old Hank as the last remaining inhabitant."

"Because Benson was part of Dr. Terrance Storm's group. The Oriel Biological Research team. He was one of the guys who came and scoped out Oriel before Storm bought it. Guess Benson wanted the Sanitorium even before Storm came to a decision," Elena said as she tore off the map and held it out to Sage. "That's where Dante's was located. Is that close to where you and Tim found the underground lab?"

Sage studied the drawing. "Yes, it is. Right up against the edge of the mountain face on the North side of the valley. But what I don't understand is what an old silver and uranium mine, a sanitorium, marmots, and genetic mapping have to do with each other. And why are the stakes so high? Why is whoever's running things in Oriel willing to kill for this stuff?"

If Elena had an answer, she didn't offer it. Instead, she walked over to the refrigerator and pulled out bread, cheese, and lettuce.

Sage played with the handle of her mug until she registered its honey-coated stickiness and set it down. Was Elena having second thoughts about helping her? Or wondering how she could contact the police? Sage pushed back her chair just as Elena turned around to face her.

"The sanitorium is where they started collecting data." Elena jabbed at the air. "Don't you see? They'd have unlimited access to a controlled group of subjects in the people of Black Mills, since they were the only ones who even cared about its existence. And who, primarily, visited the sanitorium?"

"Sick people?" Sage answered when Elena pointed at her.

"And what did they want from the sick people?"

"Umm ..." Sage felt like she was in school again. "Germs?"

"No, information! The field of genetic research was being pioneered right at the time that Benson and Storm bought Oriel. They'd be able to get reams of data from subjects with potential genetic disorders at the sanatorium, but no one would suspect anything. People wouldn't even be careful about that sort of thing then because they'd have no idea about medical privacy issues, especially up in a little town in the middle of nowhere."

"But that still doesn't explain what's going on now. Why are they trying to kill Tim and me?"

After Elena placed the sandwiches she'd made in a plastic sack, she washed off several pieces of fruit and placed them in it as well. "That's the million dollar question, isn't it? But my guess is, if you've got a secret research station in a secluded mountain town, the answer probably isn't pretty. Or legal. And that's why they're trying so hard to pin everything on you and Tim before they kill you."

A bag of chips and bottle of water followed the fruit into the bag before Elena handed it to Sage. "And that's why you'd better scoot right back to Tim and figure this out, or neither of you are going to make it."

The thought of reuniting with Tim made Sage's stomach clench. "I'm not sure if dragging Tim—"

"I don't care what's going on between you two," Elena snapped and slapped the counter. "You've got a duty to this town. The rest of its population is probably in danger or the Oriel Research Station wouldn't be so desperate. You have to find out what they're doing. If they're going to hurt the people in this town. You have to stop them, Sage." Elena grasped the table with white knuckles.

"I *knew* Tabitha and Shaun. Watched them from the time they were babies coming to the library reading group, giggling in the stacks first with friends, then with boyfriends and girlfriends. They had their whole lives ahead of them. And Sheriff Davis too. He was a good man and didn't deserve that kind of death. His wife and boys didn't deserve it either."

Sage let the librarian's words sink in, while Elena pulled a paper towel off the roll and hastily dabbed at her eyes.

Sage swallowed and stood. Elena was right. She was being a coward. And Sage wasn't the only one who would suffer if she messed this up. "Thank you for the history lesson. I'd better get back to Tim so we can figure this out."

"Take my car." Elena handed Sage her keys. "The sun's almost up, and you won't make it out of town on foot. Police are looking for you everywhere, and evidently, all of Oriel is too. Your house is barricaded behind a mile of sawhorses and crime scene tape. They even found your Jeep yesterday.

The Jeep was her baby. It made her sick to think of Officer Olson crawling all over it, looking for clues. "How on earth did they find it?"

Elena shrugged. "I don't know. Yesterday I saw it parked in the spare lot behind the city hall. That's why you've got to take mine."

"Thanks. But what about you?"

"I've got Bob's old Subaru in the garage. It still runs. If anyone asks, I'll tell them I needed to change the Honda's oil. Should keep you incognito enough, at least for a few days."

As Sage stood, Elena walked over and pulled her into a hesitant hug. "You've always held everyone in this town at arm's length, but I've watched you, Sage. I know you're brave. You couldn't have survived the system you grew up in without grit. Use that now to protect this town and find justice for the dead, but be careful ... it would kill Liddy if something happened to you."

"I will," Sage choked. She grabbed the lunch Elena held, then ran to the Honda parked behind the house.

Time to find Tim. And if her instincts were correct, he'd be one pissed off priest.

CHAPTER THIRTY

Aided by one of Elena's floppy garden hats and a large pair of sunglasses, both of which she'd found in the garage, Sage drove through town without arousing the suspicion of any of the numerous squad cars or big FBI SUVs she encountered. She'd also grabbed last week's newspapers out of Elena's recycle bin, so she could find out what lies were being fed to the media.

On the outskirts of town, as she waited for a freight train to pass, Sage skimmed the papers. Most of the national ones had already moved on to new stories. If they mentioned anything at all, it was a repeat of the official soundbites: Tim was a shady ex-Episcopalian priest suspected of illegal and despicable acts in Sudan. Sage was a now-grown foster kid with an obscure background accused of stealing high-priced equipment from the Oriel Biological Research Station.

She was pleasantly surprised, however, when she scanned through the local Black Mills Gazette. The headline read, *Search Continues for Tim Burgney and Sage Smith*. The journalist seemed more than a little suspicious of the police department's and OBRS's continuing claims. About halfway down the article, past the background information, Sage slowed her reading.

The paper interviewed Tim's neighbors, landlord, and friends. Across the board, all of them agreed that Tim couldn't have committed the crimes he was accused of. The information the Gazette provided about Tim's time in Sudan was even more illuminating.

He'd worked in the Abyei region for just a year before the Sudan Civil war turned to outright genocide. The reporter had contacted several village officials who praised Tim's initiatives, including an orphanage and free medical clinic, but all of them expressed disappointment that Tim never returned. The article also touched on Tim's time with a psychiatric hospital once he returned to the United States and his continuing outpatient treatment for several years afterward.

One quote in particular stood out for Sage. The head priest of the mission Tim had worked at, Father Malek, said, "Father Tim is a good man. It is our hope that someday he will come back to this mission and reunite with his brothers and sisters here." She had a hunch this wasn't news to Tim, and Sage remembered how he'd accused himself of being a coward after he'd discovered Sheriff Davis's body. Obviously, his past still haunted him.

The next paragraph revealed what the Gazette had uncovered about Sage, which wasn't much. She guessed that was one of the only benefits of being a foster kid and one that had been relocated from another state. Without her real name, the reporter hadn't been able to find any news about Sage before she arrived at Black Mills around her 15th birthday. It reiterated that she had been a foster kid and contained several effusively loyal quotes from Liddy.

Sage wadded up the paper and threw it onto the seat next to her. Glancing up, she realized the freight train had long since gone. She gunned the engine down the dusty road and drove away from town.

After a while, Sage pulled up to a crossroads. If she turned right, the dusty two-tire track road would lead her back to Liddy's cabin. The engine puttered while she leaned against the headrest and closed her eyes. Everything in her longed to turn left instead. To escape these mountains and the dangerous mysteries they held. Why was she even here? It would be so much easier to fade away and create a new identity somewhere else. Somewhere without the chaos.

Sage shook her head. Even as she fantasized about escaping, she knew she couldn't do that to Tim and Gus. Nor could she ignore the Wind.

It had been with her for so long, guiding her, healing her, teaching her secrets, letting her help suffering creatures. Sage had enjoyed this existence and been able to lose herself in it. But this time everything was different. This mystery lay heavy on her shoulders, and Sage felt helpless against its oppression.

She cut the car's engine and opened the window to breathe in the sharp, fresh air. Trees sighed in the gentle morning breeze. The rush of a mountain stream played harmony with the cries of a lonely hawk soaring above.

"Why have you kept me here in this valley? And why is this battle mine to fight? I have no idea what's going on or how to solve it. I got Tim involved too, and it's drug up all his past demons for the whole town to see." Resignation overwhelmed her. "We're both probably going to die before this whole thing is over. Not that you care."

"Broken One," the Wind brushed her cheek and

flooded the car with its presence. "Do you really think me so cold-hearted that I would lead you to a hopeless battle? And awaken pain in you and the priest for no reason? Do you not trust me at all?"

Sage considered its words. Did she trust the Wind?

A vivid memory charged through the layers of her confusion and hopelessness. She'd run away from Uncle Brian again. He'd come home drunk and ready to lash out at something. First he tried to hurt Gus, and when Sage shoved him away from the whimpering dog, Brian turned his anger on her, striking her again and again. Without their healing abilities, Sage knew, she and Gus would never have survived the first month of living with him, let alone the two years they'd suffered under his roof.

That night he'd been more drunk than usual. Once he passed out, Sage was able to escape his fists and groping hands. The ever loyal Gus trailed after her, but lonely desperation flooded her small, broken heart. A dog, even one as extraordinary as Gus, could not replace the loss that tore through her, fresh every day.

Although it was July, nights ran cold in the high New Mexican desert. Sage barely noticed as she wove her way through the arroyos, away from Brian's trailer and deeper into vast emptiness. With all her heart, she wished that some predator of the night would come and send her off to wherever her parents and Daniel had gone.

With bloodied, bare feet she pushed on, even as the sharp sobs left her breathless. But Sage didn't care; she longed for this suffering to end.

She stumbled to the lip of a cliff. The starry heavens lit dark, jagged rocks and a small stream hundreds of feet below. Sage stopped short, then inched closer and closer to the edge. She closed her eyes. "Here I come," she whispered, but her voice was consumed in a fierce gale of wind that shoved her away from the ledge and knocked her against the tall sandstone boulder behind her.

"Do not do this," a voice commanded into her ear in the midst of the roaring wind. "Do not throw away what has been so dearly rescued."

"You again?" Sage had cried. "You can't tell me what to do." Since that terrible, memory-shadowed night she'd lost her family, this mysterious voice had come to her in the moments of her deepest despair. But right now she resented its intrusion and wanted only to stop the pain that raged inside her.

As rapidly as the mighty Wind had assaulted her, it disappeared. Then a gentle sigh sounded next to her. "I know you are broken, little one, but you are also strong. And there is much to do before you begin that next journey on another road. You must gather up your courage and hold it close around you."

Sage crumpled into a ball. "No! I won't. I can't be alone. It's breaking my heart."

"You shall not be alone. You have me. Always." The Wind coaxed her chin up from her clenched body. Brushing her tangled hair off her face, Sage gasped in amazement. A shimmery presence, like stardust, glowed all around her. "And there is an old friend that would miss you very much."

A familiar bark sounded from the trail, and Gus jumped onto her lap, licking her face frantically.

Sage nodded pulling the dog into a tight hug. "At least I have Gus."

"And someone else. A man is coming who will teach you how to hear me better. He will be a grandfather to you." It stroked her forehead gently until Sage's breathing returned to normal, interrupted only by the occasional sob.

"Do you have the courage to live, Broken One? Or will you throw away a life that was saved?"

Sage gulped. "If Gus ... and if you, whatever you are, stay with me. I think ... I think I might have the courage."

"Well done. The world has much need of you," the Wind whispered. It tossed her hair over her shoulder and away from her tear stained face. "Look, a new friend approaches."

Sage's eyes strained in the darkness. Lit by the starlight, a slightly bent form appeared, walking toward her from the vast emptiness of the west. A peace, heavy and warm as a down blanket, fell over Sage's shoulders. Somehow she knew this person would bring back that feeling she had so desperately missed since her parent's death: belonging.

A dusting of pebbles and grit plinked across Sage's windshield and brought her back to the present.

"You were very brave then, Broken One, but it becomes harder. Do you still trust me?"

"Yes," Sage said with finality, realizing it was true. Despite all the pain of what had conspired in the last few weeks, despite her confusion over Tim, her horror over the deaths of the innocent people of Black Mills, she knew the Wind would guide her. Just as it had guided her since that day on the cliff.

"Tell me what I need to do," Sage whispered. "I'm ready."

"I led the grandfather to you when you needed him most, so that he could hide and protect you. He also taught you listen to both me and the many hidden voices of this world. Once again, it is time for you to meet someone who will reveal what is hidden. You cannot go forward until you understand what happened before."

Sage nodded. Emotions wrestled in a fierce tug-of-war

at her next question, but finally she forced the words out. "And Tim?"

"You must find the priest. Without him, you will fail at what is to come."

A deep sigh of release shook her frame, and Sage listened as the Wind gave her directions. Lightness enveloped her as she turned the key in the ignition. Despite her best efforts, the Wind wasn't going to let her do this alone.

THE MOUNTAIN PEAKS' SHADOWS WERE JUST BEGINNING to creep eastward through the valley when Sage spotted Tim and Gus walking along the dirt road. Even from a distance, she saw Tim's anger in his rigid shoulders and stalking gait. Gus, on the other hand, still seemed to be his good-natured, doggy self.

Overcome with a dizzying sense of elation, Sage slowly pulled over to the shoulder of the road. Despite Tim's obvious irritation, she pulsed with the desire to jump from the car and fling herself against him. Instead, she rolled down her window and tensed for what was to come.

"Hey guys," she called, and Tim's head snapped up.

He stopped mid-stride and stared at her with a stony gaze, but Gus raced across the road and leapt against the car door, begging to be let inside. She stepped out of the car and dropped down to receive Gus's adoring kisses.

"I know, I know, you were a good boy," she praised, which only increased Gus's happy whines and frantic tail wagging. "You stayed with Tim, just like I told you. Good job, buddy." When he finally calmed, Sage opened the back door and let the dusty dog hop in. Then she turned to Tim.

"How's it going?"

He stared at her.

"Get in a nice walk?" She saw the muscles in Tim's jaw clench as he fought for control.

"Yeah, wonderful, thanks," he finally ground out. "I love being stranded in the middle of nowhere, no idea where I am, ditched by my partner." He shook his head and walked past her. "Now that the two of you are united, I'll be on my way."

Sage chased after him and grabbed his arm. "Come on, Tim. Be serious."

"I *am* serious." He jerked away and continued walking. "I've had enough of you, your werewolf creature, your stupid dog, all of this. I'm sick of it."

Sage jogged to stay in step with him. "I told you, not a werewolf. Werewolves are like the G-rated version of a Skinwalker. And besides. Gus isn't stupid."

Tim stopped and rubbed a hand over his eyes. "Fine. Your dog's not stupid."

"Look, I'm really sorry, okay? It's going to take me longer than a week to get used to this *partner* thing." His clenched jaw twitched. "You're just going to have to forgive me and get over it."

A grudging smile briefly cracked Tim's lips before his scowl returned. "Oh, nice. Throw down the forgiveness card. That's a low blow."

Sage shrugged.

"Where have you been, Sage? Do you have any idea how worried--"

"Listen, we can talk about it later. Right now we need to meet with someone at the top of Dula Mountain. We'll barely make it on time if we leave now."

Emotions raced across Tim's face. Sage wondered what she'd do if he refused to come.

Finally he sighed and turned back towards the car. "Who are we meeting?"

The knot in her stomach unfurled, and she matched her stride to his. "With someone who will reveal what is hidden."

"What does that mean?"

"I'm not sure. The Wind says we can't go forward until we understand what happened before."

They were back at the car now, and Tim threw his backpack in the trunk before jerking open the passenger door. "That's unhelpfully cryptic."

"As always," Sage gently pushed Gus back as he tried to wiggle his way in between Tim and her. The dog ignored Sage and deliriously licked Tim's ear and cheek.

"Calm down, Gus," he murmured, running his hand through the dog's fur. "I'm not going to leave, I promise."

CHAPTER THIRTY-ONE

The tree shadows stretched impossibly long down the hillside when Sage, Tim, and Gus finally neared the summit of Dula Mountain.

"So why are we meeting someone all the way up here?" Tim said as they made the final steps of the ascent.

"I'm not sure. I guess it's pretty remote, which makes it safe."

"It is safe for the time being," a voice came from behind them, and the two whirled around. "But for how much longer, who knows?"

An elderly woman in dusty blue jeans and a dark sweater approached. "Shall we sit?" She pointed at an outcropping of several wind-smoothed rocks. "These legs aren't as young as they once were."

"Of course," Sage answered. "Thank you for meeting with us."

The woman nodded and sat down with grace that belied her years. The gentle evening breeze teased jet black and silvery strands of hair from the long braid hanging over her shoulder. Deep wrinkles at her mouth and eyes hinted at years of both joy and pain.

"Why are we here?" Tim demanded, and the woman turned a stern gaze in his direction.

"Tim," Sage whispered, "don't be rude. She'll tell us when she's ready." Sage turned to the woman. "You are kind to have come all this way, ma'am."

"My name is Naomi Notah. You may call me Naomi."

"Thank you, Naomi. My name is Sage, and this is Tim Burgney."

Her gaze still on Tim, Naomi studied him for a moment before speaking. "You are a holy man."

Tim hesitated. "Yes, I was a priest at one time. But not any more." He looked down. "I'm sorry for being rude. The events of the last few days have been ... hard."

"Your humility speaks well for you." She turned to Sage. "And I was told that you lived for a time with the *Diné*?"

Sage nodded. "With a man named Charles Benally. He was a *Hataɫii,* a Singer."

Naomi eyed her silently for several moments. "But you are not *Diné*."

"No," Sage shook her head. "I don't know what I am. Just a mutt, I guess. My parents didn't get a chance to make me anything."

Naomi took a deep breath. "You have visions that keep stealing your dreams?"

Sage nodded.

"Please tell me about them."

Sage closed her eyes and tried to quiet her exhausted mind. Finally she collected her thoughts enough to speak. "When I'm in the middle of the dream, it feels so real. Like it's actually happening in the present. It's always close to nighttime in a forest, so a lot of the details are hard to see, but I think it's at the old mine behind Shelton Reservoir, at the mouth of the Oriel Valley. Do you know the place?"

Naomi nodded, "Go on."

"I'm running through the woods with this group of people, mostly women and children. In one version, a child falls down. I pick her up, and we keep running. I can feel something dangerous behind us. The mothers keep whispering a phrase. *Tsxįįłgo,* I think is how it's pronounced." Sage looked up and saw Naomi nod impatiently. "Then suddenly we're at the mine, only it's a cave in my dream.

"We huddle in the depression, our backs against the cliff. Everyone is silent, even the babies. Then someone cries out, and we see dark figures coming through the trees. A bunch of men, their faces painted black. They have knives and axes. They start to kill us, even the little ones. And they enjoy it."

Sage shuddered, and this time when she looked up, Naomi's eyes were filled with compassion, not impatience. Sage took several deep breaths before continuing, "In one version, I hide the child under my body. In another, I turn and look back into the woods, then he comes out, licking his lips."

Sage's voice broke and tears traced down her cheeks. Tim pulled her hand into his strong grip, and Naomi moved closer to her. "Who comes out of the woods?" Naomi asked, her voice urgent.

"That creature, a *yee--*"

"Shh!" Naomi covered Sage's mouth with her hand and looked wildly around the mountaintop. "Only English! It is not safe to say that other name aloud." Her sharp words were tempered by the trembling, gentle hand that moved from Sage's mouth to smooth her sweat-dampened hair away from her forehead.

"Sorry," Sage gulped and took a moment to regain her composure. "As soon as I make eye contact with the *thing*, I'm carried away from the group and into the woods. It forces me to watch the deaths of all the women and children. Then it swallows me up, and I see faces. Terrible, waxy faces."

"Are any of them familiar to you?"

"Shaun, Tabitha. Oh, and Old Hank from Oriel Valley."

Naomi's nodded. "I had wondered about him."

"Wondered—" Tim started, but froze when Naomi slashed her hand once again.

Naomi turned back to Sage. "Continue."

"Well, that's all that happens. The one thing that changes is the child. Sometimes, I'm able to save her. Other times not. In the version where I save the child, I stab the *thing* in the foot with a knife."

Sage fell silent and watched Naomi process her words. The stern, beautiful face before her revealed very little of what the woman thought of Sage's story. Minutes ticked by. Sage felt Tim inch closer to her on their rock and looked up.

You okay? He mouthed. She nodded. A strange gratefulness flooded through her. Despite any residual anger he must feel at her desertion from the night before, Tim's stubborn concern trumped those feelings. His loyalty almost rivaled Gus's, she thought, something that both comforted and worried her.

Naomi cleared her throat and broke the taut quiet of the mountaintop. "What I am about to tell you has not been known for over a hundred years, a secret kept alive by a handful in my family. I trust that you will honor this information with the respect it deserves."

Sage nodded, and Naomi looked toward Tim.

"I don't break confidences lightly," Tim said. "I promise not to share it, unless it's necessary to bring justice for the recently deceased."

Naomi pursed her lips. "I am disappointed, holy man. Can you really not see that this evil stretches well beyond the moment?" Naomi raised both her hands and reached as if to embrace the vast expanse of mountains and valleys that surrounded the three of them. She glanced at Tim and then lowered her arms. "But thank you for your promise. Both of you." She bowed her head. "The thing of which you dream so often, has haunted this valley for many, many years.

"I am of the Folded Arms People Clan, born for the Red-Running-Into-Water Clan. The Bitter Water Clan are my maternal grandfather's clan, and The Tangle People are my paternal grandfather's clan. My ancestors lived near the northernmost reaches of the *Diné* boundaries, near the mountain you call Hesperus and we call *Dibé Nitsaa.*"

Naomi turned to Tim. "Perhaps you have heard of the Long Walk?

Tim shook his head. "I'm sorry, I haven't. I'm not originally from here."

"Unfortunately, even if you were, you probably would not have heard of it. Those in power always try to paint over their sins so that they will be forgotten or ignored." Naomi sighed and traced the shimmering veins of formica on the large rock where she sat. "In 1864, the United States Army went from village to village, telling all the *Diné* that they must leave and go to a new place the soldiers would show them. Immediately. There was no time to pack anything. Those who resisted were killed.

"My ancestor's village was a small, poor one, so we heard news of what was happening before the soldiers got there. The leader of the clan decided those who were able should escape to the mountains in the North. My people collected only what they needed, and traveled secretly, by night, until they made their way there," Naomi pointed over a distant ridge. "To the Oriel Valley—"

"What?" Sage interrupted, ignoring Naomi's frown. "I thought the only tribes here were the Utes. I've never heard of a Navajo clan in Oriel Valley."

"That was the point. That no one should hear. The Oriel Valley was small and deserted. The *Diné* who came here were few, and their needs were not great. They tried to live in secrecy and take only what they must from the land. They were not a mountain people and many died the first winter. It was hard, but at least they were undisturbed, for a time.

"The soldiers never did find them, but in their place came other hunters. Fortune hunters in search of riches buried deep in the mountains. When our leader saw them scouting the surrounding valleys, he knew it was only a matter of time before our secret was discovered, so he and the other men decided to try to find one of the Ute tribes to the South. Although the Utes were enemies with the *Diné*, he would take our men to ask if his small clan of survivors could join the Mountain Ute tribe. Perhaps they would have mercy.

"It was winter, so our leader thought he had time to make these arrangements before the miners came into the valley. But he did not.

"That is your memory." Naomi looked up into the deepening dusk, her eyes haunted. "Those women and children were the few remaining *Diné* who had survived first a death march and then the deprivation of living as refugees in the mountains. They discovered the white men slipping into the valley and tried to protect their little ones in a hidden place. But they could not protect themselves from so cunning an enemy."

"The miners?" Tim asked.

"Not just the miners," Naomi continued slowly, her eyes on Sage. "How would the miners know the leader and warriors were away? How would they know, in all the valley where the women and children would take refuge? How would they know that their actions, done in secret, could be hidden from the outside world with this forgotten tribe?"

"The ... thing you don't want me to say?" Sage said.

"Yes, what happened in the valley was not planned by simple miners. With this type of destruction, it never is." She looked at Tim. "You know this, I think, holy man?"

Tim nodded. "Yes, I do." He took a shaky breath. "When I was in Sudan the destruction was staggering. The Civil War, the genocide, all if it. Normal people who had gotten along fine for years and years suddenly turned on each other with what seemed like premeditated vengeance. The few I talked to afterwards seemed as shocked by their actions as the victims. They didn't understand how the genocide happened either."

"But why do I keep dreaming about it?" Sage demanded, unable to absorb Tim's words, her thoughts circling obsessively around Naomi's story.

"Because the earth longs to be free of the stain of innocent blood!" Naomi's voice rang clear through the sharp mountain air. "It poisons the land and all living in it."

"And everything that's happening," Tim jumped in, "the deaths of Shaun and Tabitha, of Ron Davis. They're all linked to this?"

Naomi nodded. "Evil does not happen in a vacuum. Once planted, it grows until it either consumes or is destroyed. You must ask, what caused these simple miners to do such a terrible thing?"

"Greed," Sage knew the answer before Naomi finished asking the question. "I saw it in their eyes. Even the twilight couldn't hide it. Greed was eating them alive, and the creature stoked it. Promising them things that weren't true. The silver mine here never even produced much."

"Yes," Naomi said. "And now that greed has grown. The Skinwalker has swallowed up so much evil that his powers are no longer balanced by the good that resides here. More lives than you realize have been lost."

"Old Hank? And all those faces I saw in the creature's belly?" Sage asked and Naomi nodded.

"But how do you know all this?" Tim asked. "I don't doubt your words, but if there were no survivors—"

"It was only the women and children in the valley, not the men." Naomi reminded him. "And if you remember, as Sage has said, sometimes she saved the child. She shielded it with her body."

"But she wasn't actually there," Tim said. "I mean, right?" He looked at Sage.

Sage turned to Naomi. "Was I?"

"I do not pretend to know how all things work in the dream world," Naomi said. "But a child was saved, found lying under a stranger no one could identify. The little girl was discovered by the men of the tribe when they returned the next morning. They took her and went to live with Uncompahgre Utes across the mountains. That woman was my grandmother."

"Your grandmother?" Tim said. "But if your family knows about this why hasn't anyone—"

"The time was not yet right. Now it is right." Naomi stood and gestured to the trees and boulders that surrounded them. "The earth groans to have this evil removed."

"But how?" Sage asked.

"You must bring all things in the Oriel Valley to the light," Naomi said. "And then the clever webs of lies will unravel."

"But what does that even mean?" Sage jumped up from her perch. "Your story's fascinating, but the Skinwalker is still out there. If its powers are growing stronger, like you say, is there any way to stop it? And why me?" Sage's voice filled with frustration. "I'm not Navajo. I'm not a Singer. I'm a nobody. We have to find a real Singer to deal with this."

Naomi shook her head. "I don't have that answer, but it seems your path and the Skinwalker's have entwined. Who knows why?" She fell silent, her gaze tracing the features of Sage's face.

"Some of the elders say there were no Skinwalkers until the Long Walk. That the evil done to us by the white soldiers was what unleashed these creatures. Perhaps it is your job to balance, to atone for a small part of that evil." Naomi reached for Sage's hand and leaned on her as she rose stiffly to her feet. "Don't allow your fear to take over. If you have been given this task, there must be a way to accomplish it, even if there is great danger."

Gus whined and shoved his head beneath Sage's hand. She glanced down at the dog and stroked his silky ears. "But I have no—"

"Good-bye, friends," came Naomi's lilting voice from the nighttime shadows at the edge of the ridge. "My people, my clan, owe a debt of gratitude to you, Sage. I hope our paths cross again."

Silence settled around Sage, Gus, and Tim once more, broken only by the gentle rustle of trees and night song of crickets.

CHAPTER THIRTY-TWO

"Did that just happen?" Tim asked after several minutes had passed, his voice intrusive in the almost holy silence. "It was like something out of a dream."

Sage forced herself from the turbulent questions that scuttled through her mind. "This whole situation feels like it's taken on a life of its own, Tim. We're just two small characters in something much bigger than we can understand." A tree shuddered next to Sage, shaken by a sudden gust of wind. "We need to get going."

"I hope Naomi gets down the mountain all right," Tim said after they began their descent. "It's pretty dark now."

"It seems like she'd be able to handle anything these mountains could throw at her," Sage said and wondered again why the older woman or someone from her *Diné* family wasn't the one battling the Skinwalker. Who were she and Tim to fight this monster? A couple of clueless fugitives.

With all that Naomi had revealed, Sage felt even more defenseless than before. The Skinwalker had been dealing death in this valley for longer than any of them realized.

Even if practice hadn't made perfect, the Skinwalker was adept at this game of destruction.

"This is the first time since I moved here that I don't trust these mountains, especially after what she said, about the evil growing in power." Sage spoke into the soft silence of the twilight, grief filling her chest.

"I was just thinking the same thing," he said as they rounded a curve and entered a dense spruce and aspen forest. "At least we've got your senses though, right?"

"Right," Sage said. But aside from her communication with the Wind, Sage knew she'd not sensed anything clearly since that night in the cave. Perhaps that gift had lessened too, along with her healing abilities, drained away with the tears that had erased Tim's injuries.

Sage kept her eyes riveted to the dog as he led the way down the trail, watchful for the slightest twitch in Gus's ears or body language that would alert her to danger. Maybe he was their last, best hope of protection.

"Tell me what you learned after you left this morning," Tim said once they reached the car.

While Sage guided Elena's Honda through old logging roads and back toward Liddy's cabin, she told Tim about her findings at the library.

"Benson's first name is Anders?" Tim asked.

"Yes."

"I think I told you that Olson mentioned an Anders when he was looking for me at the church. It's not a common name, so it stuck in my memory."

"Mine too," Sage said and finished by telling Tim of Elena's conjecture about the nature of the Oriel Biological Research Station's activities. "But I still don't understand how they're gathering their genetic data," Sage added. "Can you picture the old timers like Liddy giving Oriel scientists permission to play around with her DNA?"

After several moments of silence, Tim smacked the dashboard. Sage nearly swerved off the road. "What the hell, Tim? Do you want us to crash?"

"Is it really that simple?" His voice boomed through the car. "The free dental clinics!" From her peripheral vision, Sage saw him turn to her. "The clinics *my* church, all the churches, and the community center help to coordinate." Excitement drained away and he slumped back against his seat. "A free dental check-up and cleaning? Nearly everyone in the town does it. One cheek swab and they'd have a patient's DNA."

"Do they do the dental clinic during the Black Mills Health Fair?" Sage asked. "I've never been to one."

"The Black Mills docs organize the health fair, but Oriel runs the dental clinic that accompanies it." Tim shook his head in disbelief. "I've always thought it strange, given how all the scientists up at OBRS act like their own self-contained nation, way too important to mix with all us commoners. But I figured the clinic gave them a tax write off or something."

Sage marveled at the plan's cunning. While most of the independent citizens of Black Mills never gave any more personal information than they had to, who would turn down an offer of free dental care at a health fair?

"This is happening too fast." Tim finally spoke. "Naomi's story, the Sanitorium, Benson, the files from the cavern, the deaths—it's too much. I don't understand how it's all linked even if they are getting their genetic information from the clinics. And then there's the crap you pulled—"

"Me?" Sage guided the car around a tight corner.

"Yeah, you. Ditching me," Tim said, his voice suddenly

sharp. "Ever since I found you at the mine, this situation has been more like a nightmare than reality. I feel like I'm barely hanging onto my sanity, but then I think, 'At least Sage is here. She's real.' Then suddenly you're gone. Did you think I could do this alone? Or that you would? I'm not some expendable side kick you get to toss off when you don't need me anymore."

"That's not why I left. I don't think of you that way."

"Here's the thing, Sage, unfortunately I can't read your mind, and it's your actions that are going to get us killed. The Wind told us we had to stay together or die. How can you ignore that?"

Sage kept her eyes on the road and shrugged.

"Listen, if I've done something that makes this partner thing unbearable, I'm sorry. But for now, I'd rather not die. Naomi said the creature is getting stronger. Neither of us can do this alone, so don't ditch me again." He paused. "I thought we had become something like friends at the very least. The thing is Sage—"

"You almost died," Sage blurted out. "Do you think I could ignore that? Do you have any idea what it's like to keep living when everyone you love dies? If something happened to you too ... " Unable to finish the thought, Sage flinched as fir branches brushed the top of the car.

She glanced sideways at Tim. Moonlight dimly illuminated his face, and although the dark of night surrounded them, Sage could read understanding in his gaze. Quickly, she looked back at the narrow road before her. Tim's ragged sigh broke the silence, then she felt his knuckles gently brush her cheek. Sage leaned into his touch and couldn't help the tears that trickled down into his hands.

"Sage," Tim said, his voice little more than a whisper. "Don't you know—"

A deafening concussion crashed above them. The car lurched to the left, and Sage jerked hard at the steering wheel, barely missing a tree. A piercing howl rang out, followed by a savage hammering on the Honda's thin roof.

"Hold on," Sage yelled above Gus's snarling barks and shoved the accelerator to the floor. The car jerked wildly through several twists of the mountain road. A thud sounded near the trunk, and for a second, Sage thought they'd escaped. Then a roar of rage was joined by a loud crack. Pieces of plastic rained down from the roof and then it bowed down, nearly to Sage's head. She raced crazily down the track, just missing rocks and trees. Would the old car be able to withstand this treacherous ride? Sage's fears were interrupted by Tim's groan of pain.

"Are you hurt?" she yelled, unable to see him. The bowed roof had collapsed into a jagged metal barrier between them.

"Fine," he shouted. "Just go."

"I'm trying!" The car raced on, almost out of control. "There's an overhang up ahead. I'll try to swipe it off." Cursing, she slowed to navigate a narrow section of the road that curved along the edge of a cliff.

Ear-splitting howls ricocheted around them. The car's roof buckled another few inches, and a claw punched through the contorted metal. Tim yelled as the remaining metal collapsed between them, crushing Sage's right arm and pinning her against the window. Unable to steer, she tensed her body against the seat, anticipating a crash.

With the deafening screech of tearing metal and the pop of shattering glass, the collapsed roof was suddenly gone. Air rushed through the car, and Sage watched as the top of the Honda catapulted into the emptiness of the canyon. She glanced over her shoulder and saw the Skin-walker balanced on the sedan's trunk.

Gus's barking rose to a crescendo. He launched himself at the Skinwalker and clamped his teeth onto its arm. With a bay of triumph, the creature flung Gus's dangling body into the rocks on their left. Sage's heart tore in two at Gus's wail of pain.

"No!" she screamed. Her mind demanded she slam on the breaks, Skinwalker be damned. She couldn't leave her best friend suffering, dying alone on a deserted mountain road. But Sage forced herself to keep the accelerator to the ground, knowing she and Tim were the creature's next victims.

She glanced back again. As if reading her thoughts, she saw the Skinwalker jump into the seat behind them.

Tim lay slumped against his window. "Wake up. Wake up!" Sage tried to shake him with her crushed right arm, but the useless limb only glanced against his shoulder. Dead-ening despair, almost as debilitating as her injuries, flooded her. Then suddenly, in her headlights' beam, Sage saw the rocky overhang less than 500 feet away.

"We're almost there!" The car dipped violently, jolting Sage forward in a painful whip. She prayed the lurch had knocked the Skinwalker off its balance. But then a vicious clawed hand clamped around Tim's headrest and ripped it from the car. She glanced at the overhang in the distance. It was still too far away. Resignation filled her, and she let out a shuddering breath.

"Not this time, you bastard," she whispered as she closed her eyes and cranked the steering wheel as hard as she could to her left. The car smashed into the mountain wall, and the windshield and remaining windows shattered against her. Ricocheting from the impact, the vehicle's tail spun to the opposite side of the road where the mountain dropped away into darkness. The Honda teetered on the edge of the precipice for a split second before settling back onto the gravel.

With her last ounce of consciousness Sage forced her gaze to the passenger seat. But Tim was gone.

CHAPTER THIRTY-THREE

Voices echoed around her, and Sage fought against claustrophobia. Trapped, restrained. Every fiber of her being urged her to escape, but her limbs were leaden and much too heavy to move. Jagged darts of pain shot through her body, and her mouth felt as if it had been sucked dry by a vacuum.

Bright lights jolted her in and out of consciousness. Excited, angry voices repeated one word over and over: serum. Minutes, maybe hours ticked by, before Sage could, with immense effort, force herself to focus on the conversation around her.

"I want her screened every half hour," a deep voice came from her right. "We need to see how the serum reacts to her mutations. I'm working on it in the lab as well, but here is where we'll see the effects first. Alert me to any change. No matter how small."

"Yes, sir," came a strained feminine voice to her right. "And the other one?"

"He's not a priority," the deep voice responded curtly. "However, I will need him for information. Do you have an estimate on when he'll regain consciousness?"

"Benson ordered him to be removed from his meds nearly a day ago. Renault is keeping an eye on him now, but he's not hopeful. If the patient comes out of his coma, it will be in the next few hours."

A loud beep sounded. "Her IV bags need to be replaced. Should I page the nurse?"

"You go," the male replied. "I'll observe her until you return."

Footsteps faded away, followed by the sound of a door opening. A whoosh of air blasted her face. In the haze of her returning consciousness, Sage detected a terrible stench that seemed vaguely familiar, followed by a sharp clicking sound. She heard someone gasp and then the stench dissipated.

Where had she heard that sound before? She strained to remember, feeling the threads of recognition pricking at her memory. Then a loud, garbled voice filled the room and the familiarity flitted away. "Dr. Storm, paging Dr. Storm." The announcement blared several times.

Storm? The word worked its way into her sluggish brain. She tried to understand why it alarmed her so much. Had there been a storm? No, not a storm; an accident.

Suddenly, the details of her crash came flooding back: Gus, her dearest Gus, gone. Tim, gone. And the Skinwalker.

The announcement calling Storm continued, and Sage's brain snapped with sudden clarity. They were calling for Dr. Storm, Terrance Storm from the Oriel Biological Research Station. But what did that mean?

Sage tried to open her eyes, but they remained closed, cemented shut by a force she couldn't understand. A shout of anger and despair arose within her, but her paralyzed lips wouldn't let it escape. The beep of her monitor spiked as her pulse raced.

"Heart and respiratory rates picking up," she heard the voice say and then something rustled against her bed. "Are you finally awake?" A presence leaned over her, blocking the bright light. Sage heard a noise like panting close to her cheek.

There was another loud clicking sound as the door opened again. "They're paging you, Dr. Storm. Benson wants you to ... Dr. Storm? Are you alright? Do you need me to get you an injection?"

"No!" the voice snapped loudly. "Just hang up her IV. We can't afford any mistakes with this one." One final puff of breath landed on her eyes and then the voice adjusted back to its normal volume. "We need her functional as soon as possible. The Dental Clinic is tomorrow."

"I'll not leave the room until she's conscious."

"Good, and remember, Sue, any changes—"

"I'll have you paged." The door clicked once more as it opened and closed.

Sage felt her hand lifted and a pressure at her wrist.

"That should help you relax," the woman said, and Sage heard the heart monitor began to slow.

"Hope you enjoy your rest," the voice muttered in her ear as a blanket was pulled up and her pillow adjusted. A hand rested on her forehead before there was a sigh and the sound of distant footsteps.

WHEN SAGE FINALLY AWOKE, SHE FOUND HERSELF lying in what looked like a windowless hospital room. To her left, she was hemmed in by a wall of machines, connected to her with numerous tubes and wires. Curtains surrounded the rest of her bed, but through a gap in the fabric she could see a door to her right.

The earlier sharp pain of injuries was gone, replaced by a dull, throbbing ache in her head and chest. When Sage tried to shift her body in the bed, she found her arms and ankles tightly strapped to the frame. She swore and jerked helplessly at the restraints.

"So you've decided to join the land of the living." The white curtain was swept aside, and a hunch shouldered man with thick glasses glided next to her. "How are you feeling?"

"Who are you? Where the hell am I? Where's Tim and Gus?" Sage pulled again, the restraints cutting into her skin.

"You won't get out of those," the man said as he typed on a small tablet. "The bedframe's made out of titanium, and those straps have restrained bigger, stronger *guests* than you." His gaze met hers, and he gave her an ugly smirk before turning back to his typing.

Sage's heart raced and prickles of perspiration shivered down her shoulders and back.

"Do you remember how you got here?"

She glared at the doctor and said nothing.

"How do you feel? Heart racing? Headache? Chills? Nausea?" he asked almost gleefully.

Despite her anger, Sage did a quick check of her body. Heart sinking, she realized she had every symptom he'd mentioned, except nausea. Which was too bad. She would have loved to vomit all over this smug moron's face.

"I'll take that as a yes." The doctor chuckled and pushed a button that hung from a cord at the bottom of her bed. A voice came over the intercom.

"Yes?"

"Tell Dr. Storm that the patient is now awake."

"Right away, Dr. Benson."

He rose and studied a monitor to the left of Sage's bed.

"*Doctor* Benson? Anders Benson?" Sage asked.

The man nodded then straightened. He picked up one of the tubes that ran from Sage's body and plugged it into a machine.

"Must be hard to juggle your work at the Assessor's office and your *marmot* research here." Sage spat the words out. Her headache had suddenly intensified, and she felt as though her skull was being crushed in a vice grip.

"I manage just fine, but thank you for your concern." Benson replied and tapped the screen of one of the machines. "This should help with the side-effects. They're usually worse at the beginning, until you get used to the reaction."

"What reaction? And why am I strapped to this bed?" Pain and anger tangled in a whirlwind of adrenaline, and Sage's voice rose to a shout.

The door opened. "Sounds like she's doing well," came a voice from behind the curtain, followed by the snapping of plastic gloves. Another man came to stand next to Dr. Benson, and Sage recoiled.

Terrance Storm towered over the other doctor by nearly a foot, but despite his large frame, he didn't give the impression of strength. His skin had a strange grayish-yellow pallor, and it hung slack from his face. Dark, curly hair covered his head and arms. Bloodshot, pale blue eyes glowed from the baggy skin surrounding them. When Sage had seen him in the ORBS gift shop, he'd looked healthy and strong. What had happened to him?

"What are her stats?" he asked Benson, his gaze never leaving Sage's body.

"Above average. Heart rate is elevated, white and red

blood cell count are within normal limits. Capillary and reflex reactions are excellent even in the affected limbs."

"Good," Storm grinned. His yellowed, crooked teeth nauseated Sage, and she turned away. "You may leave us now." Storm told Benson.

"But—"

"I said leave!" Storm snapped.

"Yes, sir." Benson rushed out of the room.

Storm pulled a wheeled stool next to Sage's bed and sat. He leaned down and smelled the length of her arm. "At last. I've dreamed of this day for a long time."

Sage concentrated every fiber of her being into not displaying the revulsion she felt, but her ability to maintain a mask of control was strained by whatever cocktail they'd medicated her with. Her head and chest felt tight, like they were about to burst. "Who are you?" she forced the words out, groggy and thick.

"Introductions? Surely you know who I am. In fact, I believe we've met." He laughed as his eyes traveled the length of her body. Disgust roiled through Sage, and she wished she could manage enough saliva to spit on his condescending face.

Anger mutated into cold rage and helped sharpen her mind. "I know you're Dr. Terrance Storm. But I was thinking more along the lines of, why am I strapped to this bed, where is Tim Burgney, and why are you using the people of Black Mills as your guinea pigs?"

"Your investigative discoveries are truly impressive. How long did it take you to figure all that out?" He reached over and lightly stroked the skin on her arm.

At his touch, a ringing filled her ears, and Sage's vision blurred as unconsciousness threatened to pull her into its embrace. She forced her racing heart to slow and took several deep breaths. "Don't touch me," she ground out through clenched teeth.

"Now, that's not very nice, is it? Especially after all the trouble we've gone through to keep you and your friend alive." He stood and walked to the machines at Sage's left. Her vision slowly cleared, and she noticed he had a slight limp. "It took longer than I thought, but at this point you're doing well. Your stats have finally started to improve. That's probably due more to your *abilities* than any skill from these imbeciles." He gestured vaguely to the door behind him.

Sage strained once more at her restraints. The fabric chaffed her tender wrists and ankles. How on earth could this guy know about her abilities? Even the hospitals in New Mexico hadn't known, and she'd visited them often enough. Until she ran away.

"There are people in Black Mills who know we're here." The claim sounded pathetic even to her, but she continued, "The false information you've fed to the papers is wearing thin, and the town's getting suspicious. You have to let us go."

Storm chuckled and leaned close to her once more. "Let's not rush things. We're especially curious to follow your progress with the vaccine serum. Someone like you offers us a unique opportunity. Besides we're still missing your shadow." He pushed the button that hung over the edge of her bed.

"Yes?"

"Send in Tim Burgney." He turned to her with excitement dancing in his strange eyes. "I think it's time for all of us to get better acquainted."

CHAPTER THIRTY-FOUR

Storm adjusted various bags of medication and machines while Sage closed her eyes in the futile hope that this was one of her visions, a dream from which she would soon wake. When she blinked and found the white walls and curtains still surrounding her, she struggled not to whimper in despair. Storm studied the monitor displaying her pulse, blood pressure, and other numbers. Grudgingly she realized that whatever he'd done, the pain in her head and chest were receding, and her mind had sharpened. She almost felt back to normal.

The door clicked and a nurse pushed a wheelchair-bound Tim into the room. His head slumped over his chest and most of his body was covered with bandages and gauze. He barely looked alive.

Sage closed her eyes to hold back the welling tears, but they escaped, burning the scratches and abrasions on her face. First, her precious Gus had been taken from her, and now Tim was barely clinging to life. Sage took a deep breath. She could not afford to waste time in grief or fear;

Tim's life depended on her figuring out this madness and rescuing him, regardless of what happened to her.

What was this vaccine or serum they kept talking about? They were obviously planning to use it on the people of Black Mills at the Dental Clinic. Shuddering, Sage pictured Liddy, Elena, and the children who had clustered around the float the day she first met Tim. What would happen when they got a dose of this experimental cocktail? She considered the pounding head, aching muscles, and clammy coldness that were only just diminishing in her body. If her reaction to it was any indication, the general population was in for some serious trouble.

Storm strode to the door and flung it open where a nurse waited. He gestured angrily at his computer tablet. A rustle drew Sage's attention, and she looked at Tim. He had pulled his arm from its sling, and his eyes were fixed on her face. He winked, then silently raised his finger to his lips and gave her a crooked smile.

Are you okay? she mouthed frantically.

Tim gave a barely perceptible nod. His gaze returned to Storm, and they watched as the doctor followed the nurse into the hallway, demanding she find Benson immediately.

The second the door shut, Tim sat up straight and wheeled his chair closer to Sage. "Do you have any idea what's happening?"

"I don't know," Sage tried to reach for Tim, but her arm restraint rattled against the bed. He stretched a bandaged hand to hers. At his touch, Sage suppressed a choking sob of relief. "They're testing some serum on me. I think they're going to give it to everyone at the Dental Clinic. But it's bad, Tim, it's poisoning me. I feel so sick. If this is my reaction, it'll kill a normal person."

The door slammed and suddenly Storm was next to Tim's chair.

"So you're awake now? How nice of you to join us." He crushed Tim's bandaged shoulder with a white-knuckled vice grip, and Tim gave a sharp cry. "Did you have something to say?"

"Not to you," Tim rasped.

Storm contemplated Tim for a moment, smirked, then casually struck him across the face with the back of his bony hand. Tim's head snapped, and his wheelchair jolted backwards.

"Stop!" Sage jerked helplessly against her restraints.

Storm studied Tim, looking for a response. When there was none, he turned back to his tablet with a sneer. "Coward," he muttered.

Tim groaned but after a moment sat up straight again and turned his now bloodied face towards the doctor. "Maybe I am. Still, that's interesting, coming from you." He spat out a mouthful of blood. It fell on his chest, staining the white bandages with a fiery mark that glowed in the stark medical room. "Aren't you the one hiding away in the mountains, injecting the populace of a remote town with an untested serum, awash in your delusions of grandeur?"

Storm shuddered, and his gaze slowly travelled back to Tim. In the blink of an eye, he flung the tablet to the floor and struck Tim across the face again. Sage screamed in helpless rage and watched as Tim, more slowly than last time, returned to his upright position. Blood drenched his mouth and chin, but as his eyes met Sage's, she saw there was no cowardice in them. He nodded at her then jerked his head in the direction of Storm.

"And obviously," Sage gasped, hoping she'd understood Tim's lead to further enrage Storm, "the serum's been a raging success, right? I mean Tabitha and Shaun are doing so well ... wait, I forgot. You killed them. That's what all good scientists do when they make a breakthrough. Destroy their test subjects."

Sage watched Storm's smirk disappear, replaced by a mask of calculated indifference. But the clenched fists negated the casual facade.

"Guess the Clozapine stopped working after fifteen years of constant dosages," Tim added. "Psychotic behavior is a pretty serious side-effect, isn't it? I'm sure that whoever you're developing this for might see that as a drawback."

Storm's glanced between the two of them, then he stalked to the end of the bed and pushed the button.

"Yes?" came a tinny voice from over the intercom.

"I need a refill for my pen, now!"

A few seconds later a nurse rushed in. Hesitantly, she handed him a vial. Storm pulled what looked like a writing pen from the chest pocket of his white coat and inserted the vial into its chamber. He then jammed the tip of the pen into his neck.

"Another," he barked.

"But, sir, I can't—"

"Now!"

The nurse reached into her pocket and with shaking hands removed another vial. Storm grabbed it. "Go get me three more."

"Yes, sir," she whispered and rushed from the room.

He walked slowly back to the bed. "Interesting." He narrowed his eyes. "It appears you two might be slightly less pathetic than these greedy little scientists. But, of course, you only have half the story."

"The half with the deaths, murders, and adverse reactions to your serum?" Tim asked.

Storm smiled. "How easy it is to judge from the outside. What people like you fail to recognize is that there's never some scientific gain without sacrifice."

"Shaun, Tabitha, and Sheriff Davis are the only sacrifices we can expect then?" Tim asked. "Or will there be others?"

Storm ignored him. "We live in an age where we've finally discovered how genetic disorders determine nearly every weakness humans exhibit. Cancer, autism, diabetes, autoimmune diseases, asthma. There's even evidence to supports the hypothesis that behaviors like mental illness, proclivity to violence, alcoholism, and other addictions are all set within our genetic code.

"What if someone developed a serum, a vaccine, that could be given to all children at birth, maybe even in utero, that would turn off these mutations? Imagine a world free of mental and physical suffering. Wouldn't that be worth a few unfortunate casualties?"

"What are you saying?" Sage asked, interested in spite of herself. "That you could create *perfect* human beings?"

"Exactly." A ghoulish smile appeared on Storm's face, and Sage shuddered.

She searched to find the catch. A world free from mental and physical suffering? What *was* wrong with that?

"But what about the psychotic behaviors exhibited by Shaun and Tabitha?" Tim asked.

"And Old Hank," Sage added. "I saw the vials in his cabin." Realization dawned in Sage. "And *you!* You've given yourself the serum too, haven't you?"

"That was an earlier version of the formula," Storm said. "We think we've been able to eliminate that side effect."

"You *think?*" Sage choked. "Maybe you should *know*

before you start patting yourself on the back about saving humanity."

"Oh, we intend to know. That's what the Dental Clinic tomorrow is about." Storm smiled. "There's roughly 8,000 inhabitants in the Black Mills area. Even if half of them come to the event, that's an adequately sized test population, one made up of widely varying demographics. Their reaction should be enough to satisfy our skeptics."

The door clicked open and the nurse appeared, her hand full of vials. Storm walked over and jerked them from her hands.

Sage's gaze met Tim's. *Skeptics*, he mouthed. She nodded.

"So these skeptics," Sage asked when he returned. "Who are they?" She knew the final key of the mystery hung on their identity.

"I'm not sure that information pertains to you, Broken One," Storm said, loading his pen and giving himself another dosage.

"Here's something that pertains to me," Sage said, everything finally clicking into place. "Why are you involved in this? You may be doing a pretty good job fooling all the staff here at the Research Station, but you and I both know you're not Terrance Storm."

Tim looked at her in surprise.

"When did you kill him, Skinwalker?" Sage asked. "And how long have you been inhabiting his body?"

CHAPTER THIRTY-FIVE

"What a strange thing to say." Storm walked quickly to the machines to her left and fiddled with some of their buttons.

"How much longer can you keep this up, *yee naald-looshii*? You're obviously beginning to lose control. I imagine it's pretty hard to rein yourself in here day and night, working in a lab. Aside from killing some of your mistakes, you can't have allowed yourself many fresh victims. It would have raised too much suspicion if people were dying by the droves in a tiny mountain town."

Storm spun away from the monitors, and his face twitched, briefly transforming into the shape of the Skinwalker's. Sage forced herself to watch the gruesome transformation. As Storm fought to regain his human form, an idea took root in her panicked brain.

With the careful, calculating Storm in charge, she and Tim didn't stand a chance of escaping. But if the Skinwalker took over? More than likely, it would kill them. But maybe, in the chaos created by the enraged creature, there was the smallest possibility of escape. It was more than a long shot, but the only option she could see.

She glanced at Tim. He watched Storm carefully, but without fear. He looked at Sage, and she crooked her fingers to him. Slowly, Tim scooted his wheelchair to the edge of her bed and leaned toward her.

"Make him lose control," she whispered. "It's our only chance."

Tim nodded and straightened. "I bet that hurts. Do you need someone to call the nurse again?"

Storm writhed, his contortions growing more violent.

Sage gulped away the last of her fear. "Hey, quick question. Are you house trained? I can't help but notice this terrible smell every time you come around. Maybe you could get some of the orderlies to change your litter box."

"Enough!" Storm roared and this time his entire body wrenched.

"Don't go to any trouble on our account," Sage yelled over Storm's snarls of pain. "Looks like someone wants to come out for a visit."

The wailing stopped and a dark chuckle sounded. With the grotesque pop of bones and tendons, Storm's twisted body uncurled to a staggering height at the foot of Sage's bed. The unholy union of his face, neither fully human nor fully wolf, contorted in a vicious snarl as he ripped the torn shirt from his chest. His body was covered in mange-like fur, greasy and falling off in dark patches. The overpowering scent of decay assaulted Sage, and she gagged.

"Do you think I cannot sense your fear, Broken One? You reek of it, as the dead reek of rot. It feeds me. All of you pathetic, disgusting Broken Ones, your fear feeds me. Your father's did. And your mother's. Even your small, pathetic brother's."

"What?" Sage cried, her brain refusing to accept the words. "What are you saying?"

"Oh yes," the Skinwalker chuckled and lunged to the side of Sage's bed, knocking over several machines as he did so. "I recognized your scent when you came into the gift shop. You evaded me as I lay pinned to the ground by your protectors. I have always regretted that you escaped."

Distorted memories slashed Sage's terrified brain. A little girl, alone in a tent listening to the last agonized groans of her family. Being crushed under yards of silky fabric and unable to take a breath. Blindness. Emptiness. And dark howls of rage that echoed around her as she floated away.

A sob tore at Sage's throat. Memories long suppressed awakened the agonizing grief she had forced into deep slumber. Visceral, heart wrenching pain tore through her, and something between a wail and a whimper escaped her lips.

The Skinwalker leaned toward her greedily as if absorbing her anguish. "That you would be led here, to this town, almost like a gift? It is more than I could have hoped," he said, stroking her leg through the blanket. Sage tried to pull away, but her restraints held her steady.

"Leave her alone." Tim struggled in his chair.

"Or what?" The Skinwalker's piercing laughter echoed around the room. "What threat do you imagine you hold over me?"

Tim steadied himself against Sage's bed and swayed as he rose to stand. "Sage was led to this place because she's going to destroy you. You're fighting a losing battle. You're the smoke and mirrors of the final act, but no one's fooled. What you've hidden will be revealed. Everything you've concealed will be brought to light. Ultimately, you will fail, and the innocents you have destroyed both now and in the past will have their justice."

The Skinwalker let out a low growl, his eyes glinting red in the sickly hospital lighting.

Tim leaned over Sage's bed and rested his hand against her cheek. An eternity existed in that moment as she gazed into his eyes.

"Sage, don't listen to his words. They're lies. You were brought here to defeat him, and you will. You're the bravest, strongest person I know." With a trembling hand, Tim traced a gentle cross on Sage's forehead. "The Sun of Righteousness shine upon you and scatter the darkness from your path." Tears traced down his cheek and dripped onto her face where they mingled with hers and became one. They burned a pathway across the torn skin on her cheeks and forehead. "Don't give up, Sage, and don't be afraid. You will find your peace."

The Skinwalker's growl escalated into a roar, then in one swift motion, he vaulted over Sage's bed and lifted Tim up in his arms. Tim dangled limply before the Skinwalker sent him flying through the air. Sage heard the sickening crunch as Tim crashed into the wall and slid into a heavy heap onto the floor.

"Tim, NO!" Sage screamed.

"You are defeated, Broken One. You are mine. There is no priest, no dog, no interfering Wind to stand in my way. Your protectors have all deserted you." He moved back to Sage's side and lowered his face inches from hers. Sage tried to turn her head away, but he held it fast with his sharp claws. "Your choice in allies is pathetic. But then, the Wind has been a weak adversary from the beginning. If the Wind truly cared about you, why would it lead you here, of all places? Right to the doorstep of your family's murderer."

Sage flinched as the words hit her in waves, seeking to destroy any spark of hope or grit that remained within her.

"When I stumbled upon your family, I was far from home and yet, it was a very pleasant surprise. They suffered much. You have suffered much." He bared his teeth in a hideous smile and inched closer until his muzzle nearly touched her. Sage screamed and jerked against her cuffs until she felt the warmth of blood against her wrists and ankles.

The door crashed open. Anders Benson stood in the doorway with a look of horror on his face. "What are you doing?" he gasped, his gaze darting between the Skinwalker and Tim's crumpled body. "The final formula has to be ready in three days or else we'll lose the contract. You've got to get a hold of yourself. We can't afford for this to fall apart!"

The creature roared, sprang across Sage's bed and picked up the protesting Benson.

"Stop. You're ruining everything!" Benson screamed, but his cries were cut short as the Skinwalker flung him into the wall, only a few feet away from where Tim had crashed. Benson's body crumpled like a rag doll and thudded to the floor. Bits of the broken sheetrock wall rained down over the two bodies.

An awed horror at the creature's strength and brutality overwhelmed her. Sage knew it was close to completely losing control, but she couldn't give up yet. Either through escape or death, she was getting out of this room. "Was killing your staff part of the plan too?" she choked out. "But what's one more cover up? You've got to be an expert at that now."

The Skinwalker spun around and leapt on top of her bed. "Silence, Broken One," he snarled, his voice now barely intelligible. He grabbed ahold of the bed frame and snapped the restraints at Sage's wrists and then her ankles.

Grasping her arms, the creature flung Sage's limp body over his shoulder, and she cried out as the many tubes and wires ripped from her. The Skinwalker then gave Benson a final, savage kick before he crashed through the door.

He slid into the hall, knocking over carts, IV stands, and monitors. Medical staff first gaped, then screamed and fled through the large metal doors at the other end of the hallway.

"We've got a code red on the fourth floor," Sage heard a nurse yell frantically into a phone before the Skinwalker silenced her with a well aimed medical tray.

"Stop!" several voices shouted. The creature turned. Sage saw a few doctors and several armed security guards racing toward them. The rest of the staff escaped in the other direction.

The guards paused a few feet away and glanced at each other, obviously unsure how to proceed. One of them shouted, "Put the patient down now, and no one has to get hurt."

The Skinwalker's retching snarl filled the air, and he tossed Sage down the hallway behind him. She crawled underneath a gurney and watched the creature open his arms wide as if to embrace the guards. "Go ahead, hurt me if you dare."

Gun shots sounded for only a few seconds before the Skinwalker had either killed or knocked the guards sense-less, their broken bodies scattered across the floor. Sage cowered under the gurney, but the Skinwalker kicked it aside and tossed her over his shoulder.

"None will stop me!" he roared and loped down the hall with Sage dangling over his back.

CHAPTER THIRTY-SIX

Not again, not again, not again.

The thought thrummed through Sage like a dull drumbeat. Moments of that last night with her family flashed into her mind with gut-wrenching realism. Enveloped in the terrible memories, she found it hard to focus on the chaos surrounding her even when the creature slid into doors and crashed Sage against walls as he raced through the maze-like hallways of the research complex. She felt her weakened body becoming numb with pain and resignation.

Interwoven in her anguish were the Skinwalker's words about the Wind. She didn't want to believe him, believe that the Wind had betrayed her, or worse, maliciously lead her to live practically next door to the murderer of her family. But did any other explanation really make sense? When she was a teenager, social services forced Sage to relocate to this town after several failed runaway attempts, adamant that it was the safest place for her to live. Once Sage had reached adulthood, she could have left if she wanted to. But no matter where her missions had taken her, the Wind always led her back to Black Mills.

The creature took her deeper into the complex, down staircases and elevators, through a bewildering network of hallways. She needed to pay attention, remember the route so she could escape. But another part of her felt collapsed, incapable of caring about anything ever again. If only she and Tim... but wait. Tim was *dead*, just like Gus. How could that be?

Sage tried to replay the moment the Skinwalker had attacked Tim, but her brain wouldn't let her see the conclusion. It was as if the incident had been a dream, and Sage could change the outcome, if only she created the right alternative in her mind.

Numbness was winning. Her mind, like her body, was shutting down. Why couldn't she just let go? Let it all go. She closed her eyes, her forehead and nose chafing against the wiry, greasy hairs on the Skinwalker's back as he dashed down another set of stairs.

Tim's face filled her mind once more. She could still feel where his tears seared a path of fiery beauty down her cheeks. His last words broke through the chaos of her tortured thoughts: *Sage, don't listen to his words. They're lies. You were brought here to defeat him, and you will. You're the bravest, strongest person I know.*

The conviction of his words began to resonate through her, like a trumpet, louder and louder until finally they drowned out everything else. She wouldn't give up. She *couldn't*. Tim deserved justice. Her family deserved justice. And they weren't the only ones. A long line of people all the way to Naomi's ancestors cried out to have their suffering, meticulously orchestrated by the Skinwalker, brought into the light.

Then she remembered her whispered promise to the

Wind, right before she and Tim had gone to meet with Naomi Notah. Sage had vowed to trust the Wind. And in turn, it had promised to be with her and help her. But how could it do so here, miles underneath Oriel and probably halfway to hell? If only Tim were here. Even in the darkest parts of the underground bunker, he'd been able to sense the Wind's leading.

But Tim wasn't here, and this was her battle. Sage clenched her fists. "Wind, if you're here," she whispered, "if you're a part of all this destruction, then talk to me. What should I do? Show me what you want ... please." She felt the faint rustle of a breeze, from where she couldn't imagine, gently brush her cheek.

"Wait," It whispered. "You must wait a little longer." An electric jolt shot from her cheek and blazed a trail through the rest of her body, lighting it up with the familiar sting of healing.

As if realizing this, the Skinwalker suddenly stopped and threw her to the ground. Her head rang from the impact against the floor, but the rest of her body felt relatively pain free. The Wind's healing had worked.

Sage's senses snapped with clarity. Gingerly, she sat up and looked around. The creature had brought her back to the cavernous warehouse she and Tim had discovered just days ago during the Honey Festival. But this time, they'd come by an entrance at the back of the structure, near where she and Tim had scaled the wall.

"Why are we here?" she asked, searching for the creature in the dim light of the computer monitors.

"Because I need something from you," came a voice from behind her. Sage turned and saw that the Skinwalker had morphed back into Storm. His clothes hung in tattered shreds around his body, but Storm quickly pulled a lab coat from a small cupboard and shrugged it around his shoulders.

Sage's gaze fell on the several used vials discarded at the base of the cupboard. She watched Storm slip what she assumed was a new pen back into his chest pocket. Her hopes dwindled; the *yee naaldlooshii* was restrained once again under the controlled facade of Terrance Storm.

"I need one more blood sample. If my findings are similar to what I expect," Storm said, "I might just have time to synthesize a better version of the serum that I can use on myself and the others."

Was he delusional? Sage wondered. What about the trail of dead scientists and security guards that littered the hallways above them? Was he really going to pretend everything was business as normal?

WITH SURPRISING STRENGTH, STORM PULLED HER towards a door several yards away. He opened a metal door and pushed Sage into the room before locking it with a scan card which he quickly pocketed. Fluorescent lights slowly flicked on, and she scanned her surroundings. Carts full of stacked trays were neatly lined up against the opposite wall. Each one was filled with hundreds of squat ampoules. Overhead cabinets and countertops lined the rest of the walls, along with microscopes, refrigerators, and other stainless steel machinery.

"Why do you need my blood?" Sage repeated, her voice loud in the confines of the room. "Why not just use your own."

"Sit down," he ordered, gesturing to the chair before them. Sage hesitated. Storm grabbed her hair and jerked her into the seat. "Like your hospital bed, this frame has restraints. Shall I use them or will you cooperate?"

Sage looked at the rough bloody skin at her wrists and shuddered. No more restraints or she was no better off than back in the hospital bed. And then Tim's sacrifice would be for nothing. "I'll cooperate."

Storm tied a band around Sage's elbow and plunged a syringe into one of her veins.

"I'm sure it has not escaped your notice, my dear, that the serum has certain undesirable side effects," he said, falling back into the condescending doctor tone. "Much to my surprise, I have fallen victim to all of them, just like the other humans. Hysteria, psychosis, they are especially detrimental to my *abilities*," Storm grimaced. "My mind plays the most convincing tricks on me, and it is hard to maintain the correct facade, even with the Clozapine."

Sage studied the wrinkled, yellowing skin that hung in sickly folds from his face. As a powerful witch, the *yee naaldlooshii's* loss of control due to the serum's side effects must have come as a terrible shock to him. His desperation suddenly made more sense.

"You, however, have not," he added.

"I haven't what?" Sage asked.

"Experienced the side effects." Storm removed the now full syringe.

"Are you kidding?" Sage couldn't help but laugh as she untied the band around her arm. "My head felt like it was going to explode. I ached all over. This the sickest I've been in a long time."

"The point is, my dear, you are fully recovered now." Leaning forward, Storm eyed her greedily. "You are quite exceptional, you know."

" I don't know what you're talking about. I'm just a ...

normal person." The excuse sounded weak and feeble, even to Sage's ears.

"Now that's not true, is it? Does someone *normal,* as you call yourself, communicate with animals? Have extra-sensory perceptions about other living creature's locations in relation to herself? Can normal humans survive the many abuses and injuries you have, even the penetration of an '*adagqsh* and walk away all but unscathed?"

The creature's insight into the most private, unspoken details of her life revolted Sage. She felt violated by his attention. "I guess I'm pretty tough," she finally said, straining to sound casual.

"Tough?" Storm laughed as he walked to a workstation. He removed the needle from the syringe and put the ampoule of blood into a slot in one of the machines. After pressing several buttons, a loud whirring sound filled the room. Storm lifted a petri dish from an under counter refrigerator and set it next to a large microscope. "Either you are too stupid to realize the gift you've been given or woefully ignorant of the breadth of your powers. Of course that fool *Hatałii* wouldn't have known how to—" The apparatus beeped and Storm turned away, making adjustments on the machine's screen.

As a *Hatałii,* or Singer, Grandfather Benally had been anything but a fool. His wisdom about the unseen, both good and evil, had constantly brought healing and peace to everything in his path. Sage had seen it both in herself and others. If only he were here now, he would know exactly what to do.

But he wasn't. For some reason, the fate of the Skin-walker had come to rest on Sage's shoulders alone, and she could not fail. Taking a deep breath, Sage forced her mind to quiet.

Sounds faded and only thready images remained. Sage watched Storm limp from one machine to another. For all his invincibility when he was a Skinwalker, the man seemed disjointed and stiff in his human form. She wondered why he hadn't yet switched from Storm to another, stronger body. When Skinwalkers inhabited another animal's or person's skin, their evil quickly destroyed that creature's remaining life force. She remembered Grandfather Benally's words from long ago when he had hesitantly answered Sage's questions about the *yee naaldlooshii*.

"Death follows witches wherever they go, especially the shapeshifters, the *yee naaldlooshii*. Because they have chosen to follow the dark way, they doom themselves to a life of loneliness. Their years become a chase for more life, more power, but they do not realize they have already written the story of their own destruction. Death cannot be forever tricked and deceived. In the end, it always finds its prey."

"Where'd you get that limp?" The question shot from her mouth before she could consider its wisdom.

Storm looked up from the machine. His face contorted for a brief second, and Sage saw the enraged Skinwalker begin to emerge from Storm's features, like a hideous claymation movie.

The limp. Sage felt a jolt of excitement. She'd finally found the chink in his armor.

CHAPTER THIRTY-SEVEN

"Whoa, I didn't realize you were so touchy about the limp," Sage said. "We don't have to talk about it if it gets you all worked up."

The Skinwalker snarled, but not fully transformed, it shuddered and returned to its human form.

"I'm not worked up," Storm snapped after several deep and shaky breaths. He turned back to his work at the counter. "It's nothing. An old injury that never quite healed. It came from an unfortunate incident with a ... creature a long time ago."

"Another *yee naaldlooshii*?"

"No." Storm jotted something down on a sheet of paper. "Just some woman, bent on protecting a worthless child."

A searing flash of revelation assaulted Sage with a power so great it left her trembling. A woman protecting a child? It was her! *She* was the one had stabbed the Skinwalker in the foot when she saved Naomi Notah's grandmother. And he still suffered from her attack.

Sage tried to speak, but no sound came from her lips. She tried again, forcing the words out with feigned calm.

"How could a woman hurt you? I thought you were pretty much invincible?"

"It was more like a spirit being. It had great power, but I was still able to kill it.

"How can you kill a spirit?" Sage asked even as her mind raced. *Spirit being? What did that mean?*

Storm opened his mouth to respond, but then the machine beeped once more and he turned. After withdrawing the container, Storm uncapped it and used a pipette to suck up a small amount of the liquid. He then carefully added several drops of the new concoction containing Sage's blood to the petri dish and set it on the microscope tray. "Now we see if you live or if you die."

"What?" Sage choked. "But I thought—"

"You may be clever, but if your blood hasn't solved the protein abnormalities in the serum, you are worthless to me." Storm looked up from the microscope and smiled. "Either way, I shall enjoy the outcome." He leaned back over the eyepiece.

Sage glanced over to the laboratory door and then to Storm's lab coat pocket. If she caught him by surprise, maybe she could grab the keycard and make it to the door. But then Storm would transform back into the Skinwalker. He'd be on her in a second and this time, he might not be able to control his rage.

Her mind raced to find other possibilities of escape, but there were none. Resignation crept from her mind through every part of her being. Sage hugged her arms around her body. If her chances of getting out of here alive were nonexistent, she'd settle for at least taking the Skinwalker down with her. Figuring out a way to destroy the stacks of serum bottles would probably be a good idea too.

"Please, Wind," she whispered, knowing that she was

running out of time. "Tim and Gus are gone, and I can't do this alone. Tell me what to do."

"What's that?" Storm barked, and Sage looked up. He gazed at her with a wolfish smile. "We're alone down here, my dear. You can mutter and pray all you like, but it won't make any difference." He returned to his microscope.

A gentle breath of air whisked Sage's hair from her sweaty face. *Arrogance, pride,* A voice whispered in her ear. *He cannot resist them in himself or others.*

It wasn't much, but it would have to do. Sage stood and walked toward Storm. "I get the feeling that no matter what you find there, you're going to kill me anyway. Can I get a last request?"

"I'm not freeing you," Storm sat up and leaned back in his chair.

"Of course not."

"Then what do you want? I probably won't give it to you, but you've surprised me so far." Storm glanced at his watch. "You have exactly three minutes before my results are ready."

"This project you have going on here. From what you've said, it's a serum that eliminates all genetic problems?"

Storm gave her the smallest of nods and Sage continued. "I have to say, I'm completely blown away. Even a little bit in awe. Who thinks that big? And now with my blood, it looks like you've pulled it off."

Sage waited. A faint breath of air whispered about her shoulders. She listened then continued, "You'll have desperate parents and health organizations begging for your vaccine, happy to pay you, no matter what the cost. But I bet you won't make it available for everyone, even if the rest of these greedy, shortsighted scientists would. Why give away a brand new commodity for wealth alone? Money's the carrot for these greedy Oriel scientists, but it's not your endgame, is it?"

"Go on." Storm narrowed his eyes. "Enlighten me."

Still not enough. Sage waited. Images filled her mind. Soldiers. War. Destruction.

"You'd sell it to another country, for their military."

Storm sat up in his office chair. "How could you...?" He shook his head and a grudging smile curled his drooping lips.

Sage forced herself to return the smile, hoping that by doing so, she'd be able to discover the full extent of this maniac's plans. "Soldiers with near super-human abilities and healing powers?" She spoke as more pictures flooded into her mind. "The governments of the world would beat a path to your door, and you'd become a major power player in global politics. Which nation gets the bionic population? All you'd have to do is name your price, but you'd still be playing them all, like puppets on a string."

Storm licked his lips. "And then war, chaos ... it would all be mine to control."

"You're brilliant." Sage shook her head. "All my life, I've thought of my abilities as a curse, something I needed to disguise. But you? Instead of hiding them away like I was taught, you're using your powers to control your life." Sage pushed out a brittle laugh. "Soon your name will fill people's hearts with fear. The world will hide from you and feel cursed, not the other way around. If only I had grown up with someone like you teaching me."

The intensity of Storm's gaze grew as Sage spoke, and she couldn't tell if it impressed him that she had guessed parts of his plan or enraged him. He seemed ready to speak, but then glanced down at his watch and hastily turned back to the microscope. Sage held her breath and clenched her fingers around the back of the chair she stood behind. If these were her last seconds, she'd at least give the Skin-walker a headache to remember her by.

CHAPTER THIRTY-EIGHT

"Interesting," Storm said from his place at the microscope.

"What?" Sage asked taking a small step backwards.

"I'm not sure," he answered and looked up at her. "Your DNA. When I studied it yesterday, while you were still fighting off the serum's abnormalities, I thought your proteins might be able to correct the errors. But not this. It's quite extraordinary, actually."

Sage took a deep breath.

"I'd have to compare it to some of my other samples, but ..." He looked Sage up and down with keen interest. "There are aberrations in here I've haven't seen since ..." He stopped and shook his head. "This changes everything."

"What?" Sage asked, unable to hide the fear in her voice. "What did you find?

Gently, Storm set the petri dish on the counter then shivered as his body began to transform once more. Frozen with confusion, Sage watched in uncomprehending horror as the Skinwalker hefted the large microscope in his hand and then slammed it across her head.

CONSCIOUSNESS SLOWLY CREPT ALONG THE EDGE OF Sage's mind, and she blinked. Dimly lit dark rock walls, covered with strange markings and ancient maps surrounded her. Several metal tables held more instruments, none as expensive looking as the warehouse room, but still exuding a sterile medical aura. And cages, everywhere cages.

Sage groaned. She was getting pretty sick of waking up in strange rooms, filled with creepy-ass equipment and evil creatures.

She grasped the wired wall to her right and pulled herself upright. The effort left her breathless with ringing ears and nausea.

"Sage? Is that you?" a broken voice rasped from behind her.

Painfully, Sage shifted herself to the side. A bedraggled person, covered in filth and blood, leaned against the side of the neighboring cage. His matted beard and hair made it nearly impossible to see his face, but Sage still struggled to place his familiar features. Recognition came after several moments, hard and fast.

"Sheriff Davis? You're alive?"

"Shhh!" Davis's eyes flicked behind Sage, and she glanced over her shoulder, cursing at the pain it caused. Behind her, at the edge of the room, Storm lurked, moving objects from one side of the room to the other.

Sage turned back to the Sheriff. "What's happening? How are you alive? They found your body at the church."

"Not my body," he rasped. "Set up to frame Tim and you."

"But the screaming Tim heard on the phone?"

The Sheriff stiffly pulled the ragged threads of his shirt to the side and revealed the bloody, scabbed mess of countless gashes all over his chest. "The screams were real. The death was not."

"Is there any way out of here?" Sage asked, even though she knew there wasn't much chance of escape now.

"Out of the cages? Sure. I nearly got mine jimmied with a piece of wire I worked off that back bit of my cage where it's rusted."

"So what's the problem?"

"There ain't no way out of this room, unless you have that monster's keys." Davis gestured with his chin. "Even if I ask real nice, I'm pretty sure he won't give them to me."

Sage tried to smile at the Sheriff's attempt at humor, but could not find the hope within herself to do so. She glanced wildly around the room. Surely there was another way out. Another option for escape.

Her heart hammered against her ribs, and hysteria threatened to overwhelm her as the ugly truth consumed her. There was no escape. The Skinwalker had obviously chosen this room carefully. The black walls were of the same rock as the one she and Tim had climbed to escape the warehouse. One lone door broke their impenetrable, smooth surfaces. And as Sheriff Davis had said, only the Skinwalker had the key.

"I'll try to figure out something," Sage whispered.

"Be careful," Davis whispered back. "He's killed everyone he's brought in here. Except me and those poor kids in the corner."

In a small cage along the back wall, two young children huddled, trembling against one another. As if sensing Sage's gaze, one of the tear-streaked faces lifted up from the protective circle of the other child's arms. Sage let out an anguished cry. His face was so similar to Daniel's, her little brother, that for a moment she hoped that he, like the sheriff, might still live. The second child looked up, and his features were so similar to the other boy's that they had to be twins. Tears of rage flooded Sage's eyes and obscured her vision.

Suddenly, Davis scooted back to the edge of his cage. Sage dashed the tears from her face and watched as the Skinwalker approached them. She forced herself to stay completely still, frozen in her crouched position. The creature paused in front of her cage for a brief second then ripped the door from its hinges and tossed it aside. Sage heard one of the children whimper in the brief silence before the Skinwalker pulled her from the cage and flung her over its shoulder.

"It is time," the creature's hideous voice ripped through the small enclosure of the lab.

"Time for what?" Sage kicked against the horrific mass that held her in its vice-like grip. "Time to torture and kill more innocent victims? Time to destroy more lives?"

"Yes, all you say and more." The Skinwalker flung her onto the table, which Sage now realized was covered with straps. With ruthless efficiency, he bound her arms, legs, and neck tightly to the table. When Sage tried to move, the strap at her neck dug into her throat, and she could no longer breathe. Panic raced through her, but she forced herself to lie still and breathe as deeply as she could.

The Skinwalker took a step back, crouched on the floor and shifted back into the shape of Terrance Storm. "And now, my dear, I'm afraid we will part ways for the final time."

"You're going to kill me?" Sage spat out.

"Not quite," Storm grinned and then turned to the

small tray of instruments behind him. "I had been planning to use Sheriff Davis as my new form. Then I'd stumble back into town, saying I'd been attacked and kidnapped by you and the Priest, but things have worked out better than I could have imagined.

"While Terrance Storm's body was useful for infiltrating the Oriel Research Station and its arrogant little band of scientists, he has proved pathetically weak, especially after I injected him with the genetic correcting serum. This body has been on the verge of mental collapse since then. The Clozapine is barely working anymore. Besides, this research facility's days are numbered, and I'm ready to move on."

"If you're going to kill me, just get it over with," Sage shouted, barely able to suppress the hysteria that threatened to consume her. She heard the two children's quiet sobs in the background.

"Kill you? That would be extremely foolish. I have not lived these many long ages by being foolish." Storm turned and picked up something from the tray. It was a large knife, cruel and ancient looking. "As I said before, you have no idea what you are, do you?"

"I don't know what you're talking about," Sage cried.

"You're not human. Your DNA is completely different from any human, ancient or modern, who has walked this earth. That's why you can heal, communicate without words, talk to the spirit world."

Sage's panicked mind struggled to accept Storm's words. What did they mean? Was she an alien?

Storm raised the knife high in the air. "And that is why yours is the body I will inhabit next." Strange, sing-song words came from his mouth, and slowly, he lowered the knife toward her chest.

CHAPTER THIRTY-NINE

"Wait! One second. I don't understand. WAIT!" Sage screamed as she felt the knife bite into the skin at her throat.

Storm paused and met her eyes with impatience. "What?"

"Go ahead and kill me. That's fine. But let those children go. And let Sheriff Davis go. They've all suffered enough," Sage begged, the anguish and fear in the young boys' eyes stamped in her mind. "Even if they told the people in Black Mills everything they saw here, no one would believe them. It'll sound like they've gone crazy. And you'll be long gone."

Storm shook his head. "I told you that I am not a foolish person. I have plans for their bodies. Even with your silly Navajo Singer's reluctance to speak of me, I'm sure you know that followers of the witchery way, the *Ánt'įįhnii,* have many uses for the innocent after they are dead. You should know, I shot you with a bone bead from one of them."

"No!" Sage screamed, her grasp on sanity finally snapping as the full implication of Storm's words rolled over her in crushing waves. He had shot her with some poor victim's bone. And very soon Davis and the children would be used for the same purpose.

"No more! You've destroyed enough! " She sobbed as Storm resumed singing.

It was too much. This creature had erased so many innocent, beautiful lives. Time slowed, and the tragedy of each death weighed upon her soul. She saw futures that would never be realized, dreams dissolved into ashes, and tears, enough to fill a river of agony.

"Broken One," a soft voice threaded through her sorrow. "It is time. Are you ready?"

"For what?" Sage whispered.

"You must trust now. Are you ready?"

A feather-soft caress brushed against her cheek. Sage choked back her tears and took a deep breath. "I'm ready."

Suddenly, every cell in her body was singing with electric energy. Her heart hammered with explosive force, and she writhed against the sharp pricks of pain in her hands and feet. A roar of thunder crashed in her ears, and white light exploded around her.

"What's happening?" her voice cracked sharply with terror.

"Don't be scared."

Sage felt a snap, then another and another. She looked down and realized she'd ripped the restraints from her body. Storm stood frozen next to her, knife still suspended over her heart, and she knocked it away. Her body rose up over the table in a wave of trembling energy. Suddenly she was floating in the air, flying. Below her she saw Storm cowering on the ground, beginning his transformation back into the Skinwalker. But she barely spared him a glance. Several incandescent forms occupied the room, floating protectively in front of the cages where the children and Sheriff Davis crouched in terror.

Unable to make out their features, Sage blinked, but it was like she was viewing the beings through a shimmer of tears. She reached up to wipe her face, but instead of a hand, feathers brushed her cheek.

"Broken One," a voice interrupted. "You have done well." The presence before the children's cage was suddenly in front of her. For a brief second, its features tried to arrange themselves into a face, but then disappeared back into a iridescent, ethereal mass. "It is time to finish this dark evil once and for all."

Sage looked down at the slathering Skinwalker that leapt beneath her, shocked at how pitiful and weak it now seemed.

The presence seemed to read her thoughts. "Yes, this one has been very clever in disguising himself in terror, but he truly is as you see him now."

Sage shuddered in disgust. The Skinwalker looked like a deformed dog or coyote.

"For the sake of those who live here, you must destroy him. Now. Otherwise he will continue to bring destruction. This valley has suffered enough."

"How do I ..." Sage tried to ask, but her voice came out as an inarticulate series of high pitched cries.

"You must consume him."

The presence retreated back to the children, and Sage willed herself downward. The Skinwalker shied away, but then feinted back toward her with its claws outstretched. Sage leapt away from their reach, still unsure of how to fight back. The creature lunged toward her again, and this time Sage knocked it away. She watched in awe as the Skinwalker flew across the room, screaming in pain. The smell of burnt flesh and fur filled the air.

Sage looked down at her hands. But they weren't hands, they were wings. Black, white and azure feathers glowed with silver brilliance. Small flames leapt from the shimmering barbs and hissed as they hit the scattered papers on the floor. Sage leapt back in shock, awed by the transformation that had occurred.

A sharp, searing pain tore across her back, and she turned to find the Skinwalker, now behind her, attacking her once more, its claws covered with smoking, bloodied feathers.

Rage replaced confusion, and Sage stretched out her arms. She rose into the air then leapt upon the Skinwalker with vicious, glowing talons. Howls of fury and pain echoed about her, but Sage could not tell if they were hers or the creature's. She pulled the writhing, wild mass closer and closer; then, suddenly, blinding light engulfed both of them.

An earsplitting clap of thunder reverberated through the room and drowned out the creature's cries. Then, in an explosion of white energy so powerful it seemed it must destroy them both, Sage felt the Skinwalker disintegrate into nothingness as she clutched it against her breast. Pain seared through her, and she fell to the floor with a heavy thud.

The patter of gentle rain bathed her face, and Sage forced her eyes open into exhausted slits. Ash and feathers danced along the line of her vision. One smoldering feather landed on her cheek and rested there, like a comforting kiss.

"Sage?" she heard Sheriff Davis call. "Sage, are you alive?"

Then everything went black.

CHAPTER FORTY

The next sound she heard was the gentle beep of a heart monitor. Sage tried to move, but her limbs felt desperately heavy.

"I thought I saw her eyelids flutter," said a voice.

"I'll just check her vitals," came another.

Sage's stomach clenched. Not again! *No!* The thing was finally dead. And she was too. Sage tried to groan but something was stuck in her throat, choking her.

"I think she's coming to," the first voice sounded again.

Sage felt as though she needed to vomit and struggled against the pressure against her throat.

"Let's go ahead and remove her breathing tube."

There was a strange tugging sensation at her throat and suddenly she was gasping, gagging, and breathing on her own as the thing pulled free. Focusing all her concentration on her eyes, she forced them open.

Bright light and blurry images danced in her vision. Was it the beings again? She blinked, trying to clear the fog, but it stubbornly remained. A body leaned in close and shined something into her eyes. She flinched.

"Shhh, it's okay, Sage." She felt the gentle pressure of another hand squeezing hers. "You're safe now. The doctor's just checking to make sure you're all right.

"Doctor ... who?" Sage rasped.

"One of my favorite TV shows, but you can call me Dr. Chase. Now tell me, Sage, how's your vision?"

"Blurry," Sage croaked.

"That's to be expected with coming out of a coma. We're fairly confident it will clear up, with time."

"You hear that, honey? You just keep resting up and everything's going to be fine."

"Liddy? Is that you?" Sage turned her head in the direction of the speaker.

"Yes, of course it's me. Where else would I be but next to the bed of my girl? And the town's hero."

"Hero?"

"Don't you remember what happened?" Liddy's voice dropped to a whisper. "Is it amnesia, doctor?"

"I'm not sure," Dr. Chase answered. "Let's give her a moment. Take your time, Sage, and let your mind relax. What's the last thing you remember?"

"There was a lot of white..." Sage cleared her throat and tried again. "A searing heat. But I had to protect the children. I had to crush ..." The Skinwalker, Tim, Gus. She gasped and pressed herself back against the bed striking out at the doctor and Liddy.

"It's all right, honey. It's all right." Liddy's voice cracked, and Sage felt her sit down on the bed. "You're safe here. You know you can trust your old Liddy, don't you?"

"I'll give you two a few minutes." Sage felt a gentle squeeze on her shoulder and then heard the door open and shut.

"Honey, I promise you're safe now. Can you

believe that?"

Sage nodded reluctantly. "What happened?" she croaked out.

"Now, they're not releasing all the details of what went on up there in Oriel," Liddy continued. "So, I can't answer everything, but from what they have told us, you saved the entire town from being some sort of cockamamy medical experiment."

"The Sk— and Dr. Storm?" She corrected herself. "Is he...?"

"He's dead. Don't you worry about him. Sheriff Davis said he got burnt up, along with most of the lab. But they're still up there looking for more clues."

"Who's they?"

"The FBI, I think. I'm not exactly sure. They all drive big, black SUVs so I figure they're part of some government agency. They were already here in town with everyone thinking Sheriff Davis was killed, but now they seem to be running the entire Black Mills Police Department. Got Officer Olson under arrest too. That was the first thing Tim and Sheriff Davis saw to after they got back into town and before we knew it—"

"Tim's alive?" Sage cried. "But he was ... I thought he was dead." She let out a choked sob. Liddy bustled around the room, tucking the blankets more tightly around Sage and gently wiping her face with tissue until she calmed down.

"I'm sorry, honey. I didn't realize you thought he was dead. Aside from you, he's been the talk of the town. Sheriff Davis made him the head honcho of the mopping up operations over at Oriel. Doing a good job too, leaving no stone unturned and all that."

"The serum? No one got injected?" Sage gasped.

"No one, sweetie. You saved us all."

"But there were other things going on there." Sage pulled her hand from Liddy's. "It wasn't just the serum."

"Now, don't go getting all riled up, Sage. Tim'll make sure that everything is done properly. He's already pretty much dismantled the entire operation up there and has helped the city bring a class action suit against the muckety mucks who ran the joint."

"What are you talking about? How long have I been here, unconscious?"

"Nearly two weeks now."

"Two weeks!" Sage shouted. Her voice dissolved into a dry, hacking cough. It tasted of blood and ash.

The door opened and closed again, and Sage felt Liddy move away from her bed.

"I think we'd better make sure our patient doesn't overexert herself," Dr. Chase said and she saw his dark form move toward her.

"But I have so many more questions!" Sage protested and tried to pull away when she felt a pressure at her wrist. "I want to talk to Tim."

"I'm sure you do," Dr. Chase answered. "But I want you to get better. And even though your progress has been almost miraculous these last few days, you gave us a pretty good scare at the beginning. I want you to make a complete recovery. Rest is the best thing for that."

"But—"

"Quiet now, honey," Liddy's voice came as if from far away, and Sage felt the woman brush the hair off her forehead.

A familiar heaviness covered her, and Sage struggled against it for only a few brief moments before succumbing to the soft, warm quiet.

CHAPTER FORTY-ONE

When Sage awakened again, the room was dark and deserted. She blinked and realized her vision was practically clear, only blurry around the edges. She stretched this way and that, testing her body. Although she was stiff and parts of her, especially her ribs, felt tender, Sage knew she was close to normal.

Quietly, Sage eased herself from the hospital bed and steadied herself against the bed before taking several tentative steps. In a threadbare visitor's chair, she found a bag full of her clothes. Sage bit her lip. Liddy must have brought them in anticipation of her release.

"Sweet Liddy. I'm sorry," Sage whispered before quickly dressing. Peering through the door's window, she waited until the night nurse left her desk. Sage slipped through the night-darkened halls of the small mountain hospital until she found a back service entrance and escaped.

She trotted cautiously to the impound lot behind the city hall and scaled the chain link fence. Her heart leapt at the site of her Jeep, the lone offender in the dusty parking lot. She climbed up over the roll bar into the driver's seat and found her spare key in the glove compartment.

The night was warm, and Sage drove down Main Street breathing in the fragrant, familiar scents of the sleeping town. When she stopped at a red light on the deserted main street, she let her eyes linger over the coffee shop, grocery store, and the library. The Wind danced through her car, ruffled her hair, and whispered that it was time to go.

Sage contemplated stopping by her house, but decided against it. Everything she really needed, all her camping supplies, most of her clothes, and some food and water were still in her Jeep. Even though Grandfather Benally's rug was precious to her, Sage would write Liddy apologizing, explaining what happened, and ask her to keep the rug safe. Sage couldn't face entering her old home without the familiar jingle of Gus's dog tags by her side. She swallowed. The loss of the dog had haunted her dreams and thoughts since she'd awakened. She couldn't imagine life without her best friend.

Driving up the deserted road to Oriel, Sage marveled at how different the journey felt compared to her prior sojourns between the two valleys. The soft, peaceful quietness of the mountain forests was now unmarred by boundaries, bloody deeds, or sinister machinations. The eight miles went by quickly, and before she knew it, she was in Oriel.

She pulled her Jeep into the empty guest center parking lot and climbed out. The town was deserted. Crime scene tape floated around several of the buildings, but it seemed old, like it had served its purpose and was now merely a reminder of yesterday's news.

Sage walked slowly between the buildings, peeking in several windows only to find deserted interiors. The occasional mouse scurried across her path and several bats flapped through the darkness, but other than that she saw no one.

At last she ended up in front of the Rand Building. Shivering in the moonlight, she stared at the cabin then turned to survey the valley that surrounded it. Although the evil had not completely dissipated, it had lessened considerably. Probably no one besides the Wind would ever know the complete depths of darkness that had been committed here, and for that she was grateful.

She heard a crunch on the trail behind her, but didn't turn around.

"I thought I'd find you here," Tim's voice came from the darkness.

"Had to give it one last look."

He came and stood close beside her. "The doctors are going to have a fit when they realize you've left the hospital."

"It's all right." Sage smiled up at him, his face illuminated in the moonlight. "I know someone with a first aid kit."

"The Feds and the people of Black Mills aren't going to be too happy either. You're a pretty popular lady around here."

Sage looked down. "They'll forget about me before too long."

"I won't." Tim's fingers gently found hers, and they gazed at the building, both caught up in memories that already seemed too implausible to be real.

After a while, his voice, now a gentle whisper broke the

silence. "Sage, you don't have to go. We could figure this out together."

"All the questions, Tim, all the follow up interviews. And *I'm* not even sure exactly what happened. You know I ... can't do that."

"That's what I thought you'd say," his voice rasped with emotion, and tears welled in Sage's eyes. Tim released her hand and pulled her into his strong arms.

She buried her face against his chest and made herself memorize the feeling of this place in time, this moment of supreme peace and contentment. The steady thump of his heart against her cheek, the gentle rise and fall of his breath. An embrace that asked nothing of her, but only gave.

Finally, when she couldn't bear it any longer, she pulled away. As if by unspoken agreement, the two turned and started back toward her car. "Seems like you're doing a good job getting all this closed down," she forced out the words while wiping her eyes on her sleeve. "Making sure the bad guys get their due, right?"

"It's been pretty involved, but the sheriff and I are getting there. You'll be interested to hear there were all sorts of incriminating documents in Storm's hidden room where we found you. It was crazy to have them all in one place; he must have thought he was invincible. Information about the serum program, the pharmaceutical companies, the governments that were bankrolling it. And other older documents from when they bought the Sanitorium. Even some diaries from the original miners that first settled this valley."

"You mean the ones—"

"Yep, and with documentation about the massacre. I've turned them over to the Navajo Nation and have spoken to Naomi Notah about it several times. She and I are coordinating a day of remembrance and mourning in Black Mills and working to create an exhibit about what happened for the local museum. I know she also has some lawyers working on suing what's left of the Oriel Biological Research Station. It's mostly symbolic since everyone and their dog is suing OBRS, but I think it's a good thing."

Sage nodded. They were at the Jeep now. She leaned against the hood, and Tim did the same. "But what about you? You were already in bad shape when they brought you into my room. And then I thought you were dead when the Skinwalker ... Storm threw you against the wall."

"I wasn't doing well, but I pretended to be in worse shape than I really was. I thought maybe they'd let their guard down if they thought I was dying. Then, when Storm threw me, I guess it just knocked me out for a bit. I think I woke up not too long after he'd taken you. I pulled on some scrubs and just tried to follow the panicking staff and trail of bodies. When I found that room off the warehouse—" He fell silent, but continued after a moment. "When I found it, I wasn't even sure what I was seeing at first. It looked like there had been some kind of explosion. You were covered in ash. And feathers. You were barely breathing. What happened?"

"I'm not entirely sure." Sage paused. "Did Sheriff Davis tell you anything?"

"No," Tim answered. "He said I needed to ask you."

Sage nodded and tried to sort the memories that bombarded her. "Were the children unharmed?"

"Yes," Tim answered. "They'd been kidnapped from a family who was staying in a vacation cabin nearby."

"Do they seem too traumatized?" Sage shuddered. She couldn't imagine the things they'd seen.

"Well, Sheriff Davis talked with them through a lot of what they saw. He was there too and able to help them try to make sense of it all. It seemed to help, but I'm sure they'll need more. But at least they're alive. And with their family."

"Did you destroy everything you found in the lab?"

"We tried to," Tim said. "But when Sheriff Davis and I got into town with the twins, they took them straight to the hospital. Olson and his goons obviously knew they needed to mop up as quickly as possible. They threw me in jail for a couple of days before Davis was cognizant enough to take back over the case. Olson was arrested by the FBI soon after, but by the time we got to the lab, some of the things had disappeared. Now the Feds are working to track everything down and contain it."

Sage thought of the super-serum Storm had been looking at right before his death, the one created from her DNA and shivered. "I hope they do."

The Wind rustled between them, and Sage felt a gentle tug at her hand. "Guess I should head out."

"Where will you go?"

"Wherever the Wind leads me," she answered.

Tim hesitated, then cupped her cheek with his warm, rough palm. "Can I ask you one more thing?"

Sage nodded.

"Promise me we'll meet again?"

A soft gust whispered in the pines around them, and Sage listened. "I promise."

"I'll keep an eye out for Gus. Something tells me we haven't seen the last of him," Tim said as he opened the door.

Sage shook her head and looked down. "I think he's gone, Tim. But there's been a lot of surprises this week, so I guess anything's possible."

Sage climbed into the Jeep. She reached her hand out the window and Tim clasped it. "Bless me, Father."

"Go in peace," Tim whispered before releasing her.

Sage smiled and drove away. She watched Tim, illuminated in the moonlight until he finally disappeared. Then, she took a deep breath and gunned her engine down the forest lined road.

Can't wait to know what happens to Sage,
Tim and Gus? Enjoy this preview from
Book Two of the **Sage of Sevens** Series.

Desert of the Damned
by
K. F. Baugh

Look for *Desert of the Damned* Fall 2018.

DESERT OF THE DAMNED

CHAPTER ONE

Backlit sandy granules spread out in a vast sea of irides-
cence, enveloping Sage in a shimmering haze of heat and
light. The sun grew impossibly large as it began its final
descent over the desert's western horizon. A light breeze
peppered her face with loose sand as she trudged across the
slickrock plateau. The Earth took a deep breath of anticipation, knowing the crippling heat of daytime would soon be
replaced by night's gentle temperatures.

Sage paused to watch the distant desert arch shift color
from fiery red to glowing orange and then gentle gray-brown
- a kaleidoscope of change that filled only the space of
several heartbeats. The transient hues seemed almost
magical in their ebb and flow; it wasn't a stretch to imagine
some otherworldly creature stepping through the space
below the arch. Sage wrapped her arms around herself and
shivered.

A piercing cry sounded from behind her, and she
turned to study the eagles that glided above her on the ther-
mals. It was their last chance to get a meal before the light
disappeared and their feathered cousins, the owls, took over.

Faint starlight now pricked the deepening blue-black of the evening sky. Sage sighed and tightened her backpack. There wasn't much time before the darkness was complete. Night fell much more quickly in the desert than in the mountains. She needed to find a place to shelter overnight.

Sage trotted down the backside of the slickrock ridge, careful not to slip on the smooth, compacted sand. The desert floor lay a good thirty feet below her. The fall wouldn't kill her, but it wouldn't be pleasant either. The last part of her descent became a scramble. She moved down the face of the ridge with the aid of tiny finger and toe holds, muscles weary from a full day of hiking. Finally, she dropped to the desert floor and collapsed into the shade-cooled sand of the small arroyo.

Her fingers burrowed their way into the fine sand. The disrupted granules briefly released the cool, sharp scent of moisture. Sage rolled to her stomach and crawled along the edge of the canyon wall until she found an overhang and eased her way underneath it. Once her eyes adjusted to the darkness, she spotted what she was looking for. There, beneath the lip of a large bolder, the sand glistened with the telltale darkness of a desert seep.

Sage crawled over and dug deep in the damp sand until she had hollowed out a small basin. Easing her way out from the overhang, she removed her backpack and settled against a gently sloped rock. A small groan escaped her as she stretched her aching legs across the still warm sand. It would be at least half an hour before the basin filled with enough water for her canteen.

Hunger replaced fatigue, and Sage rummaged in the bottom of the backpack for several moments before she found the last of her rations: a crushed, crumbly granola bar and small bag of Inca corn. She returned them to the pack, knowing they would go down her parched throat much easier once she had a few swallows of water.

Something rustled in the scrub grass to her right. Turning, Sage tried to focus on the source of the sound. After a moment, revelation came. Her mind's eye quickly conjured the image of a small whiptail lizard burrowing its way into the warm sand before the desert temperatures dropped. She scanned the rest of her surroundings. Besides a few other lizards and a harmless rat snake, the arroyo was deserted.

Using the backpack as a pillow, she curled up against the large rock. Sage tried to find something to focus on, but no matter how hard she fought, exhaustion dragged her by the hand. She shifted to a more comfortable position, but it was hopeless. A tear slipped down her cheek. Maybe she was finally tired enough that the dreams wouldn't come.

Oblivion tugged at her senses, but the dream was right there, waiting. A harrowing no-man's land she would have to pass through before being allowed the sweet release of deep, dreamless sleep. As she wrestled with exhaustion, trying to stay awake, Sage wondered which version of the familiar nightmare would assault her tonight.

It always started with her driving Elena's car through the canyon. Heart racing, she knew that any minute the Skinwalker would jump on top of the roof and rip it off. In some versions of the dream, none of them survived; in others, all of them did. Those were the worst. She'd wake up, filled with relief that Gus was still alive. Then reality would break into her euphoria, and the depth of loss became a sudden, crushing weight. Gus, gone. Her home with Liddy in Black Mills, gone. Even her complicated friendship with Tim, gone.

Finally, the relentless need for sleep overpowered her, and Sage ceased to struggle against its terrible embrace.

Sage wrestled the steering wheel, trying to keep the speeding car on the narrow mountain road. After a quick glance at the passenger seat, she saw that Gus sat there instead of Tim.

Gus was safe. Her mind struggled to understand why this filled her with a rush of relief, but she couldn't find the answer. Something rattled on the roof. Sage glanced in the rearview mirror and saw the Skinwalker. Terror replaced the joy of moments before.

"Gus, listen to me. We only have a few seconds before the *yee*--"

"No, you listen to me," Gus interrupted with something between a whine and a rumble. "We don't have much time."

"I know," Sage cried, "but I can't stop the car. The brakes don't work. They never work." How did she know this?

She glanced at Gus, and he wagged his tail reassuringly. "I miss being your guardian, but you don't need me anymore." "What are you talking about? Of course, I need you!" Sage felt a white-hot rage course through her. "You're my best friend."

"It is time for you to find others like you. Suffering ones. The Wind will show you--" "The Wind?" Sage snarled, barely recognizing her voice. "All of this is because of the Wind. If I hadn't listened, if you and I had run away again, none of this would have happened."

Gus glanced out the window. "That's not true. You have been on this path since the night we died."

"*What?*" Sage cried, jerking the steering wheel to keep from going off the road. "What do you mean, the night we *died*?"

Gus placed a soft paw on her leg. "Is it really a surprise?

You know what happened the night your family died. How could we have survived that?"

Sage blinked and suddenly, the car was gone. A large fire burned before her, illuminating a voluminous, smoke-stained cave. She sat in a circle with a handful of other people, all of them rocking to the repetitive hum echoing through the chamber. They wore feathered capes and buff-colored wrappings. Geometric black markings adorned their arms and faces. All but one of them had their eyes closed in some sort of trance.

An ancient man with obsidian eyes, the only one not caught up in the ecstatic moment, gazed at her from across the fire. "It's coming." His voice rumbled like Gus's, but no one except Sage seemed to hear him.

"What's coming?" Sage whispered.

"The end of this world." The wrinkles that wreathed his face sagged in sorrow. With his chin, he gestured to the far side of a cave and the source of the strange humming. A figure with a gigantic horned mask danced in the shadows.

"What?" Sage watched as the figure drew closer and saw that heavy turquoise necklaces wreathed the dancer's neck. Bright copper bells jingled as he danced. The hum turned into a wavering cry, sending tingles down her spine.

"If their thirst is not slaked, we all die. They will swallow us all."

As the dancer's voice rose to a shout, he pulled a jagged knife from the folds of his skirt. Sage leapt to her feet. The masked figured turned toward her, and its luminescent eyes paralyzed her with their gaze.

Then she was back on the canyon floor, huddled next to her backpack. Asleep, yet awake at the same time. She felt Gus's warmth along the length of her back, lying next to her as he always had during her nightmares as a child.

"I don't want you to go," she whispered and felt Gus shift. He lay his head on her shoulder, and his warm breath tickled her ear.

"I know. But for now, sleep and be at peace. You will need your strength."

APPENDIX

While *Valley of the Broken* is entirely fictional, one of the events the story revolves around is unfortunately not. The terrible tragedy of the Navajo Long Walk did happen and has left a scar on the history of the Southwest. The relationship between American Indians and the United States Government has always been complex, and this region of the country was no different. During the middle 1800s, things went from bad to worse between the settlers migrating from the East and the many tribes and nations that lived in the Southwest.

Under their leader, Manuelito, a large group of Navajo began to raid throughout the New Mexico territory in the 1850s and 60s. This was to protest the newly erected Fort Defiance, which was within the boundaries of Navajo territory. A full-blown conflict was close to erupting when the Civil War started. The need for Union soldiers drew attention and the military away from the Western United States. With most of the soldiers gone, the Navajo and Mescalero Apache increased their raids even more.

Eventually, this drew some attention despite the Civil

War. In 1862, General James H. Carleton was put in charge of the army in New Mexico and ordered to bring security back into the region. With the help of the well-known guide and Indian agent Kit Carson, Carleton decided to confront the Mescalero Apache first. They soon surrendered and were told to move to Bosque Redondo, a remote settlement that was later named Fort Sumner. Carleton told the Apache that they would be allowed to return to their original homes in the future but went back on this promise. Instead, the Apache became forced workers. It was their job to transform the area around Fort Sumner into a huge system of farms. Even though most of them had never farmed before, they were told to create irrigation systems, agricultural fields, and permanent homes.

Once the Apache were sent to Fort Sumner, Carleton created another military settlement, Fort Wingate. This fort was on the eastern border of the Navajo territory. He then met with Navajo leaders and demanded a complete surrender and that all the Navajo people move to Bosque Redondo. This would require a journey of 400 miles away from their plains homeland and into the arid highlands of New Mexico. Not only that, the Navajo would have to live in a community with their traditional enemies, the Apache.

The Navajo leaders rejected the plan, so Carlton built yet another fort, Fort Canby, in June 1863. It was also located in Navajo territory. From this home base, Carson and his group of 700 men were ordered to ruthlessly harass the Navajo people. Carson told his soldiers to shoot Navajo men who did not peacefully surrender. They were also ordered to take all women and children into captivity, to destroy crops, and kill or capture livestock. The Navajo still refused to surrender, so Carleton told Carson to strike in the heart of the Navajo territory, Cañon de Chelly. Here

Carson's men were ordered to destroy crops, orchards, live-stock, food stockpiles, and homes.

This brutal campaign chipped away at the resilience of the Navajo people, especially as winter hit. By early winter of 1864, 3,000 Navajos had surrendered to Carson and his men. First, the captives were sent to Forts Wingate and Canby. While there, 126 of them died from dysentery and exposure. This was followed by a forced march of 2,000 Navajo people across New Mexico to Fort Sumner, an event now known as the "Long Walk." Many Navajo, especially the elderly, the sick, and the young, died along the route.

The first forced march was followed by another in April. This time, another 2,400 Navajo were forced to walk to Bosque Redondo during heavy blizzards and terrible conditions. Again, many died. One account in *Navajo Stories of the Long Walk Period* tells the tragic end of one pregnant Navajo woman:

It was said that those ancestors were on the Long Walk with their daughter, who was pregnant and about to give birth ... The daughter got tired and weak and couldn't keep up with the others or go further because of her condition. So my ancestors asked the Army to hold up for a while and to let the woman give birth, but the soldiers wouldn't do it. [One] soldier told the parents that they had to leave their daughter behind. "Your daughter is not going to survive, anyway; sooner or later she is going to die," [he] said ... "Go ahead," the daughter said to her parents, "things might come out all right with me." But the poor thing was mistaken, my grandparents used to say. Not long after they had moved on, they

*heard a gunshot from where they had been a short
time ago.*

The refugees' worries were not over once they arrived at
the camp. It became immediately clear that there wasn't
enough food or supplies to support so many soldiers,
Navajo, and Apache. Both tribes lived in near-starvation for
the entire winter and spring.

In the end, Carson and Carleton relocated between
7,000-10,000 Apache and Navajo to Bosque Redondo.
This was accomplished by 53 forced marches over a two-
year period.

Next, Carleton tried and failed to change the Navajo
and Apache refugees into successful farmers. Unfortunately, he underestimated the amount of food that would
need to be grown to feed the large population of the camp.
He also didn't realize that crops that grew well back East
would produce much less in the arid New Mexican highlands. Lastly, he didn't consider the long-standing hostility
between the two enemy tribes. During Bosque Redondo's
four short years of existence, another estimated 2,380
people died.

Eventually, word spread about the terrible conditions at
Bosque Redondo and public outcry forced officials to act. In
1866, the New Mexico Territorial Assembly, in a nearly
unanimous vote, asked President Johnson to replace
Carleton. It took two more years, but on June 1, 1868, the
Treaty of Bosque Redondo was signed at Fort Sumner. The
Navajo were then allowed to leave the camp and return to a
portion of their former territory in western New Mexico
and eastern Arizona. This is one of the only Native American tribes that was allowed to return to its traditional territory by the United States government.

My reason for including this appendix and sources for further reading is to encourage readers to learn about this neglected part of American history. I grew up in Colorado and studied Western history during my school years, but I was still shocked to learn about the suffering that happened around where I lived. The Ute, Arapaho, Cheyenne, Apache, Navajo, Comanche, Pueblo tribes, and others, all have their own unique tales of abuse, displacement, and anguish.

One thread in Valley of the Broken is that evil does not happen in a vacuum. It continues to exist and grow if it is not recognized, repented of, and atoned for. Each of us has a part to play in bringing healing to our nation and all its inhabitants. Understanding our history is a good first step.

Sources and for Further Reading:

1. Bailey, Lynn R. *The Long Walk: A History of the Navajo Wars, 1846-68*. Pasadena: Socio-Technical Books, 1970.

2. Carter, Harvey Lewis. *'Dear Old Kit': The Historical Christopher Carson*. Norman: University of Oklahoma Press, 1968.

3. Gordon-McCutchan, R. C., ed. *Kit Carson: Indian Fighter or Indian Killer?* Niwot: University Press of Colorado, 1996.

4. Johnson, Broderick H. *Navajo Stories of the Long Walk*. Tsaile: Navajo Community College, 1973.

5. Kelly, Lawrence. *Navajo roundup; selected correspondence of Kit Carson's expedition*

against the Navajo, 1863-1865. Pruett
Publishing Company, Boulder, 1970.

6. Roessel, Ruth, ed. (1973). Navajo Stories of the
   Long Walk Period. Tsaile, Arizona: Navajo
   Community College Press

ABOUT THE AUTHOR

K. F. Baugh grew up as a true Colorado girl, carted off to the mountains in the back of her parent's Subaru almost every weekend. As an adult, she served with a humanitarian aid/missions organization for most of her 20s, primarily in war-torn Kosovo after the Yugoslav Wars, helping with relief and community development projects. For the moment she resides in Colorado again with her husband, two children and two hyper huskies. The unique landscape of the American West inspires all her stories, both the ones she writes and the ones that stay in her head. Visit west-nowthen.com to find out more about K. F. Baugh and her books.

Keep up with K. F. Baugh:

Website: www.westnowthen.com
Facebook: www.facebook.com/K-F-Baugh-Books-and-Articles-310430926088631
Instagram: @kfbaugh

Made in the USA
San Bernardino, CA
15 November 2017